OBSTACLES FROM THE GODS

RED JAVELIN SAGA

BOOK FIVE

ROSS HARRINGWAY

OMEGA PRESS
EL PASO, TEXAS

OBSTACLES FROM THE GODS

OMEGA PRESS

An imprint of Omega Communications Group, Inc.

For information contact:

Omega Press

5823 N. Mesa, #839

El Paso, Texas 79912

Or http://www.kenhudnall.com

Cover Art by Gabriela Rivera

FIRST EDITION

Printed in the United States of America

OTHER WORKS BY THE SAME AUTHOR
FROM OMEGA PRESS

THE CLOVIS ACADEMY LEGACY

Reign of Death

The Forbidden Region

Shadows in the Dark

Weakness is Provocative

Illusion of Freedom

Burdened With Morality

THE RED JAVELIN CHRONICLES

Red Javelin

Shroud of Cleopatra

Doctrine of Avoidance

The Undaunted

PROLOGUE

Endless rows of grey and gold cloning canisters were hidden in the darkness of the Mansion basement. It had been built by David Rosenburg and his wives a decade earlier in Lynott's Land, Planet New Edinburgh. Since his death, the mansion had been vacant. His widows had fled with their offspring to other parts of the planet for fear of reprisals against them. David Rosenburg had been an evil man, vicious and his villainy had been played out for all to see on the Blood Moon. Since his death and the flight of his family, the eight floor mansion had been vacant. Only David's siblings knew the security protocol to access the manor. One of those siblings was Doctor Matthew Rosenburg. He took the opportunity to use the mansion of his deceased brother to begin his plan to escape his captivity from the psychotic General Leta Tan.

Matthew had exploited his Nano-technology to impress several of Tan's soldiers into service. One pilot and a squad of eleven women were his first victims. He later used them to enslave many more soldiers and a few private practitioner medical doctors, luring the unsuspecting targets into dark alleys or corner offices so that the microscopic computer chips could enter their bodies and possess their minds. Matthew directed his squad of slave soldiers under the command of Sergeant Ann Vu to assist in creating an army for him. After being transported to the far eastern area of Lynott's Land by pilot Maria Ishii, Vu led her squad to the mansion entrance and was met by the green skinned clone of the deceased assassin named Junior Ragnarsson.

He smiled and motioned for the women to enter the mansion. "I have already disabled the security protocols. It is completely safe."

Vu nodded, "Private Tiller, start loading in the specimens. Private Fong, take the others and secure the perimeter."

The soldiers dispersed to complete Vu's orders. Vu walked into the mansion with a purpose.

Adam smiled as Estrellita Calderon moved up next to his left side and took his hand in hers. "Who are they?"

"They are the soldiers that Matthew placed under our control. I told you about them, remember?"

She nodded, "Yes. But they seem to walk and act as if, as if they cannot move correctly."

"How so?"

"They walk stiffly and their head movements are jerky.

It is not natural."

"Well, my lovely darling, that is the effects of the mind control chips in their bodies. Once we get rid of Tan and move to a safer location, we will release them."

Estrellita shuddered, "You know that I am in love with you, Adam. But doing that to other people scares me. It is cruel. Please don't enslave anyone else. It is not right."

"I am a Rosenburg. I am not used to having compassion for others. It is a set of emotions I was not bred to have. But for you, I will release them after we complete our mission."

Adam had the mind of Matthew Rosenburg and thus all his intellect and his emotional deficits. She fell in love with him due to his brilliant mind and insatiable sex drive. Each time he held her and took her, he made her feel alive, desired, lusted for. The manner that he gratified himself by using her body brought her more physical pleasure than she had ever experienced. Their lust was mutual and their love making was second to none. But he was a Rosenburg and seemed to lack empathy for those that were not related to him. That part of him saddened her.

"I believe that you can learn to care for others, Adam. Deep down in your mind, in your soul, I know that there is a man of goodness. You became a doctor because your family told you to do so, but I also believe that you are a magnificent doctor because somewhere hidden inside of you, there is the ability to care. You and I have a very special relationship and I know when we make love that I see love in your eyes for me. If you can feel those emotions for me, so I know that you can feel for others."

Adam smiled and shook his head, recalling the last night he had shared with Estrellita, holding her, making love with her. "You are one of the most beautiful women I have ever had the pleasure of bedding. I know that you will produce healthy offspring for me. Yes, I do love you. But the way I love you is different than the way you love me. I am not like other men."

She smiled, "You are correct. You are better than other men. You are smart, sexy and a great lover. You make love to me and give me all I can handle. I would die for you, Adam."

He paused and looked into her eyes. He was silent for a few seconds as he contemplated her words. "I would die for you as well. I know that I love you. I would fight for you until my last breath."

"Then there is hope for you my love."

Adam took Estrellita's hand in his as they watched Vu's squad carefully carry in the equipment that Matthew had directed them to assemble. The mansion was vast and unoccupied. It was the perfect setting for Matthew to mass produce clones without detection from Tan or the MI that are unwelcome visitors to the abodes of others. The mind controlled soldiers began constructing several eleven-foot-long and four-foot-wide silver and red cloning tubes onto the many metallic tables in the other quarters of the mansion. Matthew intended to create an army of a few hundred to take on Tan and her army of thousands.

"Tan will fall and then we will take on General Sikorsky in Clovis City," Adam whispered to her.

"But isn't Kimberly Sikorsky a cousin of the Rosenburg's? I was always told that the Royals stand together. You would betray your own family?"

"The Rosenburg Clan was always special to the Glorious Leader. We were the ones that had the creativity to design weapons that assisted in keeping the masses loyal. But since the Blood Moon Incident, our family has been forsaken by the Glorious Leader. He lifted his protection over us. I lost children because of his unwillingness to embrace us and protect us. Accordingly, we will retake this planet that was promised to us and make a new pact with the Glorious Leader. Kimberly and the other Royals that are present here on New Edinburgh will be given a choice. They can join us or perish."

Estrellita nodded slowly, "Sounds fair to me. And what plans do the Rosenburg's have for us commoners once you regain control? What will happen to my family and friends?"

"Your sister is building an army as we speak," Adam revealed to her with a smile. "She is very resourceful. If she succeeds in getting to Tan before we do, then we will have to bargain with her to become a part of the new planetary order. She is intelligent, just like you. I believe that one of my clone brothers would enjoy breeding with her. I surmise that she would create amazing offspring."

"You mean Reynita?" Estrellita held back her desire to laugh. "Yes, she is very smart and tough. She cannot be tamed. She will fight Tan to the death if need be. She will side with us, I guarantee it. She will come up with a plan to eliminate Tan and take control of her forces. You can trust her, Adam. By the way, she has a boyfriend, so you might want to let your clone brothers know that she won't be 'breeding' with any of them. But I do have other sisters and cousins that will gladly breed with your clone brothers. That is, after I brag to them how amazing you are as a lover. Don't worry, there are plenty of Calderon girls on New Edinburgh to take care of that."

The couple grew silent as Matthew, Maggie and Jamie Rosenburg walked through the grey and white double French doors of the mansion. Private Lexi Fong was at their side, with a laser pistol in her right hand as if she was expecting a fight.

Matthew smiled at Adam and Estrellita, "Things are going as planned. Soon we will take back our world."

General Leta Tan had proven to be an unmitigated bitch in the mind of Matthew Rosenburg. She had constantly demanded reports, sometimes two to three times a day. Matthew was cognizant of the fact that Tan did not trust him. In fact,

Matthew was certain that Tan intended to kill him and his two daughters the moment she no longer needed them. So, Matthew worked hard at keeping her in the dark while he organized his plans for escape from Tan's Palace of MI soldiers.

Part of his plan began when he had been able to get eleven of Tan's soldiers and a pilot alone. Using mind control nano-technology, Matthew now had the ability to use those eleven soldiers and the pilot on the mission to do his bidding. In addition to taking over the free will of the twelve women, Matthew drew blood from each of them and used their DNA to clone them. He had left one thousand cloning tubes at the Rosenburg Ranch mansion of Cush Rosenburg, each of them with clones of the women gestating, growing and developing into duplicates of their originals. But those clones were over a thousand miles away. He needed immediate backup inside Tan's Palace.

That was where the clones of Junior Ragnarsson came in. He had forty-nine of them to use. Tan expected them all to have her memories programmed into them. Matthew used forty-eight of them for another purpose, downloading his own memories into them. The forty-ninth clone of Junior Ragnarsson was given the mind of Leta Tan. Matthew hoped that when he eventually turned the clone with her mind inside of it over to her, that she would be placated with her new toy and leave him be for a short time. He only needed a few days to use the empty fifty clone tubes to create more clones of the eleven soldiers and the lone pilot so that he would have a fighting chance to save his daughters.

He had the forty-eight Ragnarsson clones pretend as if they were asleep so that Tan and her minions would not become suspicious. But to Matthew's chagrin, the green-skinned clones had enormous sex drives and would sneak out of the large laboratory Tan had provided for him to seek out a partner. Some of the clones had been successful in finding willing partners. Matthew had ordered Sergeant Ann Vu, Private Lexi Fong, Private Jawalla Tiller and the other eight squad members under his control to regularly have sex with the green-skinned clones. They would mate behind the doors of storage closets or bathrooms. Matthew was pleased that the clones seemed to be satisfied with the arrangement. He wondered how the clones with his brain imprinted inside of them could be so different from him. Matthew had a strong sex drive, but he was normally driven by his work, not his prurient instinct to breed.

He had been occasionally keeping the company of one of his loaned computer technicians named LeVega Farley. She was attractive enough and Matthew enjoyed having sex with her. Her skin was almost a tint of pink, possibly from her years of exposure to the sun that warmed planet Athena.

Matthew had observed that one of the Ragnarsson

clones, which referred to himself as Adam, was in a sexual relationship with another of the computer technicians named Estrellita Calderon. Matthew was unaware of how the two began their relationship, but he had observed many tender moments between the two, gentle kisses, soft holding of the hands and knowingly looking into each other's eyes. Matthew concluded that Adam and Estrellita were in love.

Matthew looked off into the distance at the green and blue Super-Raumschiff that was being unloaded by his minions. The top of the ship was relatively flat although the remainder of the space craft was oval shaped. He calculated that he would need about twenty such ships to transport his clones once they were completed. Parked next to the Super-Raumschiff were two of the standard, wide "V" shaped Allen fighter ships. Each had one seat and capable of unleashing deadly R-5 Rockets and a barrage of rapid laser bursts. Matthew knew where he could procure more of those ships. He would have to seize them from his father's underground hangars.

But he needed more pilots. Many more pilots. He smiled in the direction of pilot Maria Ishii. She would be his DNA donor and he would scan her memories to implant into the bodies. He would use her to make his space pilot force and to bring General Tan to her knees.

But he was wise enough to recognize that he needed

more to crush Tan. He needed allies. He had one in Reynita Calderon. But the two of them, despite all of their mutual savvy and intellect, would not be able to beat Tan and General Sikorsky. They must find a way to recruit others, many others, from the masses.

"Come on, Raynita," Matthew whispered to himself. "Where are you? What are you waiting for?"

CHAPTER ONE

Reynita Calderon was torn. She had given many decisive orders that only seemed to anger those that sought to follow her. She found herself second guessing many of her decisions based on the cacophony of opposition from the cadets, civilians and soldiers that had willingly agreed to join her uprising against the government in control of planet New Edinburgh.

Reynita first sent six of her brothers to assist John Gauthier, James Cobb and other members of the Bragg Gang to protect the pilot instructors at the Academy. Her second directive was to send Elektra Papinakilaou, Arch Frazier, Derek Regehr and three other cadet volunteers on a mission to attempt to convince the naval command to join the rebellion. Those two decisions drew several cries of resistance, but those ordered to go into action complied with her orders.

It was when she ordered the pregnant women to report to the hospital and avoid any combat that she received the majority of her disapproval from the others. April Mejia was in no shape to participate in battle, but she and her husband protested in any event. Eventually the expecting couple agreed to depart and avoid any of the inevitable combat. Reynita recognized that Klaus Rhinehard was a very talented cadet pilot and his presence in combat would have been useful. But he would be better served by the side of his wife while she gave birth.

Reynita received dissent when she ordered that all of the Evart girls retreat into hiding along with Piotr Gorski. Reyntia made that decision based on the governmental edict that all Evart's and Gorski be shot and killed on sight. Fortunately, some members of the Andolini family backed up Reynita during the debate and agreed to assist the Evart girls and Piotr in locating a safe place to hide.

Reynita ordered Cadet Dino Black to embark on a secret mission to obtain weaponry. That order was not questioned by those assembled. Reynita decided to select a team of women to travel with her on a mission that she dared not identify to those present for fear they might inadvertently reveal her master plan. The cadets that she left out of her plans were irate.

"What are we supposed to be doing?" Bret Bragg echoed the sentiment shared by many others in the cramped military office.

"I could be useful, too." Mia Nguyen spoke up.

Reynita held up her hands defensively, "I need the rest of you to help Sergeant First Class Lund and my remaining platoon members in gathering weaponry and arming the cadets for war. When I return with my small group I hope to lead an army so large that victory will be ours."

Mark Lund looked at her with concern, "And just where do you think you will find that, Reynita? There are only a few small squadrons of fighters in some of the other territories."

Frank Preston had been silent during the entire meeting. He looked at Sergeant Benjamen Zhao and they both nodded in unison as they had figured out Calderon's master plan without her even verbalizing it.

"Lieutenant, are you planning on challenging General Tan for command of her MI army?" Preston asked out loud.

Reynita ordered that all of the cadets leave the room save the women she had already told to remain with her. Bragg and the numerous others slowly departed and Lund sealed the door behind them.

Satisfied that only her platoon members and the women she selected remained, Reynita pointed to the map of the northern continent. "Jen, Harumi, Miyu, Sara, Supreet, Melissa, Elsa, Blossom and I will be first going to the two territories that house the fighter squadrons. From there, I will challenge General Tan and fight her to the death. That is why only women can come with me. If I fail, Tan will probably order anyone with me executed. So, I will not demand that any of you join me on this quest. I only want you to come from your own free will. Jen?"

Staszko smiled and licked her lips. "You don't ask for

much, do you? I'm in."

Harumi nodded, "Me too. I won't sit this out for anything."

Blossom Li smiled. "It is my duty to my family name to fight for others. I will follow you, Reynita Calderon."

Supreet Patel said nothing but shook her head indicating that she was willing to take the risk and go to Lynott's Land and fight against General Tan.

Elsa Regher shrugged, "I guess if I die here or in Lynott's Land it matters not. I don't know what I can offer, but I am in."

Melissa Harcourt remained silent. She listened in as Miyu Tamura and Sara Stewart told their platoon leader that they volunteered for the mission. Melissa realized that all the others had spoken up and Reynita was staring at her direction. Melissa was terrified of the idea of facing Tan. As a Child of Atherna, Melissa possessed many special abilities. One of her powers was to read and link with other people and read their minds. She could also control any person's actions, make them do things that they would not otherwise do. She had used her powers to lure Drayton Love-Easter and other men to her bed. She had once caused one of her Professors to change her grade from average to a much higher number. Despite her innate abilities, Melissa feared Tan as she had witnessed Tan's cruelty on a few occasions. Melissa had read the minds of people Tan tortured to death and she linked her mind with those that were being executed. Melissa had felt their fear and saw them die as she tapped into their minds.

"Mel, are you with us?" Patel asked.

"Fine. Yes. I will go." Melissa said softly. She did not want to receive another tongue lashing from Staszko like the one she had the other day.

"Then let's move out," Lund yelled at the remaining group and pointed his thumb over his shoulder in the direction of the exit. "We have work to do."

As the meeting was breaking up and the individuals were heading toward their directed destination, Lund approached Reynita. He stood behind her and whispered into her ear.

"I don't like the idea of you taking on Tan. She is vicious," Lund hissed. He was worried for her safety as he had seen Tan in action. "She is a trained professional in the martial arts. She has some of the best trained sets of assassins on the planet. You go there and do this and she will kill you."

Reynita faced Lund. "Not if you get those children freed from the orphanage. If you do anything, Mark, make certain you get all of those children turned over. The father of those children is a man that can help us. He has an honor to him that I cannot explain. He will side with me if we give him his children. Please, Mark. Everything depends on it."

"I will do my part," Lund promised her softly. "I don't want to lose you. Please come back to me."

"You be careful too," she told him. "I want to kiss you good bye, but we both know we can't be giving any PDA's here in front of everyone."

"PDA?" Lund asked.

"Public displays of affection. Now go. When I get back I will let you mount me in my office as often as you want to."

Lund smiled, "I will hold you to that promise."

As Lund motioned to Zhao, Preston and the remainder of the platoon, Jen Staszko approached Reynita.

"We're ready to go," Staszko reported. "Sara and Miyu are armed. The rest of us will need some weaponry if we are going to take on Tan."

"Upstairs is the armory," Reynita informed her as she motioned for her small squad of women to follow her up the stairwell. "Unfortunately, it only has a few laser pistols and stun darts. We'll take what we can from here. The MI Raumschiff that I have waiting for us has much more firepower."

Blossom Li followed one step behind Reynita and Staszko. "We can steal one of the cadet training Raumschiff's and Melissa and I can fly it to the first squadron. Commander Rendon is in charge there. She is a Royal and she will never side with us. My sister Emerald is a pilot there, too. I know she will be willing to fight in our side."

"I am aware of Rendon. But the other squadron commanders are not Royal's," Reynita remarked. "Aura Lynda Glenn is serving there and so are my friends the Brock's. We will have to eliminate Rendon and her command staff. You have any problems with that?"

Staszko laughed, "I think you picked the right women to follow you on this mission. Sara and I know each other from when she was assigned to protect me and Elektra. She has guts. Harumi and I are fully capable of taking care of business. Blossom and Supreet are tough as nails and will keep their heads when things get rough. We get Lynda and Emerald on our side with a bunch of good pilots then we will be hell on wheels. Rendon and Tan are not going to know what hit them."

Reynita gave Staszko a hug, "That is what I am hoping for. Surprise is the best element in a rebellion."

"So, who do we go after first?" Staszko asked, even though she was certain of the response. Reynita would want to go after the control of the skies and space first. The Planetary Defense System had the majority of the Squadrons of the Wide "V" shaped one-person Allen fighter ships. That would be the first target of the small group of women that had volunteered to fight beside Reynita.

"We take out Rendon and convince as many of her Squadron Leaders possible to join us," Reynita told her the obvious. "Once we secure the power to control the air and space, then we go after Tan. Tan will be the most difficult since we have few allies there."

Staszko's smile faded, "We have no one in Lynott's Land that would be willing to help us?"

Reynita smiled, "I have a few tricks up my sleeve. Come on, let's get everyone outfitted and armed. We have to steal ourselves a Raumschiff."

"And then off to war?"

Before Reynita could respond, Supreet Patel approached them. She held up her hand-sized communication device. "Reynita, my sister and I recorded what happened at the Church. We uploaded to the satellite broadcast system the murder of the priest and the others. I hope that was fine with you."

Reynita nodded, "It will help us recruit more rebels. Killing a religious leader will prove to be a horrible PR move by the Royals."

CHAPTER TWO

The penalty for stealing a privately-owned space ship ranged between fifty to one hundred years of confinement on the prison planet called Cootron. It was essentially a death sentence as the living conditions for the inmates that were incarcerated there were atrocious. But if one had a death wish, they could opt for attempting to steal a space craft that belonged to the Space Command. Just the attempt was considered an act of treason against the government and warranted and automatic death sentence.

The range of sentences for such a criminal act weighed heavily on the mind of cadet junior Elektra Papinakilaou Frazier. When she left her home on Corinth over three years ago to attend the Clovis Academy on planet New Edinburgh, she never dreamed that she would get caught up in any form of conflict with the government. Despite her efforts to live on the right side of the law, Elektra had been targeted for death several times. The first event was on Space Station Cy-7 when some crazed serial killers attempted to rape her. She was saved by a dear friend before the killers could get very far. The second was during a dust storm when some highly trained inter-solar system assassins arrived in the dormitory rooms with bad intent. Elektra and her friends were ready that night and captured the would-be killers. The third time, Elektra almost died. She had lost an arm when she was hit with a laser blast fired by an assassin named Dell Ragnarsson, Junior.

She almost died.

Due to the marvels of modern medical science, she now sported a mechanical arm that enabled to complete actions that she never thought possible. She could crush metal, lift a thousand pounds without trying and take off an opponent's head with one hit. Her husband, Arch Frazier, nick-named her "the Cat" due to her many near death events. She prayed to Hera that she did indeed have a few lives left as she was now embarking on committing a criminal act that would get her the death penalty if caught.

She was helping a group of fellow cadets steal a space ship from the Space Command. But this was not any ordinary ship. They were searching for a specific model of ship that was code named the Orka. The Orka was a space craft that was similar in size to a Raumschiff, with three floors, modern weapons systems and decent medical and living facilities. The Orka can transport up to fifty crew members with comfort. The difference between the Orka and the Raumschiff was that the

Orka was designed for flying in the deep oceans while a Raumschiff was for deep space. The engines were different for that purpose. Before beginning the quest to locate and steal such a craft, Elektra borrowed an advanced computer security hacking pack from the MI headquarters of Reynita Calderon. Elektra had studied the intricate protocols of how to hack into the security systems of any space craft as part of her Academy studies. She had envisioned using the skills on some future mission to rescue some stranded civilians in deep space. Now she was faced with the prospect of hacking a ship for personal and treasonous reasons.

Elektra had agreed to lead an expedition, to the deep ocean floor of planet New Edinburgh, for the purpose of facing her aunt, Admiral Themis Zachariades, and her cousin, Captain Drimios Zachariades, to plead for their aid and assistance. Both were highly decorated naval officers and had seen combat. Their experiences would make them valuable allies. But they also commanded large Unter-See Boats that had nuclear weaponry on board. Those offensive weapons had the potential of stopping any opponent from attacking, at the very least. At their worst, the weapons could destroy an enemy Battle Cruiser or wipe out an entire city.

Some of the cadets at the Clovis Academy had become targets for assassination by the new government that had been forcibly installed on the planet. Most of the cadets were running off to hide in some safe location. Some had been caught and were awaiting their trial. Others had already been killed. Some of those cadets that were being sought out by the Military Intelligence were individuals that Elektra considered as he good friends. Many cadets and soldiers that were like minded joined together to fight back. Lieutenant Reynita Calderon had split up the forces of the little rebellion with specific tasks in mind to build up to the final confrontation against the new leaders.

The mission assigned to Elektra by Reynita was simple. Contact Aunt Themis and cousin Drimios and convince them to join the cause to oust the new military government. Elektra felt she could be successful if she could speak with aunt Themis face to face. The two had shared a close bond. Aunt Themis had practically raised Elektra and there were no secrets between them. Theirs was a relationship that transcended politics. But to reach her aunt, Elektra needed an Orka as Admiral Themis Zachariades was under the oceans of the planet, charting the currents and the ocean floor.

In addition, she needed a pilot with specific experience in operating an Orka. Calderon selected one for her. His name was Derek Regehr, a member of the rival Bragg Gang and a senior cadet astronaut. Regehr had no love for Elektra or her husband as they were both members of the Gorski Gang. Their factions had rumbled on many occasions. But now the two groups were united in a common goal, to eliminate the new military leaders and free their friends. Regehr agreed to go along and pilot the Orka, if one could be found. Regehr was light skinned with blonde hair and light blue eyes. He was forced to wear glare resistant sunglasses while on the surface of the planet due to the bright orange yellow glow from the sunlight.

Regehr had taken along with him another cadet pilot, named Sanjeeta Nehwal, who was in her second year. Elektra deduced from their body language that Regehr and Nehwal had been sleeping together for some time. They seemed to genuinely care for one another as they ran in between the sky scraper buildings of downtown Clovis City. Nehwal was not a member of the Bragg Gang and had been a loner at the Academy. She was suspicious of others due to her negative experiences growing up in an abusive orphanage. Nehwal had learned survival skills as a child in that environment. She had been the victim of sexual abuse by one of the therapists that worked at the large group home for abandoned children. She had also learned how to steal and hide food when the adults were not watching. She was caught once and beaten severely. She still had scars on her back, buttocks and legs from that incident which served as a constant reminder to her what the cost of being caught could be. She vowed to never be caught again and taught herself how to become not just a child that stole food, but to become an exceptional thief. She would take things from her professors and fellow students when they were not paying attention. She never felt remorse at her thefts as she viewed her acquisition of money, clothing and other items as a skill to help her advance herself. She obtained entrance to the Academy by changing her average grades by threatening the therapist that had used her for sex when she was a child. The therapist used his position to change the orphanage records making the substandard Nehwal a straight "A" student.

As a cadet astronaut candidate, she had to learn the laws of physics. Since her mathematic knowledge was below average, she sought out a tutor. She found that Regehr was a willing assistant as long as sex was a part of the interaction. Knowing how to please men and the importance of using sex to obtain what she wanted, Nehwal seduced Regehr so that he would help her with her class work. The relationship between the two was a loose association for the first year. During the passage of the previous twelve months, she had grown to care about the man in a way she never felt possible for her. He seemed to understand her and never made any judgmental comments about her scars or her negative behaviors. Regehr and Nehwal had grown into an item around the campus and she found that having him around to be a pleasant thing.

Nehwal would follow Regehr anywhere he directed. He was the only person that she trusted enough to follow. When he was asked to fly the Orka ship into the ocean, there was no question in her mind that she should be by his side. She had been at the funeral wearing a tight red and yellow leather suit with black boots that came up just under her knees. She had taken a red back pack from the storage room of the MI platoon commanded by the Calderon woman. She stuffed two hand lasers into the pack along with a knife and a garrote before throwing the straps over her shoulders.

There were hundreds of civilians walking here and there as if it were another ordinary day. The group would slow their pace whenever they noticed any soldiers wearing the solid black Military Intelligence or Marines uniforms. They could not afford to take the chance of calling attention to themselves.

Elektra's husband, Arch, was holding her hand in his as they pushed through the crowds. They witnessed the soldiers in black shoot down a young couple simply because they resembled members of the Wyclyffe family. When the soldiers learned that the victims had been innocent, they continued their harassment of others, with little care that they had just killed two people without just cause.

Although Arch Frazier was a geology major and was working on a minor in explorations, he had proven himself to be an excellent hand to hand fighter. They had been involved in several bar fights and each had demonstrated that they had the mettle to meet any challenge. He had taken a laser pistol and hid it under his dark sweater to avoid detection.

Walking quickly behind the Frazier family were two other cadets, sisters that had decided on committing treason named Zorana and Jasna Mikec. Zorana was twenty and Jasna eighteen, that had been part of a large Serbian family that arrived on New Edinburgh ten years ago. Their family had stayed out of political life and concentrated on being farmers. The Mikec Poggie farm was one of the largest suppliers of bacon, ham, fruits, vegetables and grains on the planet. The Mikec family had three dozen children, most of whom worked on the farm. Zorana and Jasna chose a different path from most their siblings and opted to attend the Academy. Both girls were good shooters with a laser and were taking martial arts classes. Zorana was the Captain of the Academy Tennis team and Jasna was a member of the swimming team. They wore blue and silver civilian clothing when they had attended the funeral of Lupita Calderon. Zorana had a silver half-shirt with tight black shorts and tennis shoes while Jasna was wearing a black and dark blue striped tube top with white shorts and flip flops. Both girls had on fairly expensive silver hoop earrings and matching necklaces that were given to them as birthday gifts from their doting father. They were both stunned when the soldiers invaded the sanctity of a funeral to arrest several of the attendees. Based on the abuse of power that they observed, Zorana and Jasna were resolute in their decision to participate in the coming fight.

In the distance, Elektra could see the large landing strip of the New Edinburgh space port. There were thousands of space craft of varying sizes, makes and models that were sitting inactive as their owners would venture off to the big city for shopping or eating. For the most part, the ships belonged to deep space travelers. But there were some military style ships and those owned by local families that had the financial means to afford one. Elektra allowed Regehr and Nehwal to take the lead on selecting which space craft they would steal. They all observed that there were several soldiers patrolling the long strip, occasionally stopping pedestrians and asking them questions as to their reason for being on the strip.

The Mikec sisters were keeping up with them, bringing up the rear. If the soldiers caused them any pause, they were not showing it. Some of the soldiers were looking over at the tall and slender Elektra, the striking and exotic looking Nehwal and the scantily clad Mikac sisters as they passed by. The presence of the four ladies gave Frazier and Regehr enough cover to pass on by without a second look. The six cadets stepped onto the transparent metal and concrete landing strip and could easily see the shades of purple rock and sand underneath. They walked as if they knew exactly where they were going. After walking a quarter of a mile on the strip, Regehr smiled and nodded his head to the left.

Elektra and Frazier followed his gaze and saw it. A large solid black Orka style space craft. The husband and wife squeezed each other's hands as they followed the cadet pilot.

"This is too easy," Arch whispered to his wife. He had expected a laser battle for certain. But the soldiers seemed to be occupied with other citizens and they were fortunate enough to pass through without interrogation.

Elektra stopped in her tracks when she spied upon the two Babbcottiatta that were approaching from the east side of the large runway. "You spoke too soon, love."

Arch followed her gaze and swallowed hard when he saw the giant aliens walking in their direction. Each of the creatures had one of their dreaded laser spears in one of their large fists. The energy was crackling at the tips of the metal staffs, warning one and all that the creatures would use deadly force if necessary.

"Crap," Arch whispered to himself.

"Holy Hera! They are coming right for us," Elektra whispered back. "Do you think that they know what we are up to?"

"How do you communicate with one of those things?" Arch whispered as the giant aliens grew closer with each step.

"Hell, I don't know. Tell them welcome to our planet?"

The Mikec sisters were standing by the Frazier's. Their

eyes were wide with fear. They had seen news reports of the aliens and how they could rip a man or woman apart with their massive arms using little effort.

"Should we run?" Jasna asked Elektra.

"No, that would only make us look guilty." Elektra warned her. "Keep walking like we have the right to be here."

The four cadets breathed a sigh of relief when the giant aliens walked past them without incident. They watched in silence as the Babbcottiatta walked in the direction of another cluster of civilians wearing bright silver business attire.

"I almost peed my panties," Jasna whispered.

Elektra did not want to waste any time. She moved quickly to the Orka ship and removed the pack from her shoulders and set it on the transparent concrete below her. She unzipped it and pulled out wiring that had small attachment cables at the ends and fastened them to the rear of the space craft. She looked out of the corner of her eyes to see that her husband and the Mikec sisters were keeping watch around her. Regehr and Nehwal were walking around the space craft, inspecting the hull for any obvious breaches.

Arch thought he saw Liam and Sean Cormac Collins with the woman that had changed her name to Mary Sierra walking toward a large, oval shaped, gold Super Raumschiff. They were leading several young girls to the boarding rear ramp and were quickly ushering them aboard the craft. Arch squinted his eyes, looking for any sign of the lawyer Sean Collins and could not see him. He wondered where the father of the Collins children was. Had he been killed like Major Evart and Admiral Seward, he asked himself. The events had unfolded so quickly that none of the cadets had any chance for reflection. First the Fenster siblings were kidnaped and Lupita Calderon was murdered. Then the military takeover of the planet occurred with lightning fast precision. Many good people were killed. Many others were being held in prisons awaiting their public execution by decapitation. Then the soldiers attacked the funeral for Lupita and the world seemed to change forever.

As his wife continued to attach the small wires to the metal hull of the Orka ship, Frazier tapped his left foot on the ground impatiently. He prayed that no soldiers or aliens caught them. Elektra now had her small computer pad out and attached the cables to it. She gave a verbal command for the small computer to attach itself to the computer inside the space craft. The technological ability to hack a ship computer by using an interface with the metal hull and nothing more had been perfected by the Rosenburg scientists several decades ago. She looked over her shoulder and noticed that Jasna was watching her progress. Elektra smiled at the girl and she smiled back. A few moments passed and Elektra heard the small computer in her hacking pack indicate that she had access to the Orka on board computer.

"Computer, order a shutdown of all security measures and then open the rear access doors." Elektra was calm in her delivery of her instructions. Her heart was pounding as she waited. Every second that passed could be the moment that they were discovered by a passing soldier or nosey civilian. The rear loading ramp began to lower and the back hull for the ship began to slide open from left to right.

"We're in," she informed the others.

Zorana and Jasna were the first to jump onto the loading ramp. They had already drawn laser pistols and were inspecting the rear of the ship as the hull opened. Zorana was the first to board the craft; her sister was a few paces behind her. The Frazier's were next, running up the ramp quickly. Elektra was thanking Hera for watching over them. Regehr and Nehwal were the last two to rush up the ramp. After the six were safely inside the ship, Nehwal pressed the bright red button on the side wall to close the ramp and the hull. They waited as the ship sealed shut.

"Now what do we do?" Zorana asked.

"Sweep the ship," Elektra pointed to the Mikec sisters. "Derek and Sanjeeta will take the pilot section. Zorana and Jasna, take the lower level. Arch and I will take the second floor. Shoot any occupants with a stun blast. No unnecessary killing."

"Can you give that last order to any other people on this

ship?" Jasna laughed nervously. She was scared, which did not surprise any of the others. Jasna was the youngest of them and she had led a relatively sheltered life, until now.

"Stick with me, sis." Zorana pointed the barrel of her laser down the right hallway and began walking. Jasna followed her with her laser in her right fist.

Regehr made no comments as he drew a laser pistol from under his sweater, removed his dark sunglasses and walked toward the north small ramp that was inclined upward at a twenty-five-degree angle. Nehwal followed him up.

Elektra leaned over and kissed her husband on the lips. "Love you."

Arch smiled and ran his fingers through her long dark hair. "I love you too. Let's go."

The couple followed Regehr and Nehwal up the ramp. Within a few seconds, they heard the sound of laser fire ahead of them. Arch ran quickly onto the second floor and saw seven figures on the metal landing, all unconscious. Each of the prone individuals were clad in dark blue, one-piece Space Command uniforms with black boots that were a few inches below the knees. The majority of the seven were women. Nehwal and Regehr were gingerly stepping over them as they made their way toward the ladder leading to the pilot's section.

Elektra and Arch knelt next to the seven and inspected them. There were five women and two men. Each was armed with laser pistols on their web belts. One was a Lieutenant Commander; the rest had rank insignias indicating that they were Lieutenant Junior Grades. Arch handed a handful of plastic twist ties to Elektra and the two methodically bound the seven officers' hands behind their backs and then secures their legs together at their ankles.

"All clear in the pilot section," Nehwal reported to them from above.

"I am going to go check on the Mikec girls while you strap these seven in," Elektra told Arch as she stood upright.

"Be careful."

Elektra checked the charge level of her laser pistol as she descended the ramp. "Count on it."

She ran down the ramp and turned to the left when she reached the lower level. She noted that there were no bodies on the floor as she quickly moved down the hallway. Her first stop was the small medical facility to her right which had no visible signs of any occupants. She kept moving to the other side of the hall where the engine room was located. She saw that the Mikec sisters were inside, binding two civilian women that we lying on the floor.

"Is this as far as you got?" Elektra asked them.

"These two gave us some trouble," Zorana responded defensively. "All that is left is the personal quarters and the cryo-sleep chamber down the other end of the ship."

"Fine. Jasna, you're with me." Elektra ordered. The young girl dutifully followed her down the hallway and they cleared each of the ten by ten square foot living quarters, one by one. The cryo-sleep chambers were empty as well.

"Only nine on the crew. That is odd," Elektra told Jasna thoughtfully. "Normally there would be scientists and a few MI soldiers. Very odd."

"Perhaps they were not going on any type of mission?" Jasna speculated out loud.

Before either Elektra or Zorana could respond the ship's computer began warning that the back entrance to the ship was opening.

"Holy Hera! The rest of the crew is returning!" Elektra barked at the Mikec girls. "Lock and load! This could get ugly!"

She led the two women from the engine room to the hallway that would lead to the rear loading ramp. They heard the hull doors sliding open and the ramp lowering. Elektra had her holographic-communicator in her left hand and contacted her husband to warn him of the possible in coming mass of soldiers.

The three women stopped at the end of the hall and Elektra slowly mover her head around the corner to give herself a good angle to see what was coming. As she had feared, there were twelve soldiers dressed in solid black uniforms of the Military Intelligence Branch. Fortunately, each of them had their laser rifles slung over their shoulders and their laser pistols in the holsters hanging from their web belts. Elektra nodded to the sisters standing on either side of her and she stepped out from behind the wall and began firing her laser pistol at the dozen new soldiers. The first soldier that Elektra shot had a look of dismay on her face. The last thing they had suspected was the possibility of being ambushed on board their own ship.

Jasna and Zorana followed her lead and were firing their laser pistols at them. It was almost impossible to miss as the targets were a mere twenty feet distance from them. The soldiers fell backwards as they were hit by the lasers fired by the women. The soldiers hit the metal floor causing a clanging sound. One of the MI soldiers, a female Sergeant, tried to pull out her holographic-communication device, but she was hit in the back by a laser blast fired by Zorana Mikec before she could send any messages. The sergeant and the communication device bounced on the metal floor.

Frazier ran as fast as his legs would carry him when he received Elektra's call. He had a laser rifle in hand and came to a complete stop when he reached the end of the ramp. He smiled when he saw his wife and the Mikec girls searching twelve soldiers that were lying on the metal floor.

"Looks like this was a job for ladies only," Arch remarked. "You three trying to win the war all by yourselves?"

"Stop complaining and help us secure them," Elektra was twisting plastic ties around one of the unconscious soldiers' wrists as she spoke. "We have places to go. This should be all of them. Once they are secured we can get out of here."

"How did you know that they would be soldiers?" Jasna wanted to know.

Elektra finished with her first prisoner and moved toward another prone MI soldier. She pulled out another plastic twist tie and knelt. "In your military tactics course that you will take in your next semester you will learn that all Space Command Raumschiffs and Orkas have a security detachment assigned to it. That rule is true even in port, loading dock, landing strip or on a Battle Cruiser. That was why I thought it odd that there were only nine crew members. Now we have twenty-one prisoners. That is about right."

"So, you want to take them with us? Under the ocean? With all those large creatures?" Jasna's eyebrows were raised in disbelief.

"What else can we do?" Elektra shrugged. "If we leave them here, then the soldiers and giant aliens outside will see them, realize that we stole this ship and then they will quickly dispatch a few squadrons to shoot us out of the sky. We could drop them out the air locks while in the air and let them all become Cawler bait. But that somehow sounds inhumane and we would be stooping down to their standards. So, yes, Jasna. We take them with us. We can put them to sleep in the cryo sleep tubes below and wake them after the mission is over."

"Including the seven pilots above," Frazier added.

"I like it," Zorana nodded in agreement with Elektra's plan.

The three set out to drag the twelve unconscious soldiers down the hallway to the cryo-sleep chamber. One by one they locked the soldiers into the ten-foot-long tubes and froze them. Once they completed the task, the four cadets marched up the ramp to the second level to find that Regehr and Nehwal had already strapped the seven pilots into some of the leather seats.

"I injected them all with stun darts," Nehwal informed them as she motioned with her left hand to the unconscious officers. "They won't be able to bother us for the duration of the trip. If they wake up, we will just stick them with another dart."

"I already finished the safety checks for the ship," Regehr added. "We're ready to go. You all need to secure yourselves to your seats. When we hit the ocean, there will be a jolt and I don't want any of you twisting your necks. Any idea which area of the ocean floor your aunt was going to survey first?"

"The south," Elektra told him. "She was going to start with the southern continent and the islands around her."

"Which is quite dangerous because of the large predator

ocean dwellers that could swallow our ship in one bite." Zorana warned them. "Does this ship have any weaponry?"

"Does it?" Nehwal put her right arm around Zorana's shoulders. "I just checked that out. We have rockets, lasers, electrical bursts, bright light flashes, heat bombs and other useful stuff to help us repel any inquisitive creatures. Derek will get us there and we'll protect the ship."

Regehr began climbing up the ladder. "Then strap yourselves in, ladies and gentleman. We have a long flight ahead of us."

Arch sat down in one of the large leather seats next to his lovely wife. After securing their seat belts, and their over the shoulder harnesses and head braces, he reached out and held her hand in his. "I love you, Elektra."

"I love you too, Arch." She was smiling at him. He wanted to kiss her, but the head brace prohibited it.

Their flight to the southern continent would take about two hours. To their mutual elation, the trip was completed without incident. The military did not suspect that the Orka had been stolen and no ships were sent in pursuit. The first part of their mission had been easy. Frazier would later recall that moment as one of the most serene in his life.

As the time passed, the Frazier's and the Mikec sisters listened intently to the instructions given over the ship intercom by Regehr and Nehwal.

"When we go under the water we will be facing many dangers," Regehr told them. "The worst among them is the creature called the Britva. It has razor sharp fangs, is larger than any other of the aquatic life on the planet and it has no fear. Their mouths are so wide that they can swallow a Raumschiff whole and have done so in the past. If that happens to us, and believe me it can, do not panic. Sanjeeta says that we have enough fire power that we can blast our way out of the belly of one of those things. But if the creature tosses us around or somehow finds a weakness in our hull integrity with its fangs, we might suffer water leaks. With the pressures of the ocean depth that will be dangerous. The Orka was designed with several safety measures in which we can seal off any area that has been compromised. If we have to do that, you need to get out of the area or you will drown. I won't sacrifice the rest of us because one person was lollygagging behind."

"The Britva love eating meat and they have been known to enjoy humans for food. But if there is a breach in the hull, there are thousands of other species under the ocean floor. Many of them are predators. If you somehow get swept out into the ocean, you most likely will drown or be eaten. Probably both." Nehwal told them. "I only tell you this because the hull breach issue is one that deserves extra caution. Do not be left behind. If we have to seal off an area of this ship, get the hell out."

"Now, when we approach the ocean I will initiate the ski legs of the Orka so that we can surf the top of the ocean and decrease our speed." Regehr continued his Orka initiation speech. "We will dive under the water while going at a speed of approximately sixty kilometers an hour. That is why you must wear your head brace at that moment. Also, the Britva have been known to swim up out of the water to attack its prey. If one of them attacks us, the impact will send the ship out of control. You need to be strapped in."

"Jasna and Zorana got a crash course on how to operate the weapons systems. So, if a Britva strikes us, fire at it without hesitation," Nehwal added.

"I have scanned the computer memory on our craft and found that Admiral Themis is on board an Unter See Boat called the Irkutsk. Captain Drimios is on the Kirov. We can dock with either ship quite easily, if they allow it. My question is which of the two ships do we approach first?" Regehr was speaking as he continued to guide the Orka ship with his right hand on the half-moon steering column and his left hand was typing on the large control panel before him.

"We go to my aunt on the Irkutsk first. My cousin will follow her lead." Elektra said with conviction. "Let's pray to Hera that they agree with our position."

"Well, I downloaded and saved the current events news broadcasts to show to her." Jasna jumped into the conversation.

"They killed all of the flight instructors at the Academy."

"Admiral Seward?" Regehr asked quickly.

"Yes, he is confirmed dead. The cadets that were helping him were shot down over the Forbidden Region. Were they friends of yours?" Jasna asked.

Regehr had a solemn look on his face. Calderon had sent in several of the Bragg Gang members to get to Admiral Seward before the invaders. Based on the news report Jasna was giving to him, they had failed. "Yes. James Cobb, Basil Varek and John Gauthier went in to find the Admiral. They were all some of my best friends."

"Derek, perhaps we should turn back and see if we can locate their wreckage in the Forbidden Region," Arch suggested. "Some of them might still be alive."

Regehr had considered doing just that without Frazier suggesting it. He was silent for a few seconds as he thought it over. "No. We are already approaching the ocean. If we know they crashed, then so do some of the others. The Cobb family is one of the largest on the planet. Most likely they will send out help if they have not done so already. With the loss of the Admiral and the flight instructors, we need to get help from Admiral and Captain Zachariades even more than before. If John were here he would say the same thing."

Elektra had never liked the Cobb family based on their

deep ties to the Bragg Gang. Varek and Gauthier were equally despicable in her mind. But they were all on the same side now. She understood that Regehr was suffering emotionally from the potential loss of three close friends. She knew she would have felt terrible had it been her friends that were the ones that had crashed into those dense forests filled with all those dangerous creatures. The rest of the cadets on the Orka understood Regehr's pain and remained silent for several minutes. Zorana whispered to her sister that anyone in the Forbidden Region without shelter and fire power would be as good as dead.

CHAPTER THREE

Cadet astronaut Basil Varek was left with numerous feelings due to the deaths of all the flight instructors at Clovis Academy. He had looked up to each of them as teachers and mentors. He had learned from them the skills necessary to fly a space craft. He had also learned military discipline and ideas such as loyalty, duty, service and honor. Varek was certain of one thing and that was that the murder of Admiral Seward and the other teachers had no honor in it. It was a barbaric act, one that cried out for vengeance. Varek vowed to himself to seek out those that betrayed Seward and the others and kill them.

But he had another issue to deal with. Several of his closest friends had been shot down over the Forbidden Region. Varek had no idea whether they all died in the crash landing. The idea of loyalty to his friends that Seward had instilled in him kicked in. He had to help them. The Forbidden Region was the term used for all the virgin forest areas of planet New Edinburgh. The large land masses were populated with thousands of species that lived off the basic instincts of breathing, sleeping, breeding and hunting. Those creatures had hunted humans in the past. The original human settlers of the planet had an eighty percent rate of loss of life. The Marines and the Army took on those creatures. They were able to protect the civilians and the colonies on the northern continent were built.

Varek and his family moved to the planet twelve years back. He became a member of a gang and was instant friends with the membership. The Calderon siblings were fated to become some of his closest friends. Varek had watched as many of the Calderon boys rushed in on motorcycles to rescue Admiral Seward and get him to safety. And, sadly, he saw them fail as a sniper from one of the buildings had fired one shot at them. The sniper had taken out Seward with that one laser blast. The Calderon brothers and some other friends of Varek attempted to escape capture from the invading forces by stealing a space craft and getting to a more neutral location. They failed in that task as well. The armed forces loyal to the Glorious Leader shot the stolen ship out of the sky and it plummeted to the surface and crashed in the Forbidden Region.

Varek had spent several minutes trying to contact the pilots of the stolen ship. He was distressed that his com-device calls were not answered by either John Gauthier or James Cobb. Varek was led to believe that his friends were either dead, seriously injured or unable to contact him. Or their predicament could be a combination of all the above. There were several other cadets that were on the stolen ship. He decided that he would attempt to contact them and hope for the best.

He ran down the transparent concrete streets, away from the flight academy sky scraper building where the battle had taken place and toward the cadet landing strip. He could see that there were numerous MI soldiers arriving at that location and interrogating other cadets. Some of the cadets were being hit by the soldiers. Others were being slapped in the face. The situation was out of hand and someone had to do something. The cadets were all losing faith.

Varek still had a laser sniper rifle slung over his shoulder and two laser satchel charges in his back pack that he fully intended to use. He also had a fully charged laser pistol and a twelve-inch-long standard issued military knife. And he was not alone. Running by his side were two other cadet pilots named Franco Vezpucci and Adia Kazembe and a cadet computer technician named June Colan. Vezpucci and Kazembe were armed similarly to Varek as they had fully participated in the attempted rescue of Seward. Like Varek, the two younger cadets were livid at the cowardly way Seward had been killed.

Colan had witnessed the events while working at the sky scraper building, earning Academy credits toward graduation. After living through the battle, Colan decided to stay by Varek's side no matter what. She was not certain who was right or wrong, but Varek had proven to be a competent leader. Plus, she found him attractive and wanted to see if their chance meeting might lead to something more.

Varek counted three solid black Raumschiffs that had landed on the cadet strip. There was just a tad over one hundred MI soldiers interrogating the cadets. He became infuriated when he observed three MI male soldiers tearing the clothing off an attractive cadet engineer. They were slapping her and forcing her to the ground. Varek knew that the soldiers intended to rape the girl. He glanced over to where Seward's body was lying on the landing strip. One of the MI soldiers was laughing to his platoon members and stood over the body. He whipped out his penis and began urinating on Seward's corpse.

"So much for the great Admiral!" The soldier was laughing as he emptied his bladder on the bloody corpse.

"Bastards!" Kazembe hissed.

"Adia, take Franco and save the girl. June, stay close to me. All of you stay away from the closest military Raumschiff. It won't be here much longer." Varek warned them all as he pulled out a laser satchel charge from his back pack.

He had counted no less than thirty cadets being abused by the soldiers. He hoped that an explosion would cause enough of a distraction to free them from further harm.

Varek had always prided himself on his good throwing arm. He had pitched baseball before joining the Academy and had been on the Academy team for three years. He only started twenty-three times and had recorded a record of nineteen wins, two losses and two no decisions and racked up one hundred sixty strike outs. He pulled the cord to the satchel charge and tossed it toward one of the MI solid black Raumschiffs. He pulled Colan close to him and behind one of the "V" shaped Allen Fighter ships. The charge landed on the concrete and slid just under the belly of the large space craft. The explosion was deafening.

The laser charge erupted and sent the Raumschiff several feet into the air, splitting the hull in half. Some of the shrapnel and laser energy spread out and hit a few of the abusive MI soldiers. As the explosion occurred, Vezpucci and Kazembe fired their hand lasers at the three MI soldiers that were attempting to rape the engineering cadet. All three of the soldier's bodies twisted to the concrete with holes in their chests. Kazembe rushed to the naked girl, grabbed her hand and pulled her up to her. The girl was still sobbing and had visible scratches and bruises on her from the beating the men were giving her.

Varek wasted no time. As soon as the satchel charge destroyed the one ship, he began firing his sniper laser rifle at the soldiers. Colan was behind him, with her hands over her ears and closing her eyes. Varek lost count of how many soldiers he killed after the fifth one. He was aiming for them just above the abdomen to ensure that they would be dead within seconds of being hit.

The other cadets that had been slapped and beaten rose. They began tackling the other soldiers and beating them over their heads with closed fists. Some of the cadets were able to wrestle weapons off of the soldiers and use them with deadly force. Other cadets died when the soldiers either shot them at point blank range or stabbed them with their knives. It was a fight to the death and all involved seemed to grasp that grim reality.

Vezpucci recovered a sawed off shot gun laser rifle and began firing laser slivers into crowds of confused soldiers. The majority of them had panicked when Varek's satchel charge erupted. He fired, pumped in another shell, fired and repeated the motions. He killed several dozen soldiers all by himself.

Soon it was over. There was smoke and fire everywhere. The injured and the dying were moaning in agony on the ground. Varek grabbed Colan's left hand and pulled her with him. He found a laser pistol on the ground and handed it to her.

"Use it next time," Varek barked at her.

Colan took the laser in her hand and swallowed. She was terrified that Varek seemed so certain that there would be a next time.

Kazembe gave the female cadet that had narrowly escaped being gang raped a jacket to put on. Kazembe noted that the woman had a great body which was probably why the soldiers decided to rape her as opposed to the other females present.

"Thank you," the girl told Kazembe.

"What is your name?" Kazembe asked her.

"Wanda. Wanda Essex."

"From the Essex family on New Edinburgh?" Kazembe was made aware of the fame of the influential Essex family when she attended her first orientation lecture for the Academy. They had been in the middle of the political campaigns and military expansion of the early history of planet New Edinburgh.

"Yes."

"Well, today was your lucky day," Kazembe said as she walked away from Essex to stand near Varek. Kazembe could not come up with anything to say to a member of a legendary family. As she approached Varek, she could hear him barking at the cadets that had just been rescued.

"These soldiers were criminals!" Varek yelled at the other cadets that were present on the landing strip. "It was right to kill them and it is right for us all to fight back! Take their weapons! Go to the cadet dormitories and free your fellow students! They are being treated badly, just as you all were! Go and help them as we helped you! Go!"

There were approximately twenty cadets that began picking up laser rifles and pistols to do as Varek instructed of them. Some of the cadets were firing laser blasts into the corpses of the already dead or injured MI soldiers on the ground.

Varek turned to Colan, Kazembe, Vezpucci and Essex. He was glad that they had been able to rescue the girl. He smiled at her reassuringly. "I am taking one of these MI ships to the Forbidden Region to find my friends. You are all welcome to share the risk with me or go your own way."

Vezpucci looked at the two remaining ships and pointed at the one that was furthest from them. "I say that one is in better shape. I would be honored to roll the dice with you, Basil."

"Then let's move it!" Varek urged them. His friends were in danger and time was not a luxury when fighting off hungry Dozal or Verburgt.

The five cadets ran up the rear ramp without incident. Varek, Vezpucci and Kazembe were certain that there would be officers on the space ship as they had killed only MI soldiers and no Space Command officers were part of the visible body count. Their speculation proved to be correct. They saw that there were two female Space Command officers standing in the rear loading section with their hands raised over their heads. One was an Ensign and the other a Lieutenant Junior Grade. Varek read their name tags to himself.

"We surrender," Lieutenant Junior Grade Meelia Bonn Nuzzpel announced out loud. "All we did is fly them here. We had nothing to do with the beatings or the rapes."

"We are disgusted by what is happening out there,"

Ensign Kia Marble added as she looked in the direction of Wanda Essex. "We have clean clothing that might fit you in the lockers down the hallway."

Kazembe and Vezpucci searched the two officers and began removing their weapons from their web belts.

"Is there anyone else on board?" Varek asked as he slammed his palm on the red button on the left wall to close the bulkheads and the rear ramp.

"No, we are the only two left," Bonn Nuzzpel answered quickly as she watched Vezpucci remover her laser pistol.

Varek, who was not in a trusting mood, smiled at Colan and Vezpucci. "Search the rest of the ship. Kazembe, bind these two to the metal enlisted soldier's seats on the right wall."

"What should I do?" Wanda Essex asked. She had a flight jacket on which left her buttocks exposed and plenty of cleavage. She seemed to not care that so much of her flesh was showing.

Varek grunted and pointed down the hallway, "Get to the lockers and get dressed. After that come see me in the pilot's section."

"Thank you," Essex said softly as she walked down the hall in search of an outfit. She was just happy that the cruel men that had attacked her did not succeed in raping her. She found that the metal floors of the ship were cold on her bare feet and hoped to find some shoes or, at the bare minimum, some socks.

Varek was already racing up the ramp and toward the ladder leading to the pilot section. He now had a fully stocked Raumschiff with a crew of four cadets to operate the weapons systems. They would be able to mount a defense if necessary unlike the ship Cobb and Gauthier had taken. Varek decided that time was of the essence and did not conduct the normal safety protocols before liftoff. He began typing on the command keys before him as he sat down in the pilot's seat. He could hear the engines rumbling in response to his efforts. Without fastening any safety belts, Varek grabbed the half-moon steering mechanism and moved the large space craft off the long landing pad and up into the sky line.

Varek was flying for less than five minutes when he heard someone climbing up the ladder. He looked to his left to see Wanda Essex join him through the entrance and sit down in the co-pilot seat next to him. She was wearing a skin-tight silver half shirt with a black mini skirt and boots. She had combed her long hair that had been tussled by the soldiers that had attempted to assault her. He had to force himself to take his eyes off her. She was drop dead gorgeous.

"The clothes fit a little tight," Essex stated the obvious. "I don't know how to fly a ship, but I can manage some of the computer stations and weapons controls."

Varek looked into her eyes and quickly concluded that

he wanted her to stay with him. But her talents demanded that she go to the second level. "Go to weapons. Can you operate the laser controls?"

"Yes."

"Good," was all Varek could manage to say when she stood up and descended back down the ladder. He then pressed the intercom buttons on the panels above his head. "Cadet Colan, get on the computer and start scanning the Forbidden Region for any evidence of fire, smoke, explosions or displaced trees or foliage. Let me know immediately if the computer locates anything."

June Colan frowned at that. She had been sitting in the computer command section of the military ship, waiting for him to call for her. She noticed Varek first. He was hers. But now he was calling her cadet and making eyes at the Essex girl that just joined them. Colan felt a tinge of jealousy overcoming her. The Essex girl was a cheap slut in her view. How could Varek like Essex more than her? Colan grinded her teeth together and began typing on the computer pad before her to follow Varek's commands. She would find his friends for him and prove that she was the woman for him. After she found his friends she would search the lockers for a more sexually appealing outfit to demonstrate she is just as, if not more so, worthy for the man than the Essex slut.

Colan glared at Essex as she climbed down the ladder from the pilot section.

CHAPTER FOUR

The oval shaped cadet training ship *Clovis 21* had crashed into the deep jungles of the deadly Forbidden Region. Many cadets had been on board when the military ships fired upon her and blasted her from the sky. The ship and her occupants were left for dead by the military pilots as their conclusion was that if the crash landing did not finish them, then the monstrous creatures on the surface would.

Cadet astronaut Tara Haddad was one of the first to regain here senses after the ship slid to a stop. She was certain that they had crashed into several large trees as the space craft had rolled to a stop. She went about the first order of business which was to help the others with her. She was grateful that the six Calderon brothers were unharmed, awake and alert. The six brothers had been astute enough to strap themselves into the safety harnesses prior to the space craft impacting the surface. Haddad took Manuel Calderon to the pilot section above them and found that Winter Truang, James Cobb and John Gauthier were also alive. They had each experienced some bruising from the impact and subsequent rolling, but nothing serious.

One cadet was dead. She was lying on the second level of the space craft with a large shard of metal impaled through her abdomen. Her name tag read "Chin" and she had the insignia on her shoulder of the weapons program at the academy. Haddad closed the deceased Chin's eyes and wondered if anyone else on the ship had perished in the crash.

Haddad climbed up the ladder to the pilot's section and Gauthier smiled at her. He was sitting in the black leather swivel chief pilot seat. Winter Truang was in the co-pilot chair.

"Tara, check the space craft hull and see if there are any breaches. The computer is indicating that the hull is intact but it is also showing some bizarre inconsistencies." Gauthier spoke as he stood up and began checking the transparent metal observation window before him. He noted that they were facing a vast valley with a tall hill before them. There were no predators in his view, for which he was grateful. But his main concern was what might lie in wait for them over the hill.

"Such as?" Manuel asked.

Gauthier looked at them all with concern evident on his brow. "I was doing a quick safety check to determine if we could lift off again. The computer cannot even give us the correct date, time or year. It cannot even give us basic answers as to solar cell levels, weapons availability or the ambient temperature outside."

"And we asked the computer the same questions several times," Truang chimed in. "It gives us a different response each time. The computer suffered damages to the program in the crash. We cannot trust the readouts."

"Got it," Haddad responded tartly. She understood the stress of the situation. Just one hull breach meant that flesh eating creatures would be able to set upon them all within seconds.

Cadet astronaut LaTania Serpas was not seriously injured. She complained of some dizziness but little else. She had used a strip of clothing to tie her dark dreadlocks back into a pony tail so that it would not obstruct her vision. Her Clovis Academy uniform was torn over her left shoulder and split up the seam of her left leg. She had been on the second level of the space craft at the time of the crash landing. She checked the weapons defense system to determine if they would receive the appropriate warning in case the MI attackers returned to finish them off. She was relieved when the three-dimensional view of the sky above revealed only orange and yellow skies and some deep purple clouds forming to the east.

"There were seven or eight others in the lower level," Xavier Calderon reminded everyone of the engineering students and computer technician candidates that had joined them on what he believed to be a doomed flight. Haddad sensed that Xavier was filled with distress in relation to their present predicament. She placed her hand over his shoulder and squeezed it in a reassuring manner.

Haddad drew her laser pistol as she walked away from Xavier. It was odd that the other cadets had failed to check in. The computer system had not detected any hull breaches so Haddad hoped that they would be safe for the time being. "Let's go."

She led the six black and red leather clad Calderon brothers and Serpas down the ramp from the second level of the ship to the lower level. The emergency lighting had flickered on and was a bright red color. There was grey and black smoke that grew thicker as they descended. Pepito Calderon threw a glow light down the ramp which lit up the area through the smoke. They could see that there was a fire in the back-storage area. Serpas and Juanito Calderon found fire extinguishers on the wall and began spraying the white foam on the flames. Serpas coughed from the smoke that she inhaled into her lungs. She wanted to order the ship computer to open the vents, but recalled that even the smallest insects in the Forbidden region could be deadly. One bite from some of them would send the average human into anaphylactic shock at best while others would cause an immediate reaction that could include flesh being melted off the body.

Haddad led the others down the hallway toward the rooms that had the engineering, sleeping quarters, showers, gymnasium and medical sections. They found that the other seven cadets were slowly getting to their feet. Some of them were coughing. The only one that Haddad knew by name was Leeanne David, an engineering student.

Haddad helped her to her feet. "You alright?"

David nodded and wiped a small trace of blood from her forehead. Her bottom lip had a gash in it and was bleeding. "What hit us?"

Manuel handed David a white handkerchief so that she could wipe the blood from her bottom lip. She smiled at him for the act of kindness.

"Rockets from the rear. I think our engines are damaged." Haddad watched as the Calderon brothers helped the other six female cadets to their feet. She noticed that Pepito seemed to know the names of the three computer sciences students. The girl named Barbara was hugging Pepito as she wept.

Haddad turned her attention back to David. "Do you think you and your friends there can fix it?"

"We need to see what it is before I can answer that one," David responded as she coughed some more.

"Leeanne!" Engineering cadet Nikki Blomquist blurted out as she pointed to the floor. She was moving her long silver hair from her face and blinking in disbelief as she looked down. She has a full head of long silver hair over her clear, white skin with light blue streaks in the pigmentation. Her lips were natural dark blue as were her eyes due to her being born and raised as a third-generation member of a colony on an ice moon. Her childhood had been in underwater dwellings of dark water covered with ice. All of the offspring on her home world had the mixture of blue in their skin color, which many scientists believed to be a human adaption to survive the environment that they lived in. She was wearing a purple half shirt that had the Clovis Academy logo etched on it in gold letters and white shorts with purple tennis shoes. She was allowed to dress differently due to her need to be cool at all times. Blomquist had a twin sister back at the Academy and it was well known that they frequently took baths in tubs of ice water. Her vision was far better than the average human and she could see perfectly in the dark. "I saw purple sand in the engine room! We have a hull breach!"

Haddad glanced over at Pepito. He had his arms around the computer student named Barbara and was comforting her. "You got any more of those glow sticks?"

Pepito moved his left arm from around Barbara's back, nodded and pulled one out of his pocket. He twisted it and threw it to the ground. Everyone took in a deep breath as they saw that Blomquist had spoken the truth. There was a gaping hole in the bottom of the space craft. The light purple sand of the planet surface was evident.

"It must have split on impact," David speculated. "The trees we hit weren't thick enough to cause that much damage."

"Everyone get out of here! I am going to seal off the room!" Haddad barked. Her biggest fear was that one of those disgusting large worms would pop up through the breach and pull one of them underground for a meal.

"But this is the engine room! We need access to it if we are to obtain the tools necessary to fix the outside engine," Cadet Fara Kiesbye protested.

"I am the fuck out of here," computer technician student Dominique Raklitz declared as she stormed out of the room with engineering cadet Nina Eklund right on her heels.

All the cadets, save Fara Kiesbye, began leaving the room through the only exit. Kiesbye began to search the far wall for tool kits. She found a large red and black tool kit that was three feet long, two feet wide and two feet deep. Kiesbye opened it and inspected the contents.

"This one has a blow torch, solar powered screw driver set, magnetizers and some other useful gear that we will need to fix the damages." Kiesbye closed the kit and secured the lid. She grabbed it by the handle on the top and began walking for the exit. Leeanne David was waving at her to walk faster.

"Fara, hurry up! We have to seal this off!" David was raising her voice at her.

Kiesbye handed the tool kit to David. "Here, take this one. There's one more on the back shelf. I will be right back."

"Fara! No! We have to go," David yelled as Kiesbye walked back toward the other toolkit.

Haddad heard the commotion behind her and turned around to see David standing in the doorway holding a large tool kit in her right hand.

"Leeanne! What is the hold up?" Haddad demanded as she began walking back toward the engine room. In the smoke-filled hall lit by the red emergency lights, Haddad swore she saw movement on the ceiling of the hallway about twenty feet from the engine room entrance. She aimed her laser pistol upwards and squinted her eyes. She did not see any further movement. Perhaps she was seeing things, she thought to herself.

Kiesbye retrieved the second tool kit and lifted it up into her arms as it was too heavy for her to carry with one hand like she had the first kit. She failed to recognize that the purple sand on the floor of the ship was moving when she stepped over it. As she began walking back to David she was smiling. "Leeanne, you are always such a worry wart. If there was something in the ship with us it would have attacked already."

A thin brown leg, only about two feet long and an inch and a half thick, with small hair follicles all over it pushed through the purple sand. It had no foot at the end. A second and third similar leg followed just before the head of a brown sand spider stuck its head above the purple granules. The dark eyes scanned the room and stopped when it saw the human female standing nearby.

"Can we go now, Fara?" David asked.

Kiesbye did not get the opportunity to respond. Several three-foot-long sand spiders began pushing through the purple sand. Two of the spiders were brown with poisonous stingers on the ends of their eight legs. The third spider was dark purple. Their long fangs and rear sharp stinger were dripping with deadly venom. Their eyes were black and seemed to reflect their prey in them. Kiesbye did not see her death coming. The two brown spiders leaped onto her back. One of them impaled her with its hind rear stinger. Kiesbye screamed in pain just before the second brown spider sunk its fangs into her supple neck. Kiesbye dropped the second tool kit to the floor as the poison entered her body. The first stinger from the first spider was protruding out Kiebye's chest. Leeanne David screamed as she watched her friend fall to her knees as the spiders began to spit out a cotton substance to cocoon her for a later meal.

David turned to run but the purple spider leaped several feet into the air and landed on her back. David's eyes were wide with fear as she dropped the large tool kit and reached out with her left hand to the charging Tara Haddad. "Help me!"

Haddad tried to get a good aim at the spider with her

laser pistol as David screamed. The spider's rear stinger penetrated David's back and out through her chest. Haddad stopped running and grimaced at the sight of the poor girl suffering the fatal wound. Haddad grabbed for the tool kit as David screamed again as the purple predator sank its sharp fangs into her right shoulder. Haddad could see herself in the reflection of the cold black eyes of the purple spider. David was screaming in pain and some blood mixed with a thick yellow liquid was spewing from her mouth. Haddad began dragging the tool kit backwards as Manuel Calderon showed up to help her.

"There's more on the ceiling!" Computer technician cadet Barbara Villandiego warned them from the hallway door, pointing upward.

LaTania Serpas and Pepito Calderon began firing at the ceiling with their laser pistols. Several hideous looking giant spiders began falling to the floor, their legs twitching. One large black spider fell from the ceiling and slammed on Haddad's back. She screamed and batted it off her with her left arm. She felt as if she was about to have a heart attack at that moment. She took a deep breath when she realized that the large spider had been dead before it landed on her back. She saw that it was lying upside down with its' eight long legs in the air. As Serpas and Pepito provided laser fire cover for them, Haddad and Manuel continued their escape. Down the far end of the hall there were more shadows rushing toward them. Haddad deduced it was more of the deadly spiders. She barked at the others to seal the corridor off to avoid any further loss of life.

Haddad and Manuel pulled the second tool kit out as Juanito Calderon sealed the hallway doors behind them, leaving behind numerous sand spiders and the corpses of David and Kiesbye. As the door sealed they could still hear David pleading for help. Her voice was soon silenced by the sealing of the large metal doorway.

Haddad noticed that Xavier, Jose and Jorge Calderon were looking up at the ceiling of the loading bay of the space craft with their laser rifles aimed upward. Neither of them detected any other large spiders on the ceiling.

"Why didn't the damn computer detect those things?" Manuel demanded.

"The computer was damaged in the crash. Or the rocket explosion might have done something more to the wiring of the ship that prohibited any kind of computer analysis of the hull integrity." Cadet Maria Haake responded, attempting to be helpful. Her voice was stammering due to her shock at witnessing two of her friends killed in such a horrific manner.

The other two engineering cadets, Nikki Blomquist and Nina Eklund were in tears over the death of their two friends. Haddad had little patience for their hysterics. She pointed at the large tool kits. "Your friends died making sure we would have these tools. Inventory them so we can determine if we have what we need to repair the damage to this thing and get out of here."

Eklund nodded and opened the tool kit and began looking over the contents.

"If those spiders got in through that hull breach, what else could get through?" Serpas asked out loud in the direction of Haddad and Manuel.

"Deadly insects, poisonous worms, even a Dozal could find a way through that hull damage." Manuel informed her. "We need to burn that hallway and the engine station along with the medical area. Right now, those things will be putting a cocoon around the bodies of Kiesbye and David so that purple spider can plant eggs inside of them. When those eggs hatch they will produce about fifty or more newborn spiders. My guess is that David is still alive. Those younglings will eat her alive. We have to torch the area."

"You are talking about our friends!" Blomquist yelled at him.

Manuel sighed and walked over to the woman. He looked her in the eyes for a moment and then put his hands on her shoulders. "Yes, I am speaking of your friends. Either we make sure they have quick deaths or those spiders will give them long painful deaths. Do you want those two girls to suffer any further? Do you?"

Blomquist looked at the floor of the ship and shook her

head side to side. "No."

"All right, listen up!" Haddad bellowed. "I need for each of the computer majors to see if you can repair the malfunction to the computers. We lost two because of it. I don't want any more deaths. Get to it. After that is done I want a diagnostic on the damage to the space craft and an estimate of what time frame we are looking at to repair it."

Serpas holstered her laser pistol and walked over to Haddad. "Sorry about that large spider. It was getting ready to jump on you. I had to shoot it down."

"Scared the crap out of me." Haddad laughed. "Thanks for saving my life."

"My pleasure."

Winter Truang stayed in the pilot section with James Cobb and John Gauthier as they were working the computer panels to determine their location and what possible damages they might have to face. As the two men were conversing, Truang screamed out loud and backed up against the wall. She was shaking with fear and pointing at the transparent metal observation window before them. Cobb and Gauthier looked in the direction that she was pointing and saw that a muscular seven-foot-long black and white furred Dozal was on the front of the Raumschiff, gazing into the window and hissing. It was bearing its' large fangs at them as it paced back and forth. At one point, it jumped onto the window and began clawing at it with all fours. Truang screamed again.

"Winter calm down," Gauthier told her. "Those windows are one way. It cannot see you. It cannot smell you. It is only curious as to why this ship is here."

Truang grunted as she observed the cat like Dozal glaring through the window in her direction. "Can't see me? Really? That thing is looking right at me."

"I sent out an S.O.S. to Reynita, Zoe, Brett and Basil." Cobb informed them, ignoring Truang's angst. "I hope one of them respond to us. Otherwise we may very well be trapped here. At least we have enough food to last a few months in the lower level."

Haddad climbed up the ladder and heard Cobb's comment. She stuck her head through the entrance. "Forget the food reserves. That entire section has been overrun by sand spiders. They killed two of our engineers before we could seal the hall door. Manuel wants to burn them."

"Shit!" Cobb slammed his fist on the computer panel when he processed the news. The engineering cadets were their most valuable cargo if they hoped to successfully repair the damage and escape the Forbidden Region. "So, if we can't fix this ship and no rescue comes for us then we have to move out on foot?"

Gauthier looked at each of the cadet pilots, "Yes, James.

That is exactly right."

Truang looked at the menacing Dozal on the hull of the ship. "Then we're all dead."

"No, we can incinerate the spiders in the lower level and use the blow torches to fix the hull breach." Haddad informed them. "Once we do that we secure the lower level and use sheet metal to patch repair the hull."

Cobb grunted at that suggestion, "So we kill the spiders inside the ship. Great. What's to stop more from coming in through the hull breach after we kill the ones in here by fire? Your plan sounds like we would just be spinning our wheels."

"What does spinning our wheels mean?" Truang asked.

The others ignored her question.

"We send in just four of us in enviro-suits. Two to shoot anything that comes through the hole. The other two to seal the breach," Haddad told them.

"That is just crazy talk," Cobb scoffed at her suggestion.

"I will be one of the ones to go," Haddad volunteered. "Manuel and Pepito already told me they would do it. We'll take one of the engineering girls and we can get this done. If we succeed, then we save the food reserves and retake the engine room."

"No way, Haddad. You are out of your mind." Cobb was pointing his index finger in her face as he challenged her.

"Those spiders are predators. If they get through the hull and kill the four of you then our numbers are depleted and our ability to fight back lessens. We should plan on going to the nearest major population center which is Lynott's Land only fifty-eight kilometers from our current position."

"That plan is even worse than mine!" Haddad was now in Cobb's face, stabbing her right index finger into his chest. "How many of those Dozal are out there? They run faster than humans and would be on us feasting within five minutes of us stepping foot off the ship. And the bodies of water we passed when we were flying have those Great Lakes Crocs that can smell human flesh. And fortunately, none of the Verburgt have come knocking on our door yet. Those giant tails of theirs could do major damage to the ship and force us outside. We have to repair the damages and get out of here."

Gauthier put his hand on Cobb's shoulder and shushed him. "James, Tara is right. We must repair the breach so we have control of the engine room and the food reserves again. Then we can have our engineer students and the Calderon brothers repair the back-thruster damages. Since no one is answering our pleas for help we are on our own. We have to think smart if we are all going to survive this. The smart play is repair this ship and fly out of the danger zone. So, Tara is correct. We fix the hull damage and then we repair the engine propulsion system. After we accomplish those tasks, we make haste for Lynott's Land."

Cobb glared at Gauthier for a few moments before responding. "Fine, do what you want. I'll stay here and keep trying to raise help."

"Tara, stay here and take charge." Gauthier checked his laser pistol energy level. "I'll go in with the others to fix the breach."

"You're putting her in charge?" Cobb challenged him.

"Yes. She has the most level head of anyone else on this ship." Gauthier glared at Cobb for daring to criticize Haddad. "So, until I return, Tara makes all of the decisions. Got it, old friend?"

Cobb nodded in agreement and sat down in the pilot seat. He was clearly angry but said nothing else as Gauthier climbed down the ladder. He saw that Manuel and Pepito were already in enviro-suits. They were both armed with laser rifles, which were slung over their shoulders, and laser pistols strapped to the white web belts around their waists. Nikki Blomquist was also in an enviro-suit with a back pack slung over her right shoulder. Inside the pack were a hand-held blow torch and other tools.

"I cannot stay in this enviro-suit for long," Blomquist told them. "I need to keep my body temperature low and these suits do not allow for me to properly cool my skin. So, I will need some breaks to cool off."

"Understood," Gauthier told her. "Just let us know when you need a rest."

"Where's Tara?" Manuel asked.

"I am going in her place," Gauthier informed them and walked over to one of the lockers in the hexagon shaped control room. He pulled out an enviro-suit and began dressing. "Who is going to burn those critters in the lower level?"

Maria Haake heard the question from the adjoining computer room. She pushed her light blue rolling chair back away from the large computer panel she was sitting in front of and rolled to the connecting doorway between the two rooms. "That would be me. I found some damage to the computer but the security fire mechanisms down below will work. I will get them all for you before you go in."

"All right then," Gauthier was connecting the gloves to the sleeves of the space suit. He smiled at Haake and realized he had never met her before. She was plump, had blonde hair with blue eyes and an interesting accent. He hoped that he would have the opportunity later to get to know the girl better later. "Let's get this show on the road. What is your name?"

"Maria Haake."

"Nice to meet you. Burn those arachnids in five minutes. Let the fires burn for about two minutes then douse them." Gauthier picked up a transparent metal helmet and placed it over his head and connected it to the neck of the suit. "You all ready?"

"Ready," Blomquist said nervously.

Sensing that she was apprehensive, Gauthier turned in her direction. "Nikki, you let Manuel and I clear the hall before you come in. Stay close to Pepito and don't leave his side for any reason. You are the most important participant in this task, so we are going to protect you with our lives. You understand me?"

Blomquist nodded and pulled the visor of the helmet over her face. Somehow Gauthier's tone of voice calmed her nerves. "Yes sir."

Gauthier led them down the ramp to the loser level. They stood at the door to the hallway that led to the engine room, medical facilities, cryogenic-sleep tube section, food reserves section and the sleeping quarters.

Manuel looked through the observation window of the thick metal door that separated them from the spiders on the other side. He could see several dozen of the sand spiders on the ceiling, the walls and the floor. They were all brown save the purple one that was on top of Leeanne Davis. It was moving up and down on Davis, as if it were having intercourse with her. Manuel speculated that the purple spider was implanting eggs of babies inside Davis so that the newborn could feat on her body when born. He recalled his uncle and father telling him that the spiders would plant their eggs inside the carcass of a person or other animal so their hatchlings could immediately feed after birth. Davis was still alive. She was moaning in pain. Her arms and legs were stuck to the metal floor by thick webbing that the spiders must have spun over her to keep her from moving while the purple spider conducted business.

"Your suffering will soon end," Manuel whispered to himself as he looked at David. He wished that they could do something to save the girl but he knew it was not possible. Once some of those spider eggs were implanted in a body it would take the most gifted of surgeons to safely remove them. The one thing that their marooned troop was missing was a doctor. The best thing for her was to die quickly in the fire.

Like clockwork, Haake had the security system operate the torches that were hidden in the ceilings and the walls of the lower level hallway. The flames burst into the rooms and hall incinerating the spiders. Manuel observed them running in circles as if they were searching for some salivation from the searing heat in some corner. But the flames engulfed every square inch of the hall. The spiders made a high pitched shriek as they burned. The purple spider tried to run from the flames toward the engine room. Manuel wondered if the creature was attempting to escape through the hole it had entered the ship from. David mercifully passed as the flames engulfed her body. She screamed for a second before she succumbed to the intense flames. Her flesh melted away along with the spider eggs that were inside of her. The spiders in the engine room also perished. There were others in the individual sleeping quarters that died as the fire took them. Soon the ship was free from any living sand spiders. The flames began to subside.

"It's done," Manuel told Gauthier.

"Let's go. I'll take point. Pepito, you bring up the rear with Nikki. Watch her like a hawk." Gauthier had a laser rifle in one hand a laser pistol in the other. He nodded to Manuel who ordered the computer to open the door.

The hallway door slid open to reveal steam due to the ceiling spouts that were spraying water onto the fire. There was smoke everywhere as Gauthier rushed inside. He moved down the hall and stepped past the charred skeleton of Davis. He found the engine room and looked up and down before stepping inside. There were about fifteen burned spider bodies around the room. He moved inside followed closely by Manuel. Blomquist and Pepito were soon in the room with them. Manuel had gone to the racks of supplies in the engine room. He located a sheet of light metal that he slid on top of the purple sand and smiled. The sheet metal covered the gap in the hull. Pepito found a blow torch and stood on the other side of the sheet metal from Blomquist. The two began to melt the sides into the floor of the engine room. Manuel and Gauthier kept guard as the two worked.

When they were about halfway finished with the task,

something underneath the metal sheet was pushing on it and making an angry shrieking noise. Manuel saw the sheet lifting so he stood on top of it, hoping his weight would keep the creature below from being able to gain access. Blomquist was used her hand-held blow torch with precision. She was faster that Pepito with the tool and finished her half before him. She kept working on his side so that they could finish and recover the food reserves. She screamed when she saw one of the arms of a spider pushing through the side. Gauthier stepped on the leg and fired his laser pistol at it, severing the limb from the spider.

The metal was soon bonded and the hole was covered. The entire job took twenty minutes.

Gauthier removed the helmet form his suit. He walked over to the southernmost position of the engine room and found the ship wide communication system. He pressed the red metal button and addressed the others on board. "Good job, people. Maria, has the computer detected any other movement down here other than us?"

"No, we got them all," Haake assured him from her seat in the rectangular shaped computer room. "Barb, 'Nique and I repaired the damage to the computer system while you were down below. We should have complete online computer integration within the hour."

"Hull breach is repaired," Gauthier told them.

Blomquist pulled her helmet off and was smiling from

the relief she felt. She had been terrified that the spiders would get them. She realized for the first time since the crash landing she was breathing normally. Jorge Calderon offered her a tall glass of ice water which she drank like a college fraternity boy would chug a pitcher of beer. She handed the glass back to Jorge and winked at him. Jorge was the only one that seemed to care about her physical needs.

Up above on the second floor and the upper level pilot section, the others were celebrating the success. Everyone was exchanging hugs and high fives except for Nina Eklund. She was sitting in a chair in the weapons section, crying. All she could think about was her two dead friends, Fara and Leeanne.

CHAPTER FIVE

Basil Varek flew his stolen space craft toward a set of coordinates given to him by June Colan. Her scans of the planet surface revealed a possible crash site in the Forbidden Region near the western coast line. He hit a speed of five hundred thousand kilometers an hour and arrived at the location quickly. He desperately hoped that the crashed ship was the one his friends Gauthier. Cobb and the Calderon brothers had been aboard. Varek had the computer place the ship at full stop and hovered sixty feet above the surface of the location.

"Computer, magnify the area below." Varek ordered.

The screen before him enlarged and he could see clear evidence of a rectangular shaped space craft that had crashed in that location. There was evidence of the first impact of the crashed ship in an area of dense eighty-foot-tall multicolored trees, split and crushed from the impact of the metallic craft. Varek concluded that the crashed ship impacted the surface and slid for several thousand feet based on the tress that were crushed under the impact. His eyes followed the line of splintered trees and purple sand that had been parted by the craft.

"Computer, please scan the space craft below," Varek requested. "Confirm that it is the cadet space craft that was commandeered by Gauthier."

"Negative," the computerized voice responded. "The ship below is a civilian transport Raumschiff. Ownership of the craft cannot be confirmed as the serial numbers have been wiped from the hull in the impact from the crash landing."

Varek cursed when he gazed down at the ship on the surface and confirmed visually that it was a red-yellow color mixture civilian transport ship.

"It isn't them?" Vezpucci asked. He had been silently sitting as his co-pilot on the flight. He had been drawn into committing treason when he opted to help rescue Admiral Seward. The attempt failed with Seward's death. Since then, Vezpucci had decided to follow Varek where ever he would lead him to.

"No, dammit." Varek's voice was full of despair. "Computer, scan the wreckage below. Are there any signs of life?"

"There are numerous life signs down there," Colan reported as she climbed up the ladder. "I already scanned it. There are two dozen Dozal, some Tree Spiders within the radius of the craft and inside the ship are thirty civilians. The ship was a private transport that left Clovis City in a hurry. It failed to make the proper security code clearances. Computer scans indicate that the solar engine malfunctioned and the ship crashed here. There are thirteen dead bodies inside."

Adia Kazembe, who had been listening to the discussion by way of ship wide intercom, decided to add her thoughts. "We are going to help those people down there, aren't we? They are surrounded by all those creatures. They can't hold out forever."

Colan nodded in agreement, "We should rescue them."

Wanda Essex, sitting in the second-floor weapons section of the military style Raumschiff, and listened intently to the discussion. "I vote we save them. I can stun all those Dozal and Tree Spiders from here."

Marble and Nuzzpel were bound with their hands behind their backs on the metal chairs in the lower level of the ship. But through the intercom they heard what was being said. Even though they were prisoners of Varek and his fellow cadets, the two women were not the sort to turn their backs on civilians in need. Their desire to escape Varek would have to wait until after the civilians below were saved.

"If you attempt a rescue you will need our help." Nuzzpel called out from the third floor of the space craft. Her wrists were bound by an electrical wire to the side wall. If she attempted to free herself, she would receive an electrical shock that might be terminal. She dared not try. "We can go down there and cover the civilians as we get them from the wrecked ship to this one."

Varek cursed again and ordered the computer to cut the intercom off to the lower level. He had momentarily forgotten that they had prisoners. Although his number one goal was to locate and rescue his missing friends, he could not turn his back on civilians at risk.

"They could help," Kazembe added. "There are only five of us. Two more sets of hands won't hurt."

"And they would be foolish to try to escape here," Vezpucci stated the obvious. "This area of the Forbidden Region is full of carnivores. We are also so close to the ocean and there are sure to be some giant creatures around looking for food."

Varek pinched his nose with his index finger and thumb. He did not want to delay finding his friends Cobb and Gauthier. But he could not abandon people in danger.

"Basil? What are we going to do?" Colan prompted him. "We could leave them and come back after we find your friends."

"No," Varek said after a few seconds of soul searching. "No. We don't leave anyone behind. Adia, release the two pilots below and arm them. Wanda, get ready to stun all those flesh eaters down there. I am going to land as close to the transport ship as possible. When I do, I want the two officers to go with

Franco and Adia to escort those civilians out of there. Get all thirty and do it quickly."

"Yes sir," Vezpucci smiled as he stood from his seat.

"What do I do?" Colan asked.

"Help down below, June. You need to get us an accurate head count as the civilians come on the ship," Varek ordered her. "Wanda, use the weapons section scanners to keep watch for Cawlers or other flesh eating creatures. We will be relying on you to protect our rears."

Essex approached Marble and Nuzzpel with a pair of large clippers. The two pilots became alarmed at the sight of the lovely woman holding such a weapon in her hand. They wondered if she was coming for some revenge on them for the attempt by the MI soldiers to rape her. To their relief, Essex used the clippers to cut the plastic ties from their hands and legs.

"We have to trust the two of you," Essex told them. "We are going to try to rescue those people below. Our computer scans indicate that the ship is a civilian transport and there are survivors inside. No telling if they have any weapons or how much food or water they have left to sustain them."

"What do you want us to do?" Marble asked.

"We are landing next to the ship. Varek is trying to contact the occupants to let them know we are coming. Once we get the civilians out of their transport we will run them over here.

I will get rid of the creatures, but be careful. There could be others nearby and they run and fly fast." Essex dropped the clippers on the metal floor as she walked toward the ramp to take her seat back in the weapons section. "Thanks for volunteering."

"You're welcome," Nuzzpel said as Kazembe and Vezpucci ran down the ramp and faced them.

"I see she already told you what we are doing," Kazembe said as she tossed Marble a hand laser.

The two officers nodded. Vezpucci handed a laser pistol to Nuzzpel.

The four waited as Varek landed the space craft. Once the ship touched ground, Essex sent out a three-hundred-foot radius stun blast from the weapons section. All of the Dozal in that area fell to the ground without even a scream. The weapon had done as expected, neutralizing the brain waves of the giant creatures to include their nerve endings. Many Tree Spiders fell to the purple ground as well. After scanning the grounds that were around the crashed transport, Essex announced that the coast was clear.

Kazembe ordered the ship computer to open the rear loading bay doors and lower the walk ramp. The four brave souls waited as the ramp hit the ground revealing multicolored trees and vegetation over the purple sand. Vezpucci ran out first with a laser rifle in his hands. He looked up and motioned for the others to follow. Varek landed the ship about fifty feet from the wreckage.   The two cadets and two officers ran as fast as they could to the ship. When they reached the rear of the craft, Vezpucci used his personal holographic-communication device to contact Varek,

"Any response from them?"

"None!" Varek responded as he inspected an older model Fenster Corporation brand double barreled laser rifle to ensure that it was loaded. He was concerned that the lithium based laser cartridge might overheat or explode as they did from time to time in the older laser weapons. "They might be unconscious or their communication system on the ship was damaged in the crash."

Kazembe began attempting to hack into the transport's computer system using a small hand held computer. She attached thin wires to the hull of the ship and began speaking commands into the computer. Marble and Nuzzpel kept staring into the sky, wary of Cawlers swooping in to make one of them dinner. Colan watched from the back of the Raumschiff as the four were attempting access to the ship.

After what seemed to be an eternity, the back doors of the ship opened. The four rescuers expected to be welcomed as heroic saviors. Instead they received a rude awakening. Nuzzpel took a point-blank range laser blast to her chest. The entry wound was small, but her back was blown out. Her corpse flew backwards to the purple sand covered ground. Marble dived to the side in time to avoid a laser blast fired in her direction. Kazembe and Vezpucci did the same and ran to the side of the ship.

"You won't take us like you did the Goldsmith's and Wyclyffe's!" a desperate sounding, male voice was screaming from the inside of the wreckage.

"We're here to help!" Kazembe screamed.

"Fuck you! You're here to finish us off!"

As the standoff was occurring, Essex asked the computer to scan the face and voice patterns of the man that had killed Nuzzpel. She waited for only three seconds. His name was Jason Ward, former United Nations Representative for Clovis City and member of the Security Council. He had a warrant, dead or alive, issued by the military command of New Edinburgh for treason. The warrant wasn't just for him, but for his wives and children. There were sixty-three wanted in all. Essex asked the computer to broadcast the information to Varek and the others.

Upon receiving the computer text on his four-inch-long, three-inch-wide communication device, Vezpucci realized what was happening. The Ward family knew that they were targeted for execution and fled. They crashed here. Seeing that the ship attempting to rescue them is a black MI ship, they feared the worst. That would explain their failure to respond to Varek and Kazembe.

Marble leaned against the right side of the hull of the damaged transport. She turned her head away when she saw a large pink earth worm rise from the ground and wrap around to legs of Nuzzpel's corpse. It began to pull what was left of her carcass under the purple sand. Marble closed her eyes and began to wonder if volunteering to help was worth it. They were untied but now Nuzzpel was dead.

Jason Ward stood back behind the metallic walls of his ship, glancing left and right at the different views from the three-dimensional security cameras. He cursed as he tried to count how many potential assailants might be waiting outside the craft. He had been able to round up most his family when he learned about what happened to Goldsmith. They fled the city but failed to conduct the safety checks on the ship. The engine failed and they crashed landed near the coast. He lost thirteen in the crash, including his two loyal pilots. One of his wives and a son disobeyed his orders and ventured outside to become Dozal food. Ward would not allow his remaining twenty-nine family members to be killed by the Rosenburg's. They would fight to the death.

"Jason Ward!" Vezpucci called out to him. "My name is Franco Vezpucci! I am a cadet at the Clovis Academy!"

"Go fuck yourself Franco!" Ward screamed back, wiping perspiration from his brow on his torn white sleeve. He glanced at his compliment of daughters and sons to see that they all had fear in their eyes. They all looked up to him for leadership and seemed to be unwilling to take any action without his direct command.

"Sir, I am going to throw down my weapon so we can talk!" Vezpucci yelled back to him. "If I walk up the ramp unarmed, will you promise not to shoot me?"

"What are you doing?" Kazembe hissed.

"We got to calm this situation down, Adia. Any minute now this place will be crawling with creatures," Vezpucci whispered to her.

"Yeah? Well that idiot on the transport is crazy!"

"Sir, do we have a deal?" Vezpucci yelled, ignoring Kazembe's last comment.

Ward thought for a few moments and decided to take a chance on the prospect that the person speaking to him might mean them no harm. "Okay. Just you and no weapons!"

Vezpucci quickly pulled off his web belt full of laser pistols and knives. He handed them to Kazembe along with his laser rifle. "Watch my back."

"He is gonna blast you back to hell," Kazembe told him.

"We already are in hell," Vezpucci winked at her.

"Don't say I didn't warn your ass. He's crazy and you are crazier for going in there."

Vezpucci ignored Kazembe's warnings and slowly

walked out into the open with his hands over his head. He began walking up the ramp, his eyes darting up and down. He observed Ward and five women with laser rifles trained on him. As he neared the top of the ramp Ward instructed him to stop.

"Speak!" Ward barked at him.

"Sir, we have a situation here," Vezpucci began. "We are on a rescue mission to find some missing cadets. They tried to save some of their professors from being killed and failed. They crashed somewhere in the Forbidden Region. While we were searching for them, we found you. We are not hunting you and your family. We only stopped to do what we thought to be the right thing and rescue you. That is all."

"You think I am stupid?" Ward yelled at him.

"No sir. I know who you are. You are a very important man back in Clovis City. I read the satellite news reports and I know you always advocated to maximize funding to the Academy. I really appreciate your efforts when it came to policy and education. Sir, look at my clothes. I am a cadet. I am not military. My friends and I just happened to find you here. Please, sir. Come with us before the Cawlers and other creatures start to get closer."

"But you arrived in an MI Raumschiff. You just changed your clothes to fool us. The bitch I blasted had on a Space Command uniform. She was definitely a soldier." Ward's eyes were squinting as he pointed the barrel of his laser at Vezpucci's chest. His voice raised each time he spoke the word "you."

"Yes, she was a service member. She only wanted to help you, sir. She was not MI, not anymore. She changed sides, sir. Just like we have. The MI soldiers have killed many of our friends. We are trying to raise an army to fight back. Please, sir. Come with us so we can get out of the Forbidden Region and to safety." Vezpucci could hear the shrieks of Cawlers in the distance. He felt the primal fear of being ripped apart and eaten taking him over. "Can you hear that sir? That cry from the skies? It's Cawlers. Listen to their loud hunting cry. They are hungry and you know better than me that they love to eat humans."

"He isn't lying to you, daddy," one of his daughters said from the back of the ship. "I just checked him on the computer. He is a cadet at the Academy and he has a warrant for his arrest, just like us. They have film of him killing MI soldiers. And our scanners indicate a huge flock of Cawlers flying in from the north-east. They will be on us in just a matter of minutes. Let him in."

Jason Ward and the others motioned for Vezpucci to enter the ship. He did so as the sounds of the Cawlers were growing louder.

"You really trying to start a war?" Jason Ward demanded of the cadet.

"Yes sir, more like finish it. They drew on us first and

some people I care about are now dead. My friends and I, we intend to win. But right now, I just want to get you and your family out of here to safety. Can we please go before those winged beasts get any closer to our position?"

"In a military ship?" Ward demanded.

"It's all we have, sir."

"Okay, Franco Vezpucci." Ward said and stepped into the light. His face was filled with wrinkles and his eyes looked tired. There was dried blood on his lower left lip and his left cheek had a bruise. "Lead on."

"We are coming out!" Vezpucci warned Marble and Kazembe as he turned around and began to walk down the ramp. He saw in the sky a thick dark mass approaching them at a fast speed. It was a group of Cawlers and they were swooping in for the kill. "Cawlers at one o'clock! Everyone run!"

Vezpucci ran down the ramp and held his right hand out for Kazembe to toss him his laser rifle. He caught it on the run as she joined him at his right side. Both fired into the sky at the cluster of advancing Cawlers. Marble was soon next to them firing at the airborne predators. Several of the Cawlers were struck by their laser blasts and died in midair. Their screams were high pitched. Severed body parts and multicolored twelve-foot-long wings from the creatures fell to the ground.

The surviving members of the Ward family sprinted out

of their damaged ship in the direction of the MI ship. Some of them ran with a limp or cradled an injured arm in the other as they glanced nervously at the sky in the direction of the approaching predators. Each of them was wearing civilian clothing, mostly silvers and blues with dark, knee high boots. Six members of the family were armed with weapons which they put to good use, firing at the sky filled with the winged predators. A dozen more Cawlers dropped out of the pack as they were hit by the laser fire. They spiraled to their deaths on the ground below.

"There's too many!" Marble yelled as she ran.

The Ward family had many young children and grandchildren that had to be carried which slowed the pace of the escape. Colan greeted the first of the Ward family, a pre-teen blonde haired girl with green eyes, onto the ship. "Get into the back and welcome aboard."

The Cawlers were advancing closer. Wanda Essex had claimed a seat in the weapons section of the ship on the second floor. She was surrounded by a three-dimensional view of the sky and the exact locations of the Cawlers that were swooping down at the people on the surface. Essex placed a visor over her eyes which displayed a targeting screen and allowed her to direct the computer to pinpoint the creatures. She ordered the computer to aim the ship laser batteries at the pack of Cawlers and she began firing by using the joystick that was on the computer panel in front of her. The ship laser blasts were designed to penetrate metal hulls of space craft and therefore exacted more damage on the Cawlers than the hand-held laser pistols and rifles. Several Cawlers were vaporized in the air by her shots, some shreds of wings or limbs were spared the blasts and floated to the surface of the planet like snowflakes.

Varek had joined Colan on the rear ramp and was firing his laser rifle into the sky at the creatures. He could make out their large wing spans and menacing sharp claws as they closed in on them. The deaths of the other Cawlers did not dissuade the others. They kept coming.

One Cawler flew in low and avoided being hit. It swooped down on one of Jason Ward's daughter-in-law's and grabbed her shoulders with its sharp claws. It flew back into the air with ease, carrying the screaming woman with it. The woman was begging God to help her as the creature opened its' large jaws and ripped open her neck. As it chewed on her flesh and muscle her pleas ended. Her legs and arms were limp as the Cawler flew higher into the sky to enjoy feasting on her corpse.

One of Ward's sons met a similar fate as he tried to stand his ground while firing a laser rifle into the pack of hungry monsters. The Cawler grabbed him by the top of his skull with its' clawed feet and lifted him into the air. He struggled and dropped his laser rifle as he was airborne. The claws slowly crushed his skull and his brains oozed out of his fractured skull.

His screams and struggling quickly ceased.

"Almost everyone is on the ship!" Kazembe yelled as she heard a growl from behind them. She looked over her shoulder and saw that fifteen multi-colored Dozal were digging their claws into the purple sand and hissing at them. Some of them had a reddish-brown drool dripping from their jaws. The creatures were about forty feet away from them. "Ah, shit! Run!"

The Dozal charged at them. Kazembe pushed Marble forward and Vezpucci turned in time to see the furry four-legged tiger-like creatures moving in for the kill. He fired two blasts with his laser rifle and dropped two Dozal before he turned and ran. He saw that Varek and some of the Ward family were firing at the Cawlers from the ramp of the ship. One of the Ward girls stumbled and fell to the ground. Vezpucci stopped and lifted her up and dragged her toward the rear ramp.

One of Ward's wives stopped running as her injured leg was causing her much discomfort. She was firing at the Dozal as Vezpucci, Marble and Kazembe ran past her, determined to kill as many predators as possible to protect her children. Although she hit many, one of the Dozal leaped into the air and pounced on her. Her screams caused everyone to cringe as the woman was torn to shreds by the sharp claws of the Dozal. Two other Dozal stopped their rapid charge to assist in dismembering the woman.

The Cawlers were able to grab two other Ward members

and sail into the sky as they ripped into their bodies. The screams were echoing in the ears of Kazembe as she leaped onto the rear ramp of the Raumschiff. She ran past Varek and Jason Ward who were both firing their lasers at the approaching creatures. Soon Marble was safely aboard followed by Vezpucci and the Ward girl he rescued from the ground.

Varek counted that five Ward members had become part of the food chain. The rest were safely on the ship. The Dozal were still running at them, several meeting their demise when struck by the deadly laser blasts fired in their direction. Varek yelled for the computer to seal the rear entrance as the creatures closed the distance to the ship. As the bulkheads began to close, one Dozal leaped inside the ship and was ready to leap at Varek. It was snarling and gnashing its' teeth together. Colan fired on the Dozal and it fell to the floor.

The doors slid shut and left several Dozal and Cawlers howling outside the ship.

Jason Ward slid down the left wall and was shaking his head. He was weeping openly over the loss of his five family members. "My wife. They got my last wife."

Vezpucci helped the Ward girl he had carried to safety up on her feet. He found she was not a girl but a grown woman. He marveled at her natural beauty as he considered her face. "You all right?"

"Thanks to you, yes. My name is Jessica Ward." Her hands were shaking from fear and tears were flowing down her lovely cheeks. Her bottom lip was quivering from the near-death experience. She allowed Vezpucci to hold her hands in his, or rather she welcomed the attention her dashing rescuer was paying her. She was wearing a skin-tight silver blouse and dark blue pants with knee high, black boots. Her long blonde hair was restrained by a few twist ties.

"I am happy I saved you, Jessica," he told her as he held her hands in his as if to reassure her that she was safe. He smiled as he looked into her green eyes, thinking that she might be the loveliest woman he had ever met.

Kia Marble glared at Jason Ward from a distance. He had killed her friend. She saw his grief as he wept for his lost family members and found she could not feel sympathy for him. He murdered Meelia. Marble would never forgive him for that.

Varek was already moving toward the ramp leading to the second level of the ship. "Everyone strap yourselves in! Lift off is in one minute. Those Cawlers and our laser fire will most certainly have attracted the attention of the larger creatures. Let's move!"

As everyone began scrambling for places to sit and pull safety harnesses over their shoulders, Colan brought out a cart and pushed the Dozal she had shot onto it. She wheeled it down the back hallway to the room where the cryo-sleep tubes were located. She was elated that all the others assumed that she killed the Dozal. The truth was she stunned it so she could have it for future use. Colan mused that the slut Wanda Essex would make a great meal for the Dozal.

Varek and Marble took the pilot and co-pilot seats of the ship respectively. As they began preparation for lift off, they could see that their greatest fears had become a reality. In the distance there were five Verburgt running in their direction. The large forty to fifty-foot-tall reptilian flesh-eaters made the ground shake as their large legs pounded with each leap. They each made high pitched screams as if to alert other predators to stand aside, claiming the expectant meal as their own.

"I would say to hell with the safety checks," Marble told him as the Verburgt closed the distance between them and the space craft.

"Ditto," Varek agreed and pulled the half-moon steering column to raise the ship sharply. He flew up at a ninety-degree angle which was never recommended unless it was an emergency situation. Varek believed that five hungry Verburgt would qualify as exigent circumstances. Just one of the giant creatures had been known to down a Raumschiff in the past with their strong, long tails. He had the ship accelerate rapidly and shot off into the sky, far out of the reach of the Verburgt.

"That was close," Essex told them. She was standing

behind Marble's chair as she watched the Verburgt fade from view. She watched one of the Verburgt begin to feast on the carcass of a dead Dozal, swallowing it with just two chews.

"Too close," Varek nodded. After watching the deaths of the five Ward family members he was now more determined than ever to find Gauthier and Cobb. The classroom and film can teach how dangerous the creatures of the Forbidden region are. But Varek had never fully appreciated those lessons until now. Seeing them in action up close and personal was the scariest experience of his short life. He looked over at Marble. "I am sorry about your friend."

She only nodded, keeping her thoughts of vengeance against Jason Ward to herself.

CHAPTER SIX

The large control room of Raumschiff *Clovis 21* had all sixteen of her crew members standing around a holographic display of the rear propulsion engines. There were three that allowed the pilot to steer the ship left, right or straight. The right rear propulsion mechanism had been destroyed which left them stranded in the Forbidden Region unless it could be fixed. John Gauthier hoped that the Calderon brothers or the two engineering students might have an answer on how to make the necessary repairs so that they could escape their current predicament.

"No suggestions?" Gauthier prodded them.

"The entire right side is destroyed. We cannot repair it." Nina Eklund shrugged with frustration in her voice.

"Then we need to start walking for Lynott's Land," James Cobb told them all.

An argument erupted with that as some of the other students began yelling obscenities at Cobb, accusing him of having a death wish. Gauthier and Haddad began shouting at the others to shut up. Due to the stress of the situation, the tempers between them all were clearly heightened. Manuel Calderon joined in on the cries for everyone to shut up. After a few tense moments of cursing at one another, the loud cacophony of voices began to decrease.

Gauthier noticed that fifteen-year-old Jorge, the youngest of the sixteen members, had been sitting patiently throughout the entire shouting match with his hand raised in the air as if he were attempting to gain the attention of his teacher at prep-school.

"Yes, Jorge?" Gauthier recognized him.

"Why don't we just remove the right propulsion system altogether and move the central propulsion system over to compensate?" Jorge asked with a meek voice, pointing at the three-dimensional view of the rear portion of the space craft.

There was silence for a few seconds. Blomquist and Eklund gave each other a look as they considered what the young lad had suggested.

"That is brilliant," Eklund finally commented. "We discard the damaged one, move the middle one to its place and you pilots can steer the ship again. It won't be perfect and we will lose about fifty percent of our acceleration ability, but it could work."

Blomquist walked over to Jorge and hugged him. "If you were older I would let you have sex with me."

"I have a birthday coming up soon," Jorge said with a

hopeful tone in his voice.

"Great idea little brother," Manuel said proudly.

Haddad smiled at Gauthier. She could see he was deep in thought over Jorge's idea. "We won't need the speed to get us to the private landing area in Lynott's Land. I think Jorge's plan would get us airborne at the very least. Should we do it?"

Gauthier realized all eyes were on him. He had become the de facto leader of the group based on his status as a cadet senior and his high rank within the corps. He knew that Jorge's idea was the best chance for their survival. He nodded in response to Haddad's question. "Yes. But we do this with the primary focus on safety to everyone out there. We have two engineering students and the amazing Calderon brothers that can do the work. The rest of us will have to act as guards and protect you. How many engineers can be working on the system at a time without stepping one each other's toes?"

"We would need three of us at a time," Eklund answered quickly. "Any more than that would be too many workers."

Gauthier asked the computer to display the surrounding terrain. "We know we have Dozal and Sand Spiders all around us. The Dozal normally travel in packs of twenty to thirty, sometimes packs of over a hundred have been spotted. So, this is what we will do. We send out three to work on the repairs and six lookouts. Nine total. We only work in the day light. As soon as it starts to approach dusk, we quit and come back inside. The lookouts will be posted two on the top of the ship to look for Cawlers and watch for movement in the distance. The other four will stand guard around the workers. If any packs of Dozal or Cawlers start approaching us, engineers get inside immediately and the lookouts follow. Don't take any chances. You get inside right away. Any questions?"

"When do we start?" Manuel asked the question that everyone else wanted to ask.

"First light," Gauthier told them. "Everyone get a good night's sleep. I want everyone rested and alert tomorrow. We already lost two of us to those creatures. No one else dies here. That is an order."

The meeting broke up and the cadets began to find their way to the empty sleeping quarters in the lower level of the Raumschiff. Gauthier mandated that at least on person stay awake at all times and remain in the pilot section, just in case any of the larger monsters that dominated the Forbidden Region showed up out of curiosity. He divided the shifts into four hours and, as any good leader would do, volunteered for the first slot that night.

Gauthier sat alone in the pilot section as the other fifteen were supposed to be asleep. He had the computer memory find some old rock and roll music mixes and play them to keep him awake. Maria Haake had set the three dimensional scanners to broadcast in the pilot cockpit the surrounding area so that Gauthier would be able to observe the surroundings. He had a bottle of energy water in the cup holder on the side of his pilot seat and sipped from it from time to time. He gazed out at the night sky and wondered why none of his friends had responded to their requests for assistance. Certainly Derek Regehr would be under the ocean, as per the orders he had received from Reynita, and unable to respond. But Varek, the Bragg's and Reynita would have received their holographic communications requesting support. As he mulled over that nagging question he heard someone coming up the ladder to the pilot section. He turned his head to see that Tara Haddad was joining him.

She had changed out of her cadet pilot suit into an outfit she found in the sleeping quarters. Gauthier was surprised by what he saw. She had always been conservative in the way she would present herself. But seeing her in a tight yellow tube top with skin tight black jeans and flip flops on her feet was a pleasant change from the girl that normally wore cadet uniforms and baggy civilian clothing. Gauthier had always found her attractive, with her long dark hair and light brown skin. But her uniform covered up her curves. He looked over the fullness of her breasts and her flat stomach and toned buttocks. She sat down next to him in the co-pilot seat with a smile on her face.

"Hope you don't mind a little company," she said softly.

"I couldn't sleep."

"I am glad you are here. I was getting bored," Gauthier admitted.

Haddad noticed that his eyes were looking over her chest area. That was the reaction she had hoped for when she went digging through all of the spare clothes in the empty sleeping quarters. She had never been good at interacting with men pursuant to the laws of attraction since she had always been considered one of the guys. She found the yellow tube top in one room and found that it fit her perfectly. The tight jeans she located in another room. During the times she spent with some of the female cadets they would talk about ways to seduce a man. One of the girls recommended advertising tits and ass to get the man interested. She dressed to follow that advice. She was happy to see that it had Gauthier's attention.

"Anything moving out there?" Haddad asked him with a smile.

"Nothing, thank the Stars. We have been lucky. If we survive this, it will be a miracle." Gauthier found he was smiling at her. He wanted to kiss her and find out how she felt in his arms.

"That is where you are wrong, John. If we live it will be because you kept everyone level headed. If we live it will be because of you." She turned the co-pilot seat on its swivel to face him. She wanted to jump into his arms and be with him. When the large dead spider fell on her back she thought she was dead. That experience left her with the dread of dying without ever being with a man she lusted for. She had men kiss her before, but she had never experienced the feel of a man inside of her and she wanted Gauthier more than any man she had ever been attracted to.

"Well, I appreciate the compliment, but you and Manuel had a lot to do with keeping everyone together." He responded as he looked at her bare shoulders and cleavage. "I don't think I would have been able to do this without you two. You are one amazing woman, Tara."

"You are quite amazing yourself," she could see that his eyes were admiring her body.

"Thank you."

Gauthier wanted to take her into his arms, but worried that an aggressive act by him might spoil the moment they were sharing. He found that not only was she was pleasing to look at, but she was easy to converse with as well. "Tara, why did you get yourself involved in this? I mean, you were never a part of the Bragg or Gorski Gangs, you never interacted with the Evart family or the Gorski brothers. You pretty much kept a low profile the whole two years you have been at the Academy. You are on the Honor Guard and the Fancy Drill Team. You are never late for class; you have done well in your simulator training and weapons proficiency exams. I never heard of your family until I met you. So, I have to conclude you are not personally affected by the recent military crackdown. Why would you care if the Evart's were arrested? Or Piotr Gorski or the Goldsmith's?"

Haddad crossed her arms and pursed her lips as she considered his questions. She gazed out the observation window, taking in the dark sky and the view of the stars above. "Well, first of all, you are right about most of your observations about me. I never said one word to Piotr Gorski. I never went to any of the well-publicized cook outs at the Evart family home. I avoided all the Gang stuff because one of the girls I met at the dorms warned me not to. Her name was Lupita Calderon. When I first came here from Ferro's Province, she took me under her guidance and helped me get into enough extracurricular activities so that I could avoid the hazing and other pitfalls of cadet life. She was my friend, John. When she was killed during the Fenster kidnaping, I knew something was wrong. She was too sweet a person to have enemies. When the attack occurred at her funeral, I was pissed. She deserved a peaceful ceremony and those soldiers showed up, disrupted everything and killed that poor priest. Then Reynita stood up to them and showed the rest of us we didn't have to take their abuse. I knew then that I would do whatever Reynita ordered. The fact that they killed all of our flight instructors and the Admiral pretty much made my decision final. I decided to become a rebel and betray the Royal Family. So how about you, John? Why did you get in the middle of this mess?"

Gauthier thought back to his freshman year at the Academy and his first confrontation with William Bragg and Reynita Calderon. "The Bragg Gang was the most powerful group at the Academy. We had twice the numbers of the Gorski's, maybe even three or four times the numbers. Bill Bragg and Reynita took a liking to me after I fought them. They were not used to the hazing victims to have the balls to fight back. But I did. So they invited me into their group. I joined of course, safety in numbers and all that. We did a lot of things I am not proud of. But all of the members from the Calderon's and Bragg's and Starr's and Cobb's became my closest friends. I suppose we have a few things in common. We are both angry about what happened to Lupita and we are equally enraged about what they did to Seward. I think the other thing we have in common is that we find each other attractive."

"Really?"

"Yes, really."

Haddad crossed her legs and looked out the observation window. She turned back toward Gauthier with a smile on her face. "So, I noticed that Winter has a thing for you. Anything going on there that I should know about?"

Gauthier looked away from her and looked out the window. The question was abrupt and he thought it might end any chance of sex with Haddad if he told her the truth. But if he hid the truth and Haddad became more than a fleeting interest, that lie could cause the end of something special. He didn't want to take chance on possibly losing out on a woman like Haddad, so he told her the truth. "One weekend, Winter and I hooked up. We had sex for three straight days. I think that she read too much into it and thought I was looking for a serious relationship, which I wasn't. So now she tries to get my attention whenever she can. I have purposefully avoided another sexual encounter with her so that she will be able to find someone else and move on. She wasn't the type of personality I was looking for."

"But she is pretty," Haddad probed him.

"Yes, she is. But she is lacking in maturity. I like women that are more confident and sure of themselves. Winter is not like that, at least not yet. In time she might get there. Don't get me wrong, she is a good person. Just wrong for me."

"So what else do you like in a potential breeding partner?"

Gauthier laughed. "Well, a good sense of humor, which you clearly have. I prefer a smart woman that I can spend time talking to. I have dated too many that cannot keep up with me intellectually. I suppose I am too picky which is why I am still single. Enough about me. So what do you like in a man, Tara?

Haddad looked up at the ceiling and thought that her chance had arrived. She looked at him and smiled. "I like you, John Gauthier."

"My friend James likes you."

"But I don't find him attractive. That's why I am here with you right now and not him."

His reaction was what she had hoped for. He reached over to her, wrapped his arms around her and pulled her into his lap. Before she knew it, he was kissing her passionately. She responded by kissing him back. She smiled as he began kissing her long neck and running his hands over her breasts. As he pulled her tube top off she raised her arms in the air so that he could remove it easily. As he began kissing her nipples and leaned her against the computer control panel she reached up to unzip his cadet uniform. He found the zipper on the rear of her jeans and was elated when she did not stop him from pulling it downward.

She leaned back against the control panel and opened her legs to him after he removed her panties. She took his erection in her right hand and guided it for a smooth penetration. She moaned softly as he slowly thrust himself inside of her. She looked into his eyes and softly ran her hands over his forearms as he slowly thrusted himself inside of her, over and over and over again.

As he made love to her on the computer controls she felt him explode inside of her. He then placed her gently on the floor of the pilot section and made love to her a second time. After they had finished, Haddad felt embarrassed that she had given herself to him so quickly. There had been no romance, no candlelight dinners. Just raw lust.

"I can't believe we just did this," she told him quickly. She found that although she had thoroughly enjoyed being with him, she was suddenly embarrassed that she had given her body so easily to him. "I am not like this normally. I never just do this. I mean... I don't know what came over me."

Gauthier kissed her tenderly on the lips as he lifted her up and placed her in his lap and sat in the pilot seat.

"Don't say anything yet. Just listen to me," Gauthier whispered into her ear as he ran his hands up and down her bare back. He kissed her breasts and her neck some more as he spoke. "I am glad that we did this. I want you, Tara. I mean all to myself. I don't want any other man to make love to you. Just me. And I want you in my bed every night. You think you can handle that?"

Haddad was again surprised by the man. She had expected him to move her out of his life as he had Truang. His reputation around campus was that he would sleep with a woman and then leave her. Haddad nodded her head in answering his question. "Yes. Yes, I can do that. I am all yours."

"And I am yours, too." Gauthier said softly.

The couple held each other for the next two hours, looking out at the stars in the sky as they could forget the fact that they may soon be dead.

Haddad and Gauthier were not the only two that shared a night of passion. The stress level that they had all experienced caused many of the cadets to seek out comfort with another. The cadets first began by sharing dinner and a few drinks. The Calderon brothers searched all of the rooms as the others talked. The six brothers returned carrying arms full of metal that they had stolen from a few dozen beds in the private quarters. They slid the rods onto the floor of the kitchen area and began pouring drinks for themselves.

"You boys going to keep us all in suspense or tell us what those metal bed frames are doing on the floor?" Serpas stood and pointed at them.

Manuel walked over to Serpas and put his arm around her. "They are here so that my brothers and I can do our part in protecting you ladies."

Cobb grunted at the obvious pass Manuel was making at Serpas.

"You see my tio and papa fought in the Dinosaur Wars." Manuel continued as he winked at Serpas. "My father got the Medal of Valor for a battle he was involved in. It was a situation like the one we find ourselves in now. He was a squad leader in a Marine Company. They were in a transport that crashed in the Forbidden Region. My father always believed that it had been a setup by some diamond smugglers. The point is, they were about two hundred kilometers from any colony and surrounded by hostile creatures just as we are now. My father told me his company commander, Captain Nikolai Gorski, had them blow up the trees for about a hundred yards around their ship to increase visibility so they could see attacking Dozal or Jumpers easier."

"What has all this got to do with the metal you all spent the last hour gathering up?" Eklund demanded. She was tired and wanted to try to get some sleep even though her nerves would most likely prohibit her from being able to do so.

"Because Captain Gorski knew that their power batteries for their laser weapons could run out and leave them all defenseless. He had the company take the metal frames from the beds, use blow torches to sharpen the ends and make them into spears." Manuel paused and picked up a six-foot-long metal frame piece in his right hand and twirled it around. "My father told me that the Dozal came in vast numbers. The Marines fought them off and drained most of their laser weapons. They didn't lose one soldier. The Jumpers came next and the Marines fought them off with machetes, knives and rods just like these. The third day brought in a new threat, the Dilvianna. The Marines fought them off for eighteen hours. My father told us he killed hundreds using a spear just like this. And in that battle, none of Gorski's Company died. Sure many were injured. Some lost limbs. But they all were alive when General Knox and his rescue mission arrived. It was considered the most inspirational battle of the Dinosaur Wars.   They called my father's unit the Gorski's Bears after that. All of them individually became known as the Dinosaur Hunters."

"So, we sharpen the tips of these things and then what?" Truang asked.

"Then you each have to prepare yourselves mentally to fight for your lives. Because if those Dozal that are out there attack us, they will come at us running at speeds of about fifty to sixty kilometers an hour. If there are more spiders waiting for us, well, you all saw what they can do. The Jumpers, Charzz, Dilvianna, Verburgt and Cawlers will try to kill us with what my tio called 'Jaws and Claws.' We are a part of their food chain just because we invaded their planet. If we want to get out of here alive, we need to become like Gorski's Bears. We need to get vicious and spill a lot of blood. You hesitate to use deadly force then those creatures will kill you. Leeanne and Fara found that out. So, who is ready to cut some metal?" Manuel handed the metal rod in his hand to Truang.

"I'm only nineteen years old," Maria Haake spoke up. "I'm not ready to die yet. I may be a wimpy computer nerd, but I am ready to become a Bear."

The others were nodding in agreement.

"Then let's get some work in," Pepito said.

The cadets worked for two hours using blow torches to sharpen the metal so that they could be used as an offensive weapon. As the time passed, some of the men and women began to pair off and making suggestions that might lead to a night of passion. Manuel had spent the hours working with Serpas and teaching her how to wield the metal rod as a weapon. They flirted and worked and flirted some more.

Serpas eventually succumbed to the seduction of Manuel. Given what they potentially faced in the morning, she did not want to spend what might be her last night alive by herself. She willingly joined Manuel in the room he had selected to sleep in. She smiled as he began kissing her. When he pushed her up against the wall of the sleeping area, she unzipped the front of her cadet uniform, exposing her cleavage and flat, toned stomach. Manuel pulled her uniform down and tore off her brassiere before carrying her to his bed. She laughed as he laid her onto the bed and looked up at him expectantly as he quickly undressed himself. She praised the Stars with a loud yell as he entered her. Serpas moaned with each thrust inside of her and enjoyed the look in Manuel's eyes as he continued to take her. Serpas orgasmed quickly, finding that the manner in which Manuel took charge of her enhanced her sexual desire. She did not care that what they were sharing was a moment of pure, animal lust. It was what they both needed and they fully satisfied one another to the fullest. After making love together she fell asleep in his arms, feeling the safest she had in the last full day.

Pepito Calderon had been in a relationship with Barbara Villandiego at the beginning of the school semester. They had split up for reasons neither one could remember. After finishing with the blow torches, they spent the night in bed and wondered why they had split up in the first place. Despite Gauthier's order for a good night sleep, they spent the night talking, having sex, talking some more and then having more sex. The majority of their conversation centered on the stories Pepito heard from his father and uncle about the Dinosaur Wars. He warned her about several of the species that his father fought. She hung on his every word as if her life might depend on it. In between each story he told her, he would roll her over onto her back and mount her again and again. The couple did not sleep at all.

Truang realized that Gauthier was not interested in her any longer. She was terrified of dying and even more so by being eaten by one of the creatures that were outside of their ship. She had watched some of the others pair off to have sex as if they had no other care in the world. Truang wanted to do the same so that if she died in the morning, she would have had at least one last moment enjoying a man. So she tried her hand at seducing

Cobb. He proved to be amenable to her suggestion that they have sex. He kissed her roughly and unzipped her uniform rapidly. Truang realized immediately that Cobb was not the sort of man that was willing to engage in foreplay. He did not take her to a bed. He maneuvered onto a floor in one of the sleeping quarters, pulled her underwear off and tossed it aside as if it were trash. Truang had been with Gauthier and he was a tender love maker. She had also been with Dominic Andolini, Rolf Rhinehard, Dino Black and two of her flight instructors. Each of the men that had sex with Truang in the past proved to be good lovers to her. They were gentle and made the experience memorable and enjoyable. But Cobb was all about himself. He took Truang for his own pleasure and cared little for her gratification. Although he was willing to bed her, he treated her harshly after he finished. He told her to leave and cursed at her for suggesting that she stay the rest of the night. When she hesitated, Cobb slapped her hard across the face and demanded in a threatening tone that she leave him alone. Truang gathered her clothing and, in tears, she sought out an empty room to sleep in.

Cobb was angry for many reasons. He was angry at his friend Gauthier for taking Haddad away from him. Cobb had told Gauthier many times that he was attracted to Haddad. Cobb tried to get Haddad to stay the night with him many times, only to have her politely refuse his advances. Before his sexual experience with Truang, Cobb followed Haddad from a distance.

He listened as she let Gauthier make love to her. He returned to the lower level of the ship seething with rage. When Truang was there for the taking, he led her to his room. But as he had sex with Truang he pretended in his mind that it was Haddad. The second reason that Cobb was angry was that he had lost his temper and hit Truang. He did not know why he lost his temper in such a manner. He fell asleep thinking that Truang would just get over it.

Juanito found passion in the arms of the computer programmer Haake. For him she was a desirable woman to sleep with. For her she just wanted to be with a man, any man, before the morning came. Her first choice had been Manuel but he had been taken by Serpas. So Haake settled for her second choice. Juanito proved to be a good lover to her and vice versa. In many ways she was a bit surprised that Juanito wanted to be with her. Haake was slightly overweight compared to the much more attractive engineering cadets. Plus, Juanito was handsome enough that he could, in Haake's opinion, choose any girl he wanted. After they had sex together, she felt a bit embarrassed that she gave herself to him. She did not regret it as she enjoyed being with him. But she began to stress over what Juanito would think of her in that she let him bed her so easily. She waited until he fell asleep so that she could sneak away to another room.

Xavier and Jose tried to convince one of the other girls

to sleep with them but failed. Jorge kept being reminded that he was only fifteen. The brothers found separate rooms to sleep in that night.

To Jose's elation, he was later awakened about two in the morning by Dominique Raklitz. She told him she had a change of heart. Standing next to his bed, she undressed for him, smiling as she did so. Once she was completely nude, she crawled into his bed and they began kissing one another softly. She assisted Jose in removing his cadet uniform and began performing oral sex on him. Jose relaxed as she kissed, licked and massaged her bare breasts over his erection. He orgasmed into her mouth and she swallowed every drop. Jose was delighted to have paired up with a woman of such experience in pleasing her man. They spent the next hour exploring each other until they ran out of sexual energy. Jose was surprised to find that Raklitz had many markings on her body. The most eye catching was a large tattoo of a blue and red dragon on her back. She had a number '33' on her left shoulder in black ink and the number '45' on her right. She explained to him that it was done while she was being raised in an orphanage on Sikorsky's Planet. The numbers were so that the orphanage staff could identify her. The Dragon was done by a fellow orphan with much artistic ability. Raklitz did it to scare away the managers and employees of the orphan facility that would come around late at night looking for sex with the abandoned girls. For some reason the girls with tattoos were left alone. She never learned the reason for that dynamic in her home. Jose appreciated her being so honest about her past. The fact that she was able to obtain a position at the Clovis Academy given her difficult childhood was a testament to Raklitz's ability to adapt and survive. He knew she would need that survival instinct in the morning.

Nikki Blomquist and Nina Eklund slept together in the same room. They spent a few hours talking about their fears and hope that Gauthier's plans would work out. The two girls had been roommates at the campus dormitory and became quick friends. Each girl had arrived at Clovis Academy from different worlds and full of dreams for their future. Eklund talked Blomquist out of her idea that perhaps sleeping with the teenage Calderon boy would be acceptable due to what they all faced the next day. They fell asleep in each other's arms to comfort one another from their mutual fear of being eaten by one of the monsters that were outside their space craft.

For each of the cadets, the morning came far too soon.

Gauthier woke up with the red orange glare of the sunlight hitting him in the face through the transparent metal windows of the pilot section. He moved his head and realized that he was in the pilot's seat, nude, with Haddad lying in his lap. She was asleep with her head buried in his chest. He spent a few seconds to look over her slender body with curves in all the right places. He wished he could spend the entire day with her in his arms. But duty called. He gently shook her awake. He was surprised that their replacement for the night watch never relieved them. He was grateful that the night watch had not really been necessary.

"Tara, wake up. Time to get to work."

She stretched her arms and yawned. She opened and closed her eyes several times due to the glare of the sunlight. "How long were we asleep?"

"Too long. We need to get dressed and get to work. The sooner we fix this ship the sooner we can get back to civilization."

The lovers stood up and began looking for their discarded clothing. They dressed quickly. They could hear voices below on the second level. The smell of coffee and breakfast reached them. They both realized they were hungry.

After they had their clothes back on they kissed for a few seconds before descending the ladder to see that Manuel and Serpas had breakfast ready for them. The four exchanged greetings and ate together. Serpas had found some new clothes and was wearing a dark, short sleeved t-shirt, dark red shorts and white tennis shoes that seemed to fit her perfectly. Manuel was wearing a black jump suit that had several pockets on the legs and torso. Gauthier noted that Manuel was wearing the Academy issued black boots. Serpas and Manuel were joking with one another as they filled the large blue and grey metal conference table with metal platters of pancakes, scrambled poggie eggs, bacon, sausage, biscuits and metal pitchers filled with water and juices.

Manuel shook Gauthier's hand, "Breakfast is served, my friends."

"Smells delicious," Haddad remarked with a smile.

They were soon joined by Blomquist and Eklund who were dressed in grey Clovis Academy t-shirts and dark sweat pants that they had found in the clothing lockers in the lower level. The two women were carrying tool kits and had a look on their faces that meant they were ready to get to work. Serpas handed the two girls a fresh cup of coffee as they entered the room.

"There's our stars of the show," Gauthier greeted them. "You two ready to fix this ship?"

"I was born ready," Eklund responded as she sat down to a plate of freshly cooked bacon.

Before anyone could roll their eyes at her at Eklund's sad attempt at humor, the rest of the crew walked up the ramp to join them.

Each of the cadets sat around the table accepting a cup of coffee from Manuel and Serpas. Some of them ate, others were too apprehensive to try or they had no appetite. Gauthier waited until all the crew were settled in seats before he began.

"Good morning. I trust everyone slept well. This is the plan. In one hour, we will begin. We will use the overhead bulkhead entrance to place to sentries on the roof of the ship. They will be armed with sniper laser rifles and laser pistols. Their function will be to keep an eye on the rolling hills to the south for any approaching creatures and watch the sky line for any Cawlers. The Verburgt are the tallest of the known animals here and if they come at us you will see the tops of their heads or their tales over the smaller trees. You will also feel the ground shake as they weigh over a thousand pounds. If you see evidence of either one, send out a distress call to everyone so that we can hide back in the ship. If those creatures are spotted, everyone drops what they are doing and gets into the ship. Understand?" Gauthier waited for everyone to nod that they did.

"Who takes the upper level shift?" Juanito wanted to know.

"I am getting to that. Manuel and Pepito, you will be on the ground level with sawed off laser shotguns, spears, machetes, satchel charges, grenades and laser pistols. Your only job will be to protect Nikki and Nina as they remove the damaged parts and move the central part to replace it. I want James and Juanito to take the left flank on the ground while I will be with Xavier on the right. Jose, you will be with LaTania on the rooftop. Winter and Tara, you will be in the pilot section giving us an extra set of eyes. Barbara, Maria and Dominique, you three will operate our weapons sections and computer surveillance systems. We will be relying on your life sign scans and vibration detections for any signs of trouble. I know I sound like a worried parent, but please keep your eyes open. We all will get out of this alive if we are smart, we keep our heads and we work together."

"What about me?" Jose asked, waiving his hand in the air to catch Gauthier's attention.

"You stay on the ship and be ready to retrieve our used laser charges and recharge them. You will be our weapons quartermaster. You can handle that?"

Jose nodded his head. He was elated that Gauthier chose him for such an important task. "Yes, John. I will make sure we don't run out of charged cartridges. You can count on me."

Juanito had found a pair of dark green sweats and tennis shoes in one of the rooms below. The clothing of the former occupants of the space craft fit him well. He sat down next to Haake and smiled at her. She looked down at her plate of food, ashamed that she had left him alone after they had made love. Juanito noted that Haake had also found some red sweats and white tennis shoes that seemed to fit her. He poured a portion of juice into one of the metal drinking glasses and handed it to her.

"Why did you leave me alone?" Juanito whispered into her ear.

Haake looked him in the yes and shook her head, "I was ashamed. I don't know. I just did. I am sorry."

Juanito took her right hand in his left and smiled at her, "Don't be. I really like you."

Haake smiled, "But I am over weight."

Juanito shrugged, "I like you as you are. Don't run out on me again. Next time I want to wake up next to you."

Haake blushed, "Do you really mean that?"

Juanito nodded, "Absolutely."

Manuel noticed that Raklitz and Jose were sitting close to one another and staring longingly into each other's eyes. Manuel smiled and lightly slapped Serpas on her rear end. She laughed playfully at his display of affection and continued making more coffee for the group. Manuel hoped that with all of the good feelings in the room, everything would work out well for them all.

As the cadets dined on their breakfast the purple sand spider that had been placing her eggs into Leeanne Davis was seething with rage. When the humans had initiated the fire attack, she lost dozens of her children and the unborn that were in the human called Davis. The purple spider narrowly escaped death when the fire rained down on her and her offspring. She had scurried as quickly as she could out the hole in the bottom of the space craft and suffered only minor burns. She wanted vengeance against the humans that had killed her family members and burned her. She and her remaining eighty children waited under the purple sands for the humans to give them another way into their metal ship. She wanted to plant eggs in all of them so that she could begin to repopulate her family.

CHAPTER SEVEN

MI Second Lieutenant Reynita Calderon had committed treason. She shot and killed a fellow officer in front of a thousand witnesses. Even though a huge price would soon be placed for her head, she felt justified in the killing. The officer in question had murdered an innocent priest, a man of peace. Now Reynita was working quickly to put together a team to help her not just avoid capture, but to win a war.

She had selected a group of women cadets and soldiers to go with her to gather a few squadrons of fighter pilots and then an army of fifteen thousand soldiers. Each of the cadets that she had picked to go on the mission had to dress up in military uniforms and pose as MI soldiers. The team of women spent a quarter of an hour finding uniforms that would fit them in the lockers of the basement level in the Clovis City Military Intelligence Building. Corporal Miyu Tamura helped cadets Elsa Regehr, Supreet Patel, Harumi Shigeta Andolini, Jen Staszko, Blossom Li and Melissa Harcourt with boot sizes and uniforms. Tamura ensured that the women looked the part, even giving them enlisted rank stripes on their shoulders and some ribbons to put on their chests. Sara Stewart rounded up the basic military weaponry from the supply rooms to arm the cadets.

As the team members readied themselves, Calderon contacted her father via her hand held Holographic-communication device and told him she loved him. She pled for him to leave the city and go to one of the other provinces for just a little while. She contacted Matthew Rosenburg and asked him how his children were doing. She said good bye to her lover Mark Lund. Then she received the confirmation that Admiral Seward and the entire flight instructor roster had been killed. She sat down in her black leather chair and closed her eyes. She had needed those men and women to lead the cadet pilots into battle. They had been brilliant pilots and tacticians which was probably why the new military leaders killed them all.

Further distressing to her was the news that six of her brothers were shot down over the Forbidden Region along with her close friends James Cobb and John Gauthier. Losing her brothers was enough to make her want to walk away from her plans. Adding Lupita to the tally that made seven siblings that had been killed by the Royal family in a week. She vowed to herself that she would punish those that had taken their lives. She tried her best to put their faces out of her mind so that she could concentrate on the task at hand.

Stewart and Tamura led the cadets up to Reynita's office and presented them to her.

"You all look like real MI soldiers," Reynita

commented. "It is still not too late for any of you to walk away from this. Once we leave, you will become enemies of the State and subject to torture and execution if caught. I do not want to ask any of you to do anything that you are not ready to be held accountable for later. If you stay and come with me, we might all be killed."

"Are you trying to scare us off?" Patel asked.

"The Royal Family has treated my race like lower class scum since our creation," Melissa Harcourt spoke up. "I am tired of being called names, spit on, looked on with contempt and discriminated against. I would rather be dead than spend another day going through that kind of treatment."

"Is that how each of you feel?" Reynita looked at the other women, regarding the look of confidence in their eyes staring back at her.

"I am scared to death," Elsa told her. "But my brother is on a dangerous mission to help us, so I want to try and make him proud. I will do what you order me to do."

While the others were talking, Harumi inspected her samurai sword and slid in back into a blue and red sheath that was slung over her left shoulder before looking back at Reynita. Harumi's husband was out in deep space, where she did not know. Her brother-in-law was serving on the Second Fleet and many of her closest friends were scattered throughout the Eight

Solar Systems. If there was to be a change from the leadership that the Royal Family forced upon them, then one planet had to overthrow them. Harumi was determined that the first planet to cast out the Royal Family would be New Edinburgh. She nodded to indicate that she was ready to fight.

"We're ready. When do we leave?" Staszko asked.

"Right now," Reynita responded.

Reynita had the cadet's dress in solid black fatigues so that they could pass for MI enlisted service women. She also armed them all from her small armory located at her platoon headquarters. She led her team of women to the main landing strip on Clovis City so that they could acquire a ship to take them to the other provinces on the planet. When they arrived they split up and looked for the first vacant Raumschiff.

Reynita found one after only three minutes of looking. It was a grey colored Super Raumschiff that had the name *Comen Mierda* written in red on the sides. Reynita laughed as she read the name. It was perfect. She saw that the rear loading dock ramp was down and there was a lone woman in the back of the ship, taking inventory of some plastic crates that were stacked on the floor of the space craft. Reynita looked over her shoulder and saw that Tamura and Regehr were with her, both only a few steps behind her. Tamura had her sniper laser rifle in her arms, carrying it like she was a mother with a newborn child. Regehr had a laser pistol in her right hand, pointed downwards so that she would not accidentally shoot anyone.

Reynita drew her laser pistol and moved quickly up the metal ramp of the space craft. The woman taking inventory was taken by surprise when she heard the sound of Reynita's boots clanging on the metal ramp. She stopped dictating the inventory to her hand held computer device, saw that three MI soldiers were approaching and immediately put her hands in the air.

By the time Reynita reached the woman, she could hear the footsteps of Tamura and Regehr coming up the ramp.

The woman was trembling. "Por favor! No quiero morir!"

Reynita realized that their black MI uniforms and their swift entry onto the ship had the woman scared to death. She was telling them that she did not want to die. Reynita was grateful that her father and mother forced her to learn more than one language. She decided that it would be best to calm the woman down by speaking to her in her language. "Tranquilo. No quiero molesta te. Cuantos personas contigo en esta astronave?"

The woman looked at Reynita's face and considered the question regarding how many people were on the ship with her. She shook her head.

"Ninguno," Reynita heard her answer. None. The woman was alone. Tamura and Regehr were not fluent in Spanish and had not understood a word of the conversation.

"She says that she is alone here. Search the ship anyway and be careful. Elsa, inform the others to get over here on the double. We leave in five minutes," Reynita ordered as she searched the woman and found a laser pistol hidden under her blouse. Tamura was ascending the ladder leading to the second level of the ship as Regehr followed Reynita's directives and began contacting the others on their team.

Reynita pulled the laser pistol away from the female. She needed information from the woman. She decided to admonish her for carrying the illegal fire arm and then get her name. She pointed to the seized weapon. "Muy mal. Como te llamas?"

"Mi llamo Sandra Tavera Marquez y Plata," the woman responded. She still had her quivering hands up.

Reynita questioned her as to the contents of the plastic crates and learned that they were full of illegal drugs synthetic cocaine and red dust. Reynita was a bit surprised that the woman was being so honest and that a major drug dealer like her would be operating solo. The woman confessed that she had arrived from planet New Berlin. She had two partners in her drug business and that on the flight between planets, there was an argument regarding the profits. Her two partners fought and stabbed each other to death. She dumped their bodies in space and made the only logical decision for her and that was to complete the transport of the illegal drugs to Clovis City.

As Marquez y Plata told her tale, Staszko, Patel, Andolini, Stewart, Li and Melissa boarded the craft. All of the women save Staszko joined Tamura and searched the rest of the ship.   Staszko pressed the large red button on the right wall of the receiving area so that the rear of the Raumschiff would close.

Reynita informed Marquez y Plata that she was under arrest and tossed a set of arm and leg ties in her direction. The woman put them on herself without a word. Reynita was certain that most of the story given to her was probably crap.

"Jen, keep her company and don't let her out of your sight.   She might be very tricky. She speaks primarily Spanish, but I would bet next month's salary she understands everything we say. So be careful of what you say in front of her," Reynita admonished her.

Staszko smiled at the woman. "Not to worry. She won't be going anywhere."

Reynita ran up the ladder and onto the second level where the command room, computer room and weapons section were located. She observed Regehr and Patel in the computer room, getting everything operational for a long flight. Tamura, Stewart and Harumi were in the weapons room, each typing on the computer panels around the wall.

"LT, this ship has rockets and laser capability. And some of these guidance systems are state of the art," Stewart reported when she noticed her enter the second level.

"There was an advanced weapons seminar I went to before I transferred to the unit. This ship has tactical programs that were in the planning stage just under a year ago. Whoever owned this ship spared no expense in outfitting it for defense." Tamura marveled at the three dimensional tactical screens up before her. The view of the scene was much more clear and detailed than that of an average military ship. She expanded one of the targeting screens with one of her hands so that she could gain a better vantage point of the area below. "If we get into a combat situation, these guidance systems almost guarantee we cannot miss. And the armor piercing missiles have internal heat seeking devices. This ship is full of contraband weaponry."

Stewart laughed, "Illegal drugs and weapons are all over. This ship should be seized and impounded."

"We are seizing it," Reynita barked as she climbed up the ladder to the pilot section. She smiled when she saw that Li and Harcourt were already making the safety checks before lift-off. She could hear Tamura and Harumi discussing the fire power of the ship as she slid back down the ladder.

"Lieutenant, all security checks are completed." Li reported over the ship communication system. "We are prepared for lift off."

"Get us out of here, Blossom."

"Where are we going?" Li asked.

"Flight Command Headquarters on Dakota Province. It is located just a mile off the coast of Murdock Ocean."

"I have been there before," Melissa informed Li. She had dated a pilot during her first year in the Academy that was stationed there. He had flown her to his military housing on several different weekends and even allowed Harcourt to control the ship. He had been given orders and transferred to New Sao Paolo before her second year started and she never heard from him again. "I know exactly how to get us there."

"Then you will be the ship Captain for this mission." Li told her. Even though Li had spent the majority of her young life on planet New Edinburgh, she had never visited the Dakota Province.

Harcourt took the half-moon steering column in her hands and verbally ordered the ship central computer to activate the engines. She slowly raised the controls and felt the sensation of the *Comen Mierda* begin to rise from the transparent metal landing strip. She slowly brought the craft about five hundred feet into the air before she pushed the throttle control on her left to half speed.   The ship moved forward and she continued to move it upward so that the ascension was at a forty degree angle.

As they sped away from Clovis City they could both see the Great Protective Wall in the distance. There were many MI soldiers and Marines patrolling on the top of the structure, armed with laser rifles and shoulder propelled rocket launchers.

"Better get more altitude," Li warned her. "Our flight is unauthorized and those cowgirls down there might fire at us."

"Got it," Melissa used the single hand steering stick in her hands to urge the ship higher and increased the rate of speed. Li preferred the half-moon steering column and watched Melissa with keen interest to learn her style as a fellow astronaut.

On the second level, Harumi stepped away from the computer weapons controls and attempted to contact her husband via an encrypted, personal holographic attachment. She needed to hear his voice, to see his face. She held her device in her hand and verbally urged it to locate her missing husband. The last she heard from him, he was in route to planet Cootron. She was worried about him due to the news of the demise of the Second Fleet.   She was certain that he was going through emotional turmoil over the loss of his twin brother.

"No word from Dominic?" Reynita observed her trying to use her hand held communication device and deduced that she would be trying to reach her husband.

Harumi shook her head in the negative. "It has been hours since I last heard from him. If Marco is dead, then he would really need to hear from me. I want to be there for him. But I am here and cannot console him. I feel so useless."

"Come sit down with me," Reynita offered. She had not interacted much with the woman in the past. But the last time she saw her, they had shared some drinks and a few laughs. She liked Harumi and wanted to put her mind at ease. "Come on. Miyu and Sara can handle the weapons section. Relax. You need to get your mind straight."

Harumi nodded and walked over to the metal table covered with soft black leather that Reynita was sitting next to. She pulled out a cushioned chair and sat next to her. She kept her Holographic-communication device open, just in case Dominic responded to her.

"Reynita, I love him so much. I do not know what I would do without him." She set the open device on the table top. "I loved Marco, too. He was like a brother to me. I mean in every way. Before Dominic and I let the rest of the Gang know we were involved, Marco protected me and the other Gorski Gang girls. He was like big brother; you know?"

Reynita shrugged. "I can guess. Some of my sisters were the oldest children in my family, so I never had an older brother. Did you?"

Harumi smiled. "Yes, Dominic was kind of drafted by my big brother. They are serving together under Admiral Weems. His name is James Shigeta. He and Marco treated me almost exactly the same."

"Have you received any news from your brother then?"

She shook her head. "No. I have tried and the get the

same non-responsive tone from the inter-planetary satellite broadcast system. Something is going on with them. They were in a dark stretch of space, searching for a missing ship. They found it and then went on to Cootron. Dominic was very secretive in what he told me about what was going on. I could tell by the tone of his voice that it was something serious. No telling what happened to them."

"And he was serving with Gorski and Harrison?"

"Yes. They were all on the same ship together."

Staszko walked up the ramp and sat down with Reynita and Harumi. She was grinning and tossed a set of multi-colored three-inch-long and two-inch-wide plastic security cards to Reynita.

"I put our little drug smuggler into cryo-sleep in the lower level." Staszko reported. "I had to give her a stun dart to get her in. She babbled on and on about how she did not want to die. I kept reassuring her, but it didn't calm her down. So, she will be out of commission for a little while. These are the scanner cards we will need to operate the security systems and weapons on the space craft."

"Good, because I think that girl was hiding something. She claimed her crew members got into a fight over money and killed each other. I think she killed them or made the story up to hide the true identity of the true owners of this space ship."

No one else offered an alternative to Reynita's theory of

the prior owners of the space craft.

Harumi stood up from her chair. "I think I will consult with the computer memory and find out who we really deprived of all the, um, merchandise in the loading bay."

Staszko was running her hand over the soft table top. "Now this you do not see on the standard military issued Raumschiff. This is why private enterprise is best. You should see downstairs, Reynita. The kitchen is amazing. State of the art food processing stations, freezers full of food packets of lobster, crab meat, steaks, salmon and other fish from other planets. These people had some bankroll to buy all of that."

Reynita realized she had not really paid much attention to how the ship was so much more pleasant to be in as opposed to the military versions. Before she could respond the alarms for the ship began to wail.

"Incoming?" Staszko jumped to her feet and began running for the weapons section. She sat down at an empty seat and began to type commands on the keyboard before her. Harumi was soon next to her.

Tamura and Stewart already had on their earphones and tear drop communication devices as they were scanning the area in the sky around them.

"Kuso!" Corporal Miyu Tamura hissed as she was looking over the different targeting displays before her.

Harumi recognized her native tongue of Japanese and realized that whatever Tamura saw, it was not good.

"What is it?" Reynita demanded.

"Squadron of single pilot Allen fighters are on our ass, LT!" Tamura responded loudly over the sirens. "Forty-two ships and they are closing on us fast!"

"Get ready to fight back!" Reynita ordered them and turned to her left where the large computer station was located. Regehr was staring at Reynita, her eyes wide from fear. Patel had kept her head and scanned the approaching ships.

"Report!" Reynita yelled at them, louder than she normally would have spoken. She did so partly because she needed the information. The other reason was to get Regehr to snap out of her trance and get to work.

"Forty-two Allen Type Fighters on our rear, about seventy kilometers back and closing!" Patel reported loudly. "Computer scans indicate that they are armed with eight armor piercing rockets each and fully charged laser batteries."

"I am picking up some of the chatter from the ships." Regehr reported meekly. "They have orders to escort us back to Clovis City."

"And if we refuse?" Reynita wanted to know.

"Then they are to shoot us down over the jungles so that we can all become Dozal food." Regehr responded as she gave the others a look of fear.

Reynita ascended the ladder to the pilot's module, barking orders as she climbed. "Tamura! Arm the rockets and get ready to fight! Jen, Harumi and Sara! You three take the laser canons and be ready. Lock on the closest targets! We are not going down without a fight!"

Reynita rapidly climbed up the ladder to the pilot section and saw that Li and Melissa were monitoring the conversations from the approaching ships.

Li turned her head toward Reynita. "We are over the jungles now! They are ordering us to return to Clovis City or they will burn us to the ground."

Reynita shook her head. "No. They want the cargo of this ship. They would not have sent out forty-two ships just for an illegal departure. That is only a misdemeanor at best. There is someone with a lot of rank that knew this ship had massive quantities of drugs on board. That is the only way this makes any sense."

"Lieutenant, if I may," Melissa spoke up. "There should be a small medical area below. I need you to go downstairs and get some vitamin booster shots. Get a couple of them."

"What for, Melissa?"

"Because I can do things," Melissa gave Reynita an evil smile; her eyes seemed to sparkle as she spoke. "I know my abilities are why you brought me along. Time for me to earn my keep, as they say. But I will become weakened when I begin using my powers, so please hurry. And on the way down, tell the others that they will need to be ready to light them up. Tell them to wait for my signal."

Reynita nodded and slid down the ladder without using the steps. Melissa had suggested that she was a valuable asset to come on the mission because she could read minds. Reynita made that decision to include her, but now Melissa spoke of other powers that she possessed. She told them that she could control the actions of another, through mind control, and force them to do things that they would never do on their own. Reynita had heard rumors that the Children of Athena could control minds. Some of them could use telekinesis to move objects. Another rumor was circulating that a Harcourt could cause a person's body to explode with just a though. Reynita had never witnessed any such thing. She only heard about them from hearsay statements of random astronauts that visited the planet.

She ordered the four women in the weapons section to be ready to fire as she ran past them to the ramp leading downward. She did not wait for them to acknowledge her orders as she continued running. Her adrenaline level was as high as it had ever been. Her boots were clanging on the metal floors as she ran toward the medical area. She pushed the door open, ordered the computer to turn on the lights and whistled as she saw the rows and rows of medical cabinets along the far wall.

They were full of pre-measured hyper dermic needles for numerous uses. She began to open the glass doors and read the fine print until she found the energy injections. She recalled that Julia Steiner had skillfully used the same treatment to keep the Clovis Academy team alert during the Blood Moon Incident. Reynita was not one to shy away from things, but when she recalled watching Steiner inject Gorski, Harrison and the others in the neck with the long needles, she cringed at the memory. She hoped that the dark blue liquid in the hyper dermic needles would work for a Harcourt.

In the pilot section, Blossom Li took control of the steering duties at Melissa's request. She explained that she could not fly the ship and use her powers at the same time. As Li kept the ship steady, she looked at Melissa's face. Her eyes were closed and her teeth were grinding as she was concentrating. Beads of sweat began to appear on her forehead.

Melissa scanned the minds of the pilots that were now only a few kilometers behind them. She found their squadron leader, a Lieutenant Commander named Lisa Wong Feklisov. Harcourt read her mind and found that Feklisov was a Royal Family member that had arrived on the Lysander on the mission to replace the local government leaders. She had been given strict orders to bring the ship in or blast it from the sky. As Melissa read Feklisov's memories she learned that Reynita had been correct, the drugs on board were the property of Peter Rosenburg and he was the one that had ordered the squadrons to be dispatched and recovery his stash.

Melissa began to take control of squadron leader Feklisov's mind. She began to overwhelm her free will and had her activate her eight rockets for launch. As Reynita climbed the ladder to the pilot section, Melissa forced Feklisov to arch her Allen Fighter ship upward and to the left. Her other pilots were confused by the sudden movement from their commander, but did not make any move to protect themselves.

Good, Melissa thought to herself. She compelled Feklisov to come around hard and flank her own squadron. Melissa was able to learn from Feklisov's mind which of the pilots in the squadron were the best fighter pilots. She mentally forced Feklisov to aim her rockets at those pilots that were the best. When she was only about half a kilometer from her own squadron, Feklisov fired all eight of her armor piercing rockets. Although she had tried to resist the mental command to do so, she was far too weak to fight it. Melissa smiled as the rest of the squadron began to panic and their V shaped formation began to break apart. The pilots were flying this way and that, without rhyme or reason. The last thing they had anticipated was one of their own firing on them. Melissa then had Feklisov firing her laser batteries at her own squadron members, focusing her fire power on the ships closest to the Raumschiff.

And then the explosions began. The eight rockets found targets and exploded on impact, reducing the squadron from forty-two to thirty-four. The laser batteries from Feklisov's ship also did some damage as several ships began taking hits. Some exploded; others were sliced into with minor damage. The sky was lit up like a fireworks display as the ships erupted into fireball of exploding metal and flesh. Shrapnel was flung in all directions and the sound of the eruptions were deafening.

In the weapons room, Staszko, Shigeta, Tamura and Stewart saw that as their sign and began firing. Tamura and Stewart seemed to be like two young girls at an arcade playing their favorite game. They launched a barrage of armor piercing rockets at the scattering Allen ships. Jen and Harumi fired a few blasts from the laser canons at targets coming at them from the left and right.

Several of the Allen ships took direct hits to their hulls. Over a dozen of the pilots were forced to eject from their damaged craft. Li watched the three-dimensional view screens before her as pilots were descending toward the jungle below. They each had on jet packs that would enable them to glide down. Unfortunately, they were all going to land in a densely populated jungle full of Dozal, Jumpers, Verburgt, and sand and tree spiders and about another hundred or so hungry reptilian and insect species that had grown to enjoy the taste of human flesh and bone.

One of the Allen Fighters got off a few laser bursts at the Raumschiff. The laser hit the outer hull but the metal deflected the lasers back at the Allen Fighter. The pilot screamed out loud as she saw her own laser blast coming right back at her. She covered her face as if that would help just seconds before her ship exploded. Patel and Regehr gave each other confused looks as they had never heard about any metal hull of a space craft that could repel laser fire back at the person that had initiated the attack. This was something new altogether. Patel silently decided to search the on board computer system to learn of this new technology provided they survived the encounter.

Li gasped when she noticed a pack of Cawlers began to rise from the tree line below. The Cawlers were the deadliest of the flying predators on the purple planet. They were the same species that had killed the famous war hero General Rock Murdock during the Dinosaur Wars along with thousands of other soldiers and civilians. The Cawlers had a twelve-foot-long wing span with sharp claws on their hands and feet. Their beaks were razor sharp and could split a man's skull or rib cage with little effort. The Cawlers swept in on the descending pilots and began attacking them in mid-air. Li watched as the creatures latched onto their prey with their sharp claws and began slamming their beaks into the faces and chests of the doomed pilots. Li was grateful that she could not hear their screams as most of them were being eaten alive. Li cringed when she saw a female pilot grabbed by two Cawlers that held her arms open as a third Cawler swept in and began ripping open her stomach to dine on her intestines and stomach.

Squadron leader Feklisov was shot down by one of her own pilots in the battle. Her ship was spiraling out of control when Melissa released her control over her. Feklisov shook her head and realized she was going to crash land. She ejected and looked a few hundred feet above her to see that many of her pilots were being torn apart by the Cawlers. She drew her hand laser as she was gliding down toward a clearing in the jungle. That was when she screamed and began to kick wildly. Below her was a giant Verburgt, standing on its' hind legs and its long tongue waiving in her direction. She saw it open its' massive jaws and could see the razor sharp teeth waiting for her. Feklisov screamed and fired her laser at the creature.

The laser blasts only seemed to make the giant lizard monster wince. She cried as the Verburgt moved underneath her and caught her in his gigantic mouth filled with sharp teeth. As she felt the jaws closing around her she cried out in terror. When the pressure of the jaws began to crush her and tear open her flesh her screams increased in intensity. Her screams ended when the teeth crushed her ribs and lungs. Only the lower part of her left leg fell to the ground. The rest was devoured.

Reynita injected one of the needles into Melissa's neck to give her more energy.

"More," Melissa said softly. "Hit me again."

Reynita stuck another shot into the other side of Melissa's neck and injected her. Harcourt seemed to become more aware of her surroundings after the second energy shot. She was blinking wildly at Reynita and then Li.

"It's over, Melissa." Reynita told her. "Thanks to you we got them all."

Melissa nodded. She had never used her powers to kill before. She had manipulated others before. She had used her mind control to get men to sleep with her. But she had never killed before. She found that she was drenched with perspiration and breathing heavily from the exertion of energy to cause Feklisov to turn on her own people.

"That was incredible, Melissa." Li told her with a level of newfound respect in her voice.

Reynita hated watching the pilots die, but they were foreigners. The entire squadron had been shipped to New Edinburgh from Sikorsky's Planet and Reynita recalled that her father had always warned her that foreigners would try to steal your job and anything else they could get their hands on.

Reynita had learned with experience that her father had been wrong about his paranoia regarding the immigrants to New Edinburgh. They were not all that bad. For her it was a matter of survival now. In war it was kill or be killed. That was one of the lessons of her four years at the Academy. Down in the second level of the ship, the other women were hugging and slapping each other's hands in celebration. If any of them had been apprehensive about bringing Melissa Harcourt on the mission, their concerns were no longer on their mind. They were now grateful that she was with them.

Reynita ignored the shouts of joy from below and turned her attention to Li. "Blossom, how fast can this ship go?"

"About five hundred thousand kilometers an hour," Li responded.

"Then get us to Dakota Province ASAP. We just wiped out an entire squadron. We need to land before they send out some more. I can guarantee someone at command will be really pissed off about this and they will order us hunted down. Make this ship go faster than it ever has," Reynita urged. She hoped that when they landed they would not be greeted by hostile soldiers. She wondered how many of the booster injections Harcourt could handle as her service might be required again very soon.

CHAPTER EIGHT

Cadet astronaut Dino Black led a small group to the secondary engineering school hangar area to find the dual major cadets. He was accompanied by cadets Brandon Harcourt, Trey Glenn and Stacey Stahl. The four were armed with laser pistols given to them by platoon sergeant Lund and they hid the weapons under their baggy sweaters to avoid detection by the MI forces.

Black was in his junior year and had come to planet New Edinburgh from planet Athena. He loved how he felt in the cockpit and looked forward to the day he would be a commissioned officer, flying on missions instead of practicing on flight runs that were for a grade point. He had dark hair with dark eyes and distinctive cheek bones. He stood about six feet six inches tall and was an avid marathon runner. His arms and legs were long and lean due to his daily regimen of running a minimum of ten kilometers to twenty kilometers. His siblings had been split up when his parents died in an explosion. Black was never adopted from his orphanage although a few of his younger sisters had been.

Trey Glenn was in his first year and was from one of the oldest families that had colonized the planet. He had an older brother and sister that had already graduated from Clovis Academy and were serving as pilots in the Space Command. He was short and a bit overweight which prompted some of the other cadets to call him names and pick on him. He had short blonde hair and green eyes with a double chin. He was doing his best to lose enough weight so that he could follow his siblings' footsteps and fly space ships.

Brandon Harcourt was a Child of Athena that had spent his three and a half years at the Academy keeping a low profile. He was studying mathematics and physics with a goal on moving on to earn his doctorate. Brandon enjoyed the gymnasium, especially the free weight room, as well as the basketball courts. Joining an insurrection was an easy decision for any of the Children of Athena, given how they had all been historically mistreated by the Glorious Leader and his descendants.

Stacey Stahl was in her first year as a pilot cadet. She had been born on Mars, raised on planet Athena and had a sibling group of eighteen. She was almost six feet tall, voluptuous, with brown hair and brown eyes. She had developed a crush on Black and followed him all over campus. She had selected Clovis Academy over many others due to the inspiration she found from the Blood Moon Incident. Stahl had not been the only cadet to choose Clovis which caused the Academy to increase from just under fifteen thousand cadets to a little over nineteen thousand. Stahl had a cross tattooed on her left cheek to signify that she was a Christian.

They noticed that cadet Lu Wang was at one of the many repair hangars, working on a Raumschiff along with three other engineering students.

There was room for twenty Raumschiff's to be parked in that particular hangar. Black counted only two. He nodded at Wang and the other cadets as he walked past them. With a quick glance, Black concluded that the two ships were too badly damaged to meet their purposes. He kept walking, looking at each hangar to see whether there were any ships that they could steal and use to begin to round up more cadet pilots.

Wang began following the four cadets. He had earned an amazing payday by betraying his dormitory roommate, Dirk Fenster. Wang concluded that the four cadets were up to no good by the manner that they were looking into the hangars and walking by. If the cadets were considering treason, Wang came with the idea that he could turn the cadets in to the authorities for another cash reward.

At the second to the last repair hangar, Black found a Raumschiff that looked to be in good condition. He saw about thirty cadets sitting around the ship, some in engineering uniforms and the other in cadet pilot flight suits. Black walked toward them with a quickened pace. Glenn. Stahl and Harcourt kept up with him. Black walked underneath the space craft and inspected her lower hull. He found it to be without any blemishes and walked around the left, to the front and the right. He stopped at the rear of the Raumschiff where the back entrance was wide open and the loading dock ramp was lowered to the hangar floor.

"Is she able to fly?" Black asked the group of thirty cadets.

One of the female cadet pilots stood up. "Yes, it will fly. We finished replacing the solar panels just an hour ago. Do you want to take it for a spin?"

Black ran his hands across the back of the ship. "As a matter of fact, yes. Do you think that the towing cables can handle the weight of say four Allen Type Fighters for a seven-hundred-kilometer trip?"

"That's a long way off," the female cadet responded.

"Longer than you think," Black said under his breath.

Explorations cadet Dempster Harang had positioned himself about one hundred yards from the male dormitory towers.   He had his right hand balled up in a fist and was chewing on his knuckles as he always did when he was nervous. The original two dormitory towers were still standing in their original location. Due to the expected increase in enrollment at the Academy, former Dean Harvard had contracted to have several more built around the originals. Now there were three men and six women dorms, all within a one-mile radius. They were the same size and width as Harvard had wanted uniformity.

Harang promised his friend Arch Frazier that he would help in the effort to begin organizing the other cadets to stand up and fight back against the new military leaders. As he viewed the scene before him, he worried he would have to break his promise. The military had surrounded the dormitories with large ground vehicles that traveled by hovering a few feet above ground that were named Violators. The Violators were forty feet long, eighteen feet high and twelve feet wide. They were metal shells, similar to the old tanks used in the Second World War. But instead of shells being fired from their twelve separate canons, they fired laser balls. The balls would be propelled from the canon and explode on impact. The laser would vaporize any living being within fifteen feet of the explosion. There were also machine gun laser turrets on the top of each Violator with an MI soldier sitting behind it, ready to rain multiple laser fire onto any crowd that stood against them.

There were several solid black Super Raumschiffs that were hovering above the dormitories ready to fire if need be. Harang ascertained in the far distance that the campus flag pole that had the bodies of Dean Warren and her husband, each hanging by the neck. There were several warning signs that all cadets were to report to their dormitories and remain there until further notice.   In bold red letters the signs went on to warn that failure to comply would result in death.

Harang had not worn his cadet uniform and knew he could pass himself off as a civilian, at least for a little while. He could hide out at some random hotel room or with a sympathetic friend that lived off campus. But he would eventually be forced to return. He had on a purple sweater with black slacks, black leather jacket and boots.

He watched as several hundred MI soldiers were running here and there, placing three-foot-high concrete barricades up and taking position behind them. The soldiers were all heavily armed and ready for action.

Harang had observed movement on the rooftops of the dormitory towers which led him to conclude that snipers were placed there to support the ground troops. He was not a military tactician. He was studying geology and explorations. But one did not have to be a military genius to realize that an attempt against these forces would leave behind many casualties.

He looked to the cadets that had accompanied him to the location of the dormitories. His girlfriend, Ye Yibing, was watching the events before her with a look of amazement. Her long dark hair was flowing with the wind. She often looked at Harang and blink as a Raumschiff would fly overhead. She was wearing a civilian set of clothes as well and would blend in if need be, Harang thought.

Bret Bragg stood several paces away from them. He was one of the more athletic cadets on campus and had become one of the leaders of the Bragg Gang. He grinded his teeth as he viewed the military presence in the distance. He was aware that of the group, he was the only one that had taken military tactician courses. Harang was going to be a geologist and Yibing a computer expert and mechanical engineering student which would not bode well for them if they had to fight. The other cadets present caused Bragg to be even more hesitant to take any offensive action. His twin half-sisters, Zoe and Shanna stood behind him. They were both terrified by the scene. Bret did not want to charge in for fear of placing them at risk. The twins were in their first year at the Academy. Although they had taken their first class on weapons proficiency, they were not combat ready. All three of the Bragg cadets were in civilian garb and wanted to leave the location and go elsewhere.

Bret Bragg motioned for his sisters to follow him. They slowly moved near Harang and Yibing. The five cadets watched the events before them with the hope that they would not attract attention.

"What do you suggest?" Harang asked them.

"We could go hang at O'Malley's," Zoe Bragg suggested.

"Or One Card Short of a Full Deck," Shanna added.

"No," Bret shook his head. "The military will be cracking down on all of our usual hangouts. We would be arrested in seconds. We need to go elsewhere."

"Could we get a transport and get to Cy-7 or one of the other territories?" Yibing offered her thoughts as a question.

"Or we could stay at dad's home," Shanna said as she watched a female cadet approaching from the left. She was walking toward the dormitory towers and showed no fear of the soldiers that were standing guard at the entrances. "Hey, Bret. Isn't that the girl that Gauthier dated? The one you called Big Tits Carteri? She's walking right toward the front entrance of the main dorm tower. Doesn't she know that martial law was ordered?"

Bret looked at the well-endowed cadet closely and indeed it was her. Cadet pilot Jeanna Natalia Carteri was studying to become an astronaut so that she could follow her biological father as an officer in the service. Bret recalled that Carteri had interacted with the Bragg Gang several months back when she had a short fling with Gauthier. Her mother was a lawyer and her father a naval Captain. Bret recalled that Carteri was the product of an affair and her mother had enough money to keep the child from a life in an orphanage. Recently her father had made contact with her due to his current assignment leading him to the planet. Her large breasts were the topic of Bragg Gang conversations that Shanna and Zoe had been privy to. Although

Gauthier refused to discuss his sex life, the other men in the Bragg Gang wanted to live vicariously through him and speculated often about Carteri's breasts. Bret observed that Carteri was dressed in a baggy dress that came to her knees with high heels. Her long brown hair was flowing freely as she moved effortlessly in the heels. As she walked toward the original women's dormitory some of the male soldiers began whistling at her and making vulgar comments. Carteri was used to men whistling at her and making crude comments. She acted as if she did not hear them and kept walking as she had learned it was best to ignore such men. Confronting them only seemed to encourage them. Bret recalled that Carteri's father was a high ranking officer which would explain her lack of fear of other soldiers. As a military brat, she probably had been around soldiers her entire life.

"Why you call her big tits?" Yibing finally asked with a confused look on her face.

"Look at her chest," Zoe responded. "No other girl on campus is that big."

Yibing nodded. "I see. I understand."

The five cadets watched in silence as Carteri was slowly surrounded by four male MI soldiers that were making sexually suggestive remarks and gestures to her. Carteri, used to being the object of sexually inappropriate whistles and vulgar statements, laughed off their behavior and responded to them she had to join her study group inside the dorm. She stopped laughing when three of the soldiers stopped her from moving. One of them held her still by placing his hands over her shoulders. The other two moved in front of her and began running their hands over her body. She pleaded with them to let her go to no avail. Both of the soldiers complimented her breasts while the soldier behind her demanded that she voluntarily undress for them. Carteri tried to wiggle free but the soldier behind her grabbed ahold of her upper arms and held her close to him. One of the soldiers tore the front of her dress open to reveal her ample bust. The others began ripping off the remainder of her clothes. Carteri began to scream as the men forced her to the ground. The fourth soldier unzipped his uniform so that he could pleasure himself at the expense of Carteri.

"We can't do a damn thing to help that poor girl," Harang hissed with anger.

As the first soldier set upon Carteri to rape her, there were shouts from the dormitory towers for the men to stop what they were doing. The Bragg's, Yibing and Harang saw another cadet pilot named Lee Spanic running at the four soldiers, cursing at them in an attempt to stop them from hurting Carteri. Spanic and some of the other cadets that were obeying the mandate that they remain in the dorms had observed the rape and rushed out of the dorms to lend Carteri a hand. One of the four soldiers pulled out his laser pistol and fired, blowing off the top of Spanic's skull. The corpse flopped onto the ground and the four men commenced violating Carteri without further interruptions.

"That was Lee. They killed Lee," Zoe repeated with a stunned tone of voice. Spanic had been one of Gauthier's friends that would occasionally join the Bragg's for a beer or three at the pubs. He had always been cordial with the Bragg girls and flirted with Elsa Regehr whenever the opportunity permitted. Watching the good natured Spanic be killed before their eyes was enough to cause the others to want to leave and find a safer location.

"We better get the hell out of here," Bret advised.

"Yes, best idea I heard all day," Harang added.

They walked quickly as the cries for mercy from Carteri ceased as the second soldier mounted her.

"I am so ashamed," Bret Bragg said to himself due to their inability to help the girl.

As the five cadets were walking away they heard the shots from the south of the dormitory towers. The sound of laser fire erupted and screams from people being hit by them echoed between the large dormitory buildings. Harang held Yibing's hand tight, afraid of losing her to the sadistic soldiers in the distance. The couple stopped and turned around in unison to see that several cadet pilots, along with some cadet engineers and computer science majors were charging the MI soldiers, firing laser rifles and pistols at them. Several of the soldiers were instant casualties as the cadets came to fight for keeps. All of their laser settings were on the kill or vaporize function.

"Where did they come from?" Yibing wanted to know.

"No telling," Harang responded as he began cautiously walking back toward the dormitory buildings.

The four soldiers that had been raping Carteri were pulling their uniforms back on and finding their weapons to go help in the fight. Harang began running past the concrete barricades as the attention of the forces were clearly on the rear offensive. He ran past several Violators and areas where sand bags with rapid fire laser guns were mounted behind to get to the victim. He found Carteri nude, bruised and sobbing. He knelt down next to her, removed his jacket to cover her and told her to hold onto his neck. Harang gingerly lifted her into his arms and began to move quickly back to the others. The sounds of battle grew louder. He could hear screams as people lost limbs and many lost their lives. Harang was grateful when Bret unexpectedly joined him and helped carry Carteri.

They did not know that the cadets that were attacking were the same ones that Varek, Vezpucci and Kazembe had freed from the abuses of the MI soldiers earlier. The attack by the cadets failed as the MI soldiers had superior weaponry, superior numbers and better training. Harang and Bret carried

Carteri to the location where Zoe, Shanna and Yibing were waiting for them. Carteri was shaking and clearly distraught.

"She needs medical attention," Harang told the others. "Let's get her to the ER."

As they departed they could hear the death cries of the brave cadets that attempted to stand up to the MI soldiers. In that short time, thirty-seven MI soldiers died while one hundred thirty-three cadets lost their lives. In one of the dormitory towers two cadets named Laurinda Paes and Hilda Haake filmed the events on their Holograpic-Satellite communication devices. They then uploaded their film to the campus satellite system and sent it out to many of the larger satellite service providers. They had previously done the same with the execution style murder of the Warren's. The rape of Carteri, the murder of Spanic and the brave, albeit misguided, attack by the cadets soon became big news. The recordings reached other planets and the people began to watch the horrors that were being perpetrated on the innocent citizens of planet New Edinburgh. The result was a building rage among the populace against the new occupation forces.

The Orka style Raumschiff sped along at a reduced speed of fifty thousand kilometers an hour. Regehr kept the ship thirty feet above the ocean as he listened to the scan results provided to him from Nehwal and Elektra. The two cadets were sitting next to him in the pilot's section, searching for evidence of the two Unter-See Boats called the *Kirov* and the *Irkutsk*. Arch was in the computer section along with the sisters Zorana and Jasna Mikec scanning for any sonar clues of the dangerous underwater creature called the Britva. Regehr wanted to avoid submerging the Orka near any of those large predators.

Regehr kept one of the dozen large screens in the pilot section on the current events broadcasts so that he and the cadets he found himself aligned with could stay on top of all the news. The reports of Admiral Seward were pouring in. The government controlled news media spin was that Seward was a traitor and died trying to attack an elementary school full of innocent children. Regehr knew that story was full of poggie dung. The other main article was the hangings of Dean Warren and Professor Warren. The government was blaming the murders on Cadets James Cobb and John Gauthier who were both shot down over the Forbidden Region and confirmed dead. Regehr shook his head over the way the government, the military and the news reporters deceived the average citizen. He wondered how many years it had been going on and how many stories he followed in his life that were full of lies and subterfuge.

"I am so sorry about your friends," Elektra told him. "I know we had our past fights and differences, but John and James were not cold blooded killers. The Cobb family must be beside themselves right now with one of their sons being accused of something so despicable."

"Thank you," Regehr responded as he took a drink of water from the bottle on the side of his seat. "James was a bit crazy and did some crap that I would never do. But John was more suited to be in your gang than ours. He was calmer than the rest of the Bragg's. They would never be able to make the murders of the Warren's stick on him."

"What about the Warren's children?" Nehwal wanted to know. "Some were younger and living here on New Edinburgh. What did they do to them?"

"That is something I don't want to think about right now," Regehr mumbled, using his free hand to enlarge another news report that had Professor Rand accepting the position of Temporary Dean of the Academy. He lowered the volume to drown out her speech. "That was the bitch that sexually harassed Reynita and some of the other female students. I can't believe they promoted her."

"Tyrants, Derek. Tyrants always promote the incompetent or the corruptible so that they can be controlled," Elektra told him. "They are following the communist play book to the letter. Kill all of the smart and respected people and then replace them with fools, buffoons and opportunists. People like Rand have so many skeletons in their closet that they can easily be blackmailed to do what others want. If Rand ever falls out of favor, discarding her would be simple. They bring up her past, act like they never knew about it and demand with righteous indignation that she resigns."

"You should be Secretary General," Nehwal laughed.

"Found them!" Elektra suddenly blurted out as she used her fingers on her left hand to expand the view under the ocean. Regehr and Nehwal stared at the image of the *Irkutsk* with silent respect to the size of the craft.

"She is massive," Nehwal observed.

"Arch, any sonar hits on the Britva?" Regehr asked over the ship wide communication system.

"We are clear," Arch Frazier responded.

"All right then, I am lowering the water sled legs so we can surf the ocean and they we will dive. Everyone strap yourselves in." Regehr rapidly pressed color coded buttons over his head and on the panel before him that was chest high.

The Orka responded by lowering the surf board looking legs so that the ship could glide over the water. That process took all of fifteen seconds. Once the on board computer notified Regehr that the ship was ready, he slowly lowered it onto the ocean. They were soon surfing on the ocean and marveled at how well the ship handled the waves. It was almost like a roller-coaster ride for the cadets due to the up and down motion of the waves.

"Diving!" Regehr informed them as he pushed the steering column downward and watched through the transparent metal window as the ship began to be swallowed by the deep blue water. The legs withdrew back inside the ship as Regehr took her deeper and deeper. Through the observation window, Elektra and Nehwal were amazed at the thousands of various under water life forms before them. Some were tiny worm like creatures that glowed in different colors. Others were large predator fish ranging from an inch long to forty feet long that were swimming next to the ship as if they were trying to determine what it was. They were all worried that a Britva would come near them. They were feared as they had been known to swallow Orka ships whole and even been able to grab them and damage the hull. A water leak could be fatal under an ocean, but especially so on planet New Edinburgh as the life forms were perilous. There were some of the worm like creatures that would secret a substance that would eat through human skin as effectively as the most potent acid.

Regehr hummed Beethoven's Ninth Symphony to himself during the descent. The Mikec sisters were marveling at the three-dimensional views of the ocean from their seats in the computer room. Zorana had put on a burgundy leather jacket on as she realized the temperature was dropping dramatically. Jasna seemed to not care about the cold and stared at all of the colorful life forms before her.

The descent took several hours to complete. Regehr

explained to the others that they could not drop straight down due to the pressure on the ocean floor. Elektra found that she was enjoying the ride. She had never imagined that the aquatic life could be so lovely.

"Arch, are you watching all of this?" she asked.

"It is absolutely breathtaking," Arch responded as he stared at the three-dimensional view in the computer room.

"I'm so glad we came," Jasna finally told her older sister.

"Me, too. I never knew that the Purple Planet had such hidden beauty," Zorana agreed and pulled the jacket around her chest.

The Orka eventually came into close proximity with the *Irkutsk*. The cadets viewed the Unter-See Boat that was the length of two thousand feet and about one hundred-sixty feet wide. The ship had fifteen floors from top to bottom. She was grey in color with some deep blue streaks painted into the grey to offset the color. It had no propellers as the submarines of antiquity. The ship was driven by using a system that drew in water and forced it out the rear to propel her forward. There were also some rear and side propulsion vents that used high pressure to steer the ship up, down, left and right.

Elektra knew that she was looking at one of the deadliest creations made by mankind. The *Irkutsk* could launch several nuclear devices that could reach a target at the distance of two

Astronomical Units. It also maintained a steady supply of armor piercing torpedoes and other offensive capability. Given their proximity, Elektra decided that it was time to raise her aunt Themis and dock with her ship.

She pressed the external communication button on the console before her. "Computer, patch me in to the Irkutsk. Person to person request by Elektra Papinakilaou and Admiral Themis Zachariades."

They all waited as the computer attempted to complete the request. The wait was short as they all were soon treated to the image of the Admiral in her grey class C uniform before them in a three-dimensional broadcast. She was standing in her personal quarters with her balled fists on her hips and smiling at them.

"Elektra. What are you doing on the ocean floor?"

"Auntie, I am looking for you. Some things have happened. Terrible things. I need to speak with you. I request permission to come aboard."

Themis was silent for a moment before responding. Her face did not betray her feelings or intentions. "Alright. Docking bay is opening now. I hope this is good. Your mother would be very upset if she knew that you were under the ocean with all these predators around."

"Thank you so much! I can't wait to see you and

Drimios again."

The image of the Admiral suddenly faded away.

"Not much of a conversationalist, is she?" Nehwal remarked.

"She believes that less is more," Elektra agreed as she watched Regehr slowly guide the Orka style ship to the under belly of the *Irkutsk* where the docking area was located.

The procedure to enter the bottom of the ship took all of fifteen minutes' time. The bulk heads on the bottom of the ship slid open and allowed the Orka to enter before sliding shut. The water was then drained from the room and the Orka was magnetically drawn to one of the sets of hooks on the wall. The cadets watched in awe as they were secured by the hooks and their Orka ship was held firm. They could hear the computer informing them that the docking procedure was complete and that they were free to come aboard the ship.

"Lower rear exit ramp," Regehr instructed the crew.

Zorana and Jasna Mikec were the first two to the rear of the ship. They were each excited to see the large craft from top to bottom. Arch waited for his wife to join him before walking down the ramp to the bottom of the Orka. The rear ramp lowered and touched the floor. Elektra could see a welcoming party was there, including Admiral Zachariades. She ran down the ramp and embraced her aunt and held her tight. Arch followed her with the Mikec sister's right behind him.

Arch observed that there were several Orka ships held to the side walls with large clamps. Some of them had naval markings on them. There were two solid black that signified they belonged to MI. He wondered why MI would be on a mission to map the ocean floor. He shook hands with the other members of the greeting party. Captain Geoffrey Carteri was a man that was small in stature with a shaved head, dark eyes and fit frame. His uniform was crisp and professional. He had served with the Admiral for almost a decade and had a reputation for being reliable and loyal to her. He had started his career in the naval service as a scientist and later took computer on line classes to switch to the military branch. He had several wives and children that had been left behind on old Earth while he served out the mission on planet New Edinburgh. He had a few illegitimate children in several locations. One of them was a cadet pilot at the Academy. Carteri had been trying to establish a relationship with her ever since he had arrived on New Edinburgh. She had been receptive to getting to know her father and he looked forward to the next time he would see her.

Next to him was the executive officer, Commander Krysta Vintilescu. She was a petite brunette with a scar on her left cheek and had an implanted fake left eye due to a past battle she fought in. The fake eye looked exactly like the real one and functioned even better. She could see for a mile without effort.

She had also been with the Admiral for a good amount of her career. She had been widowed many years earlier and had two children, each by a different man. The loneliness of being under the ocean for several weeks at a time could drive a person to seek out companionship in any manner. Vintilescu was a member of the ship sex club that had crew members rotate sex partners without question. Each evening, several crew members would meet in one of the recreation decks, select a partner for the evening and leave with them for sex. Vintilescu had no clue who the fathers of her children were and she did not care. She had left them in Rumania to be raised by her mother.

Arch and Elektra introduced the Mikec sisters, Nehwal and Regehr to the officers.

"You handled the Orka like a professional," Vintilescu commented as she looked Regehr over.

Nehwal could sense that the Commander was interested in Regehr for more reasons than his ability to pilot an Orka. She instinctively put her arms around Regehr's left arm and glared at Vintilescu. The Commander smiled at her as she understood that the cadet was marking her territory.

Finally, the Admiral addressed the group. "Elektra, you really should not have stolen that ship. You are in serious trouble with the authorities in Clovis City."

"But auntie, they are killing people up there!" Elektra began her prepared speech to justify her actions. "The killed the dean of our Academy and several professors. They killed Admiral Seward and Major Evart. They killed a priest, gunned him down in cold blood. He was unarmed. I saw them do it. They just cut him down like he was nothing. We had to get away."

Themis nodded as Elektra spoke. "Yes, I know. I know. I spoke with your mother after the arrest warrants were sent to us by the UN Security Council Director Rebecca Rosenburg. The Royal Family is really in no mood for any more games. I personally spoke to Director Rosenburg on your behalf. She will allow you safe passage home and will have the warrant for your arrest quashed. Now your mother is really upset with you. Your mother wants you to return home to Corinth immediately."

"She wants me to do what?" Elektra was stunned by the attitude of her aunt and the dictate of her own mother. Out of the corner of her eyes she saw three dozen MI soldiers descending the ramps from the side entrances to the docking area. They were all armed with laser rifles and had faces of stone. They quickly moved around the six cadets and surrounded them.

"The terms of your freedom and your life were negotiated by me with the new military commanders," Themis explained calmly. "They contacted me personally and I pleaded for you to live. They agreed to allow you to escape decapitation if you return home to Corinth and if I turned over your co-

conspirators for execution. I am sorry, Elektra. But it is for your own good. One day you will thank me for saving your life."

"What the fuck!" Regehr bellowed as he struggled with two MI soldiers as they began to place restraints on his arms. He fought them as best he could until one of the soldiers stunned him with a hand held Taser. Regehr collapsed to the floor, shaking from the electricity coursing through his body.

Arch Frazier turned and hit one MI soldier in the face and almost was able to swing at a second before he was stunned by a laser blast. Nehwal fought back as well, using her skills as a scrappy orphan to trip soldiers and kick them when they were down. Had there only been a few soldiers, she might have had a chance. But the sheer numbers overwhelmed her and she screamed as she was slammed down onto the metal floor. She cursed them as she felt them binding her legs and then her wrists.

The Mikec sisters did not know what to do. They were surrounded and fighting back didn't seem to go well for the others. The girls raised their hands in the air as the soldiers bound their legs. Soon their arms were bound behind their backs. All four of the prisoners were thoroughly searched and their weapons were removed.

Elektra was in tears. She could not believe that her beloved aunt would betray her in such a manner. She attempted to rush to the side of her husband but was restrained by three MI soldiers. "Why? Why are you doing this? Please, let them go!"

Themis shook her head from side to side. "You were always my favorite niece, Elektra. Your sisters were smart, cute, and fun to be around and two of them had potential. But you? None of your sisters had your potential. That is why I am stepping up now and ending your destructive patterns. You left Earth to come to this Zeus-awful planet. You marry this peasant without telling your family. How could you, Elektra? We all had such high hopes for you. You are brilliant. Beautiful. If you had to marry anyone on this purple trash dumpster called a planet, you should have gone for his roommate. At least he was a Fenster and could have given you a grand lifestyle. No, you pick a peasant from a peasant family that will never have a pot of Corinthian clay to piss in. You will be a widower after Frazier is executed. But you will be fortunate in that you did not get pregnant and thus produce more worthless peasants."

"How can you say such things?" Elektra was beside herself with grief. She watched helplessly as the MI soldiers carried Regehr and Frazier off toward one of the other ships docked there. "He loves me! We love each other! He is a good man! Don't do this! Why? Why?"

"Why? Yes, I suppose I do owe you an explanation." Themis sighed as she watched the rebellious cadets being forced aside. "You see, my dear, life is not fair. We are Greeks and we know history and politics as part of our culture. We know that kings die, queens fall from power. Presidents, chancellors, Caesars, dictators, czars and prime ministers get assassinated or removed by rebellion all throughout the history of humanity. But not Vladimir Sikorsky. He has ruled for two hundred years, Elektra. Two hundred years. He will rule for another two hundred. You and I will be dead and turned to dust before his rule will end. So, we must be smart, do we not? You and your friends wanted to fight against Sikorsky's handpicked Generals that came here to restore order. That was stupid. Let us assume, just for a moment that you would have been successful. Then what? I will tell you what would have happened. Sikorsky would have launched one of those Red Javelin weapons and wiped out all mammal and reptile life on this planet. That is what you and your misguided friends would have accomplished."

Elektra glared at her aunt as a woman in a black uniform approached from the upper level ramp. She was followed by three men in similar uniforms. She was tall, slender, with long dark hair and was wearing the rank of Captain. She stood next to Admiral Zachariades and smiled at Elektra. Her name tag read "RENDON." The men were all over six feet tall, muscular and handsome. Elektra realized that the three men looked exactly the same. She concluded that they were possibly triplets or some genetic experiment.

"So, you would have won a little war here and then died when the Red Javelin hits you. Very bad plan, my dear niece.

Very bad. No one can stand up to the Royal Family. But if you live within the confines and expectations of the regime, you can advance. Look at me. I am an Admiral in the navy. My son is the Captain of his own ship. You can achieve great success if you are smart. That means ignoring men that come from the peasant class and being loyal to the regime. Your mother agrees with me, Elektra. You will go home now and forget this miserable planet. Forget these so-called friends of yours. They are not worth it. Find a man of means, marry him, let him enjoy lusting over your body and make offspring with him. These five are already finished. Forget them. The masses that you sought to win freedom for will cheer as their heads are severed from their bodies." Themis was nodding at the Mikec sisters and Nehwal as she spoke.

While Themis spoke, Jasna was sobbing and felt her knees grow weak with the news that she was going to be tortured and decapitated. There were two MI soldiers holding her shoulders to keep her upright.

"Look at her. She is pretty with a nice body. She obviously has some smarts about her if she qualified to attend the Academy. But she just ended her life because she was stupid enough to commit treason. Her only hope now, in fact the only hope these three girls have right now, is if these three clones of the Glorious Leader find them enticing enough to use them to bear children." Themis pointed at the three identical men in black standing next to Captain Rendon. "Yes, Elektra. Yes. Your female friends here will either breed or be decapitated. That is all that awaits them until the end of their pathetic days. That is why you must avoid the peasant class. They exist only to perpetuate the herds of sheep for the leaders. These three seem to have good bodies for breeding purposes so they might be allowed to live. Now, Elektra, go home. Drimios will personally see to it that you are placed on a transport back to Earth."

Elektra watched as the three clones of Vladimir Sikorsky approached Nehwal, Jasna and Zorana. They each looked like a much younger version of Sikorsky and Elektra speculated that the clones were about twenty years old. The soldiers held the women firm as the clones began to fondle each of the captive women. Jasna cried as the clone feeling her breasts began to rip her clothing off. Zorana spit in the face of the clone that was running his hands over her body. For that moment of defiance, Zorana was slapped in the face hard enough to cause her head to whip to the side. Her lip was gashed from the impact and she had blood dripping onto her chin. She was forced back upright as the clone tore off her top revealing her breasts. The clone was smiling and began to fondle them.

Nehwal did not cry or fight back. After she was stripped down to her waist, the clone of Vladimir Sikorsky facing her turned to Captain Rendon. "Her back has scars. She is not acceptable."

Rendon shrugged. "Send her with Frazier and Regehr to be executed. The other two will be used for producing more offspring. Once we arrive in Clovis City the Mikec girls will go to the Rosenburg Ranch to breed. The rest will die."

As the three cadets were taken toward the ship only Jasna made any pleas for mercy. Elektra closed her eyes and felt for the girl. She had felt responsible for all of them as she had believed that her aunt would help them. She had been mistaken and now Jasna and Zorana would be condemned to a life of sexual slavery while the others would die.

"It is for the best," Themis said again.

"I hate you," Elektra told her aunt, glaring at her.

"You will get over it," Themis dismissed the statement. "Cheri, are you ready to depart?"

Rendon nodded and saluted her. "Yes. We will leave within the hour. The Royal Family thanks you for your loyalty."

"And I thank the Royal Family for all the opportunities afforded me." The Admiral returned the salute. "Watch my niece. She can be stubborn. Do not let her harm herself."

Rendon glared at Elektra. "You are fortunate to be well connected. It is well known that you killed my nephew on Cy-7. But your aunt has taken steps today to cleanse your sins. Do as she advised you and you will have a long and productive life.

Step out of line one more time and even she will not be able to protect you."

"When you arrive home, tell your mother and your sisters that I love them." Themis began to walk back up the ramp with Carteri and Vintilescu following her. "Have a safe and law abiding trip home."

Elektra began moving her feet as the soldiers in black were shoving her to move. At least she would return to Clovis City in the same ship as her husband and the others. She hoped that she would be able to see them on the short voyage back. She put on a brave demeanor and fought back the tears. In her arrogance she had placed her husband and the other cadets in danger. She swore to herself to make things right, one way or another.

CHAPTER NINE

The upper metal bulkhead of *Clovis 21* slid open to reveal an exit space of six feet by five feet. Jose Calderon climbed up the ladder leading to the exit and pulled himself onto the top of the space craft. He was armed with a sniper laser rifle which was slung over his left shoulder, a laser pistol that was in a holster around his waist and two satchel charges and a back pack full of grenades over his right shoulder. His face had black streaks of paint applied to break up the contours of his head. It was a trick his father and uncle taught him when he was a boy. He surveyed the sky line and saw that the red orange hue around him was clear of any packs of Cawlers. He reached down the upper bulkhead entrance and helped Serpas up. She was armed with a laser rifle, laser pistol and a knife. Once the two cadets had their feet firmly planted, Cobb passed up through the exit four of the metal spears that they had been sharpening the previous night.

"Nice day," Serpas remarked. She and the rest of the cadets had been injected in the cheek with a small communication microchip that was tapped into the ship frequency so that all could hear her. Each cadet also received a receiver in their right ear lobes so that they could hear everything being said. "All right, listen up. Maria's scans were spot on. I can see the tree lines in the distance and there is no movement. The rolling hills have no Dozal watching us. No Cawlers in the sky. All clear."

Gauthier ordered the ship computer to open the back exit and lower the ramp. He had a laser rifle over his shoulder, a laser pistol in his left hand and one of the bed frame metal rods that had been sharpened on each end. Manuel and Pepito were to his right, bearing laser rifles and large sheets over their backs holding several of the metal spears that they had worked on. Juanito and Xavier were to his left, armed in a similar manner as their brothers. Blomquist and Eklund were behind him, each carrying a large tool kit and had laser pistols in holsters around their waists. Haddad was standing by a pile of the metal spears and movement detectors with Jorge next to her.

The rear doors slid open and the loading ramp dropped to the surface full of purple sand. The group walked down the metal ramp with their eyes wide open, looking all around for danger. Haddad and Jorge carried down several of the skinny seven-foot-long metal movement detectors and began driving them into the ground. As soon as their poles were two inches into the sand, they began to blink a red light on the top to indicate that they were operational. The movement detectors could sense any activity under the ground for about one hundred feet in either direction. After they finished they returned to the rear of the Raumschiff and began carrying the spears out to the others.

Cobb joined Juanito on the left side of the ship. Each of the men were cognizant that they were the closest to any tree line than the others. They had purple sand for less than fifty feet before the multi-colored forest obscured their view. They accepted the metal spears and extra movement detectors from Haddad when she arrived with them. Cobb said nothing as he noticed Haddad was wearing a black leather pair of pants with dark knee high boots, black half shirt and a black leather jacket. Her hair was tied behind her into a pony tail. He was still angry at her for choosing Gauthier over him. He helped Juanito place the detectors close to the tree line and the two quickly repositioned themselves closer to the metal frame of the ship.

Gauthier and Xavier went through the same process. The only difference was that they were facing rolling hills for at least three kilometers. Gauthier gave Haddad a kiss when she delivered the detectors to them.

"You seal the bulkhead behind you," Guather told her.

She had her arms around his neck. "You watch your butt, lover boy. I'll kick your ass if you get yourself killed."

The two men did not wait for Haddad and Jorge to depart before they began jogging off into the distance to place more of the motion detectors into the ground.

Jorge stopped and tapped Blomquist on her shoulder. She turned and faced him with a quizzical look on her face.

"I wanted you to know that I froze several changes of clothing for you," Jorge told her.

"How did you do that? Why did you do that?" Blomquist asked him, surprised that the teen would be so considerate of her physical limitations to the potentially warm environment.

"I wanted you to be safe and comfortable out here," Jorge responded. "So, last night I went through the clothing reserves from the previous owners of the ship and found several outfits that should fit you. I dipped them all in water and hung them up in the walk-in freezer in the kitchen. When you start feeling warm, just contact me and I will bring one out for you to change into."

"Thank you," Blomquist said with a smile.

Haddad motioned for Jorge to follow her back onto the space craft as Gauthier had instructed. With all of the detectors either in place or delivered, they sealed the rear bulk head and moved to their posts on the Raumschiff.

After the rear entrance sealed, Blomquist and Eklund began unpacking their tool kits as Manuel and Pepito kept an eye out for any creatures. The two women pulled out transparent protective face masks, secured the straps behind their heads and began using solar powered blow torches to burn away the damaged metal. The two women wanted to make quick work of their task so that they could get back inside the safety of the ship.

Thirty feet under the purple sand eighty-seven brown three-foot-long spiders felt the footsteps above them. The purple colored mother spider had let the others know what she expected. She wanted the female humans alive so that she could plant her eggs inside of them. The brown worker children were ready to attack and kill the males and incapacitate the females.

Over the rolling hills a large pack of two hundred Dozal were sleeping under trees and inside caves. They had spent the prior evening hunting and stalking potential prey. One of their scouts had found the damaged space ship on the other side of the hills and reported that it smelled fresh meat inside. But there was no way to gain access to the food inside the metal shelled object. As the sun was bright in the sky an orange, black, white and red striped muscular Dozal was stretching out and smelled something in distance. He smelled fresh meat. It wasn't the normal poggie or other form of mammal that the Dozal was used to hunting and eating. This smelled different. The Dozal concluded that whatever it was, the aroma indicated that the meat would be delicious. It waited for the rest of the pack to wake up. They would hunt this new prey with the unique odor and they would feast.

The engineering students used many of the solar

powered tools to remove screws, fasteners and hand held magnetizers to remove the damaged metal parts from the rear propulsion system. Three hours passed as Blomquist and Eklund were able to complete half of their task. They removed the damaged part after restructuring the damages to the outer hull. They gratefully accepted the cold bottled water that Haddad and Jorge delivered after completing that part. Blomquist had to change twice into the frozen clothes that Jorge had been so considerate to prepare for her. Each time Blomquist stripped naked the men would turn away from her, although Pepito was sneaky enough to get a look at her from an angle. He found her to be very desirable and her light blue nipples were different.

"Now we have to carefully remove the central thruster and place it into the empty slot," Eklund told the others.

The thruster weighed nine hundred pounds and required the use of a hand-held magnetizer to move into place. The screws to fasten it onto the rear of the space craft were a foot long and an inch thick. They kept concentrating on their work, trusting in Manuel and Pepito to protect them. Both Blomquist and Eklund were covered in sweat as they continued to work on their project. Neither girl had any idea of the danger that was approaching them.

Haake heard the loud alert as she was sitting in her rolling, black leather chair in the computer section of the ship. She had her legs resting up on one of the computer panels when the beeping began. "Look sharp everyone! The detector rods have movement underground. Several objects moving rapidly toward the ship."

"Probably those damn spiders!" Raklitz commented as she sat up in her seat.

"They are moving fast!" Villandiego added as she typed up commands on her computer panel and pulled up a three-dimensional view of the objects that were moving toward them. "It is definitely arachnid in shape. They are surrounding the ship. Should we come out and help?"

"Negative," Gauthier responded. "Stay at your posts. We are ready for them."

"What should we do?" Blomquist asked nervously.

"Keep working," Eklund told her. "Let Manuel and Pepito handle them."

The purple spider led her offspring under the sand. They were closing in on their prey and they began ascending to the surface.

Gauthier and Xavier had planted a laser satchel charge under the sand about eighty feet away from them and wired it to detonate remotely. They waited until the spiders that were coming from the left to get close enough to their trap before springing it. Xavier had his holographic-communication device in his hand and pressed the 'Send' button to activate the detonation sequence. The satchel charge made a sound like a steak being seared as it erupted a yellow-orange laser brightness that traveled fifty feet in radius. The trap worked and over thirty of the brown spiders were vaporized. The purple sand above the satchel charge were burned into chunks of glass from the intense heat generated from the explosion.

Cobb and Juanito had planted a similar trap in the tree line. They also set theirs off and eliminated just over one dozen of the giant spiders. The purple spider realized that their human prey had been ready for them. She squawked out a high pitched command that the humans could not hear. She ordered the other spiders to the surface and to charge their targets.

Manuel and Pepito cursed in unison when a dozen spiders burst through the purple sand a mere ten feet away from them and began to charge at them. Both men carefully aimed their laser rifles and began firing. One by one the spiders made high pitched screams as they were blown in half by the laser blasts. One of the large brown spiders leaped in the air and dodged the laser fired at it by Manuel. It soared several feet in the air with its fangs bared and was ready to sink them into the human. Manuel turned his laser rifle around, holding the barrel and used it like a baseball bat. He hit the spider in its face with the barrel. The spider fell backwards onto the ground and rolled over several times before regaining its footing. Another spider leaped at Pepito who pulled one of the several metal spears next to him from the ground. He impaled the spider in its open mouth and flipped it aside. A dark orange liquid spilled onto the pear that Pepito was using from the wound inflicted on the spider. Manuel fired another shot at the spider that had come so close to jumping on him. His aim was true the second time around and the spider died as the laser obliterated its' head.

Other spiders began to pop up from under the sand and rush the humans. Cobb was taken aback by how fast the eight legged creatures could move. He fired his laser rifle at the arachnids. On the top of the ship, Serpas and Jose were helping out, firing their sniper rifles to support their friends on the ground.

The purple spider stood back and watched her children being slaughtered. She reluctantly commanded them to withdraw. She had observed the humans in combat and their defenses. She knew of other spider families nearby. She would return with them and attack again. But this time she would go after the two females on the ground. They were clearly trying to do something important as they did not stop their work during the attack. The purple spider hissed in anger and vowed to the survivors that they would return with triple the force and attack again.

The humans began celebrating their first victory of the day. Each of them silently hoped it would be the last attack they endured.

Serpas and Jose hugged on the roof of the ship, celebrating their success. Serpas looked over his shoulder and cursed. In the distance on top of the rolling hills she saw two Dozal looking in their direction. One was covered with white and black stripes. The other had a multi-colored fur pattern of orange, red, white and black. Jose turned and saw the animals. They were growling and gnashing their teeth menacingly.

"Look alive people," Jose warned. "The Dozal must have heard our weapons. They are coming."

All the cadets on the ground turned their attention toward the rolling hills and saw the two Dozal there being joined by dozens more. Their fur colors varied. Most of them had multi-color stripe patterns, a few had solid colors varying from red, orange, white, black and yellow. They were all growling and hissing, baring their sharp fangs.

"John, they are going to charge right at your position!" Haddad warned as she viewed a three-dimensional view from her position at the tactical seat on the pilot section. Truang covered her mouth with one hand, terrified of the large cat-like Dozal that were in the distance. She estimated that it was seven feet in length and almost five feet tall.

Gauthier glanced at Juanito and noted that he had his laser rifle at the ready. Gauthier spoke into his tear drop microphone that was sewed into his tunic: "Tara, you and Winter get up on top with LaTania and Jose. We are going to need all the firepower we can get. Dominique, get up there too."

"I am reading over one hundred of those Dozal on the other side of that hill," Raklitz reported as she stood up and grabbed a laser pistol that was lying on a computer stand next to her seat.

Gauthier knew from the inception that their plan had been risky. He hoped that with four shooters up top and two on the ground they could take out the majority of the fast moving predators. With any luck, the Dozal might be dissuaded when they see many of their pack dying and withdraw. "James, Manuel, we'll need you to give support fire from your positions. Nikki, Nina, drop what you are doing and get a weapon. We are all combatants now."

Blomquist and Eklund nodded when they heard the command and climbed down their step ladders that they were standing on to work on the rear of the ship. They each pulled out laser pistols as the joined Manuel and Pepito on the ground.

The multi-colored king of the Dozal creatures was standing proudly on the hilltop looking down at the sweet smelling prey below. The king was satisfied that the food would feed the entire pack, including the younglings that were playing back at their cave lair. It growled a command and then led the others, running on all fours at full speed. The other two hundred

Dozal followed him. They were soon running at over forty kilometers an hour. They were all growling and hissing loudly. Haddad, Truang, Serpas and Jose aimed at the middle of the charging pack of the creatures. They waited for Gauthier to give the word to fire.

Gauthier waited until the creatures would be in range for maximum use of their laser weapons. He looked up at the clear red orange sky line and took a deep breath. He was amazed that he was not scared. He thought he would be terrified by such a threatening sight. He looked at Xavier and saw that he was fidgeting and his eyes were darting back and forth. Gauthier realized that Xavier was getting nervous. Gauthier smiled at him just before he screamed out the command to fire.

The cadets began firing their laser rifles and laser pistols at the distant Dozal. The laser bursts took off heads and limbs from the furry predators but those that were not hit did not slow their gait. The shots that missed caused purple sand to fly into the air from the force of the laser energy impacting on the surface. Some of the Dozal lost limbs and slid to the ground howling in agony. Gauthier realized his hopes that the predators would withdraw when they began to take casualties was misguided. If anything, it doubled their resolve and they began to run faster. Truang and Serpas commented on how pretty the Dozal looked with all of their multi-colored patterns. Cobb barked for them to keep quiet and keep shooting.

The sounds of the growls grew louder as the creatures grew closer. Due to the howls of the Dozal, none of the cadets heard the sound of the approaching footsteps from the opposite side of the attack. In the computer room, Haake and Villandiego watched in horror the view from their three-dimensional display before them. They saw the head of a sixty-foot-tall Verburgt looking over the tree line at their ship.

"Guys! Trouble to your rear!" Haake warned. "Guys?"

None of the cadets on the roof of the ship or on the grounds answered as they were too involved in the battle with the Dozal. The sounds of the screams created by the dying Dozal and those that were in the hunt probably drowned out Haake's voice. She gave Villandiego a look of concern.

"That Verburgt is moving toward our ship!" Villandiego screamed in a panic-stricken voice. She had never seen anything so big in her life at least not live. She had seen pictures of them in posters and news reports. The sight of the giant jaws of the Verburgt opening and closing caused her to feel the icy tinge of fear in her heart.

Haake grabbed a laser pistol from the table, "Jorge, get up here and help Barbara! I'm going top side!"

Haake ran from the computer room and found the ladder that would take her to the roof of the ship. She climbed up and could see that Serpas, Haddad, Truang, Raklitz and Jose concentrated their attention on the Dozal. Each of them firing lasers over and over again. Haake pushed herself and ran to them, looking over her shoulder to see that the Verburgt was now moving at a faster pace toward their ship. She grabbed Haddad by her shoulder and screamed at her.

"Tara! Behind you!"

Haddad looked over her shoulder and saw the sixty-foot-tall, green and silver skinned Verburgt charging in. Its massive jaws were opening and snapping shut with an off-color drool flowing in anticipation of the snack that waited for it below.

Haddad hit Serpas on her shoulder and was screaming at the others to turn around and fire.

"Fire at what?" Raklitz asked as she turned her head to see what Haddad and Haake were screaming about. When she saw the giant Verburgt she cursed out loud.

Haddad, Raklitz, Serpas and Haake turned around and began firing wildly at the Verburgt while Calderon and Truang continued to fire in support of the cadets below. The laser fire that hit the Verburgt only seemed to anger it. It roared with rage as small pieces of its' scaly skin was shot off by the lasers. Down below, Gauthier and the others noticed the decrease in fire support from above. The Dozal were closing in on them quickly and another one hundred Dozal were now showing themselves on the horizon. Gauthier speculated that the new Dozals had been hiding from view in order to be protected from whatever defense the humans had to throw at them.

The Verburgt was now taking large steps with its' muscular hind legs to get to the humans on the top of the shiny space craft. It felt the bee sting lights hitting it in the chest and neck as it charged. The Verburgt had never tasted humans before, but that did not deter it. The creature fixated on the plump one to the left. It decided to feast on her first.

Jose took a chance as the giant carnivore grew closer. He pulled one of the laser satchel charges from his bag and pulled the ripcord. He threw it as hard as he could in the direction of the giant creature. It sailed into the air and landed just in front of it as it was picking up speed. The laser satchel charge erupted in a bright, blinding light. The legs of the Verburgt and part of the tail were vaporized. The giant creature screamed as it was flying out of control due to the explosion. The creature could not conceptualize how or why it no longer had legs just that it did not. The face of the Verburgt slammed hard on the far side of the Raumschiff and caused the craft to tip toward it. The cadets on the roof were screaming and trying not to fall toward the jaws of the Verburgt.

But the biggest concerns of the cadets should have been the growls from less than a mile away. Several other Verburgt heard the cries of their brother. They had been hunting all morning in the Far East forests for some of the meatier prey.

They were hungry and needed to feed. The explosion and the howls of their fellow Verburgt got their attention. They turned toward the sounds of the other Verburgt and decided to investigate.

Gauthier and Xavier felt the ground shake as the legless Verburgt smashed onto the purple sand and their Raumschiff lifted up into the air and fell back down. They were both narrowly missed by the Raumschiff as it rocked back and forth. Inside the ship, Villandiego and Jorge had not been strapped in. Villandiego hit her head on her computer panel before her and fell to the floor. She suffered a gash in her forehead and had a slight loss of blood. Jorge rolled to the ground and came to a stop when the ships ceased rocking. He checked Villandiego and found that she was unconscious. He took her place at the computer panel and began scanning the horizon. He swallowed when he saw the four new sixty-foot-tall Verburgt approaching their location. Three of them were green as he had seen in his classroom studies, but one was grey with red stripes. He began to scream to the others through the intercom system that the game was up. Four giants were approaching from their southern position. He received no response.

Jose slid off the roof and grabbed hold of one of the ladder handles on the side of the ship. He watched helplessly as the other two satchel charges fell to the purple sand along with the handmade spears and some of their grenades. He could hear the injured Verburgt howling in what he assumed was extreme pain from losing its' legs. He was cognizant that none of the others had fallen over in his direction. He swung his legs up and began climbing back to the top of the ship's hull.

Haake grabbed hold of a metallic four-foot-long antenna on the top of the Raumschiff and was able to catch Truang with her free hand as she was sliding toward the Verburgt. Haddad was able to keep her footing and caught the hand of Serpas, holding her in place. Raklitz was unable to grab any kind of portion of the ship and she fell off the side, hitting the ground with a thud. She was several feet away from the giant Verburgt. The fall caused her breath to be knocked out and she was holding her side on the ground. She was certain she might have broken some ribs. She held her sides and looked up at the giant monster and prayed that it did not see her so close.

"We lost our grenades and satchel charges!" Jose informed Haddad and Serpas.

Haake pushed herself upward and could see the heads of the other four giants over the tree line. She pointed in the direction of the new adversaries in the distance. "We better get them back up here quick! There's more coming!"

Jose looked over the side at Raklitz who was struggling to get up on her hands and knees. "Dominique! Get up! We need you to throw us the back pack with the grenades and the two satchel charges back up to us! Dominique!"

She wasn't responding. It was all she could do to suck in small breaths of oxygen. She held her side and concluded that she had broken her ribs. She looked at the legless Verburgt and could see that it was dying.

Haddad decided to take matters into her own hands. She ran to the upper hatch in the bulkhead and jumped through it and into the control room. She didn't pause to grab the ladder. She landed on her hands and feet and saw that Jorge was tending to Villandiego. Haddad ran down the ramp to the rear exit and opened the bulk heads. As soon as there was enough room to squeeze through, she did so. Her feet were soon pounding on the purple sand as she ran behind Blomquist, Eklund, Manuel and Pepito who were firing wildly at the charging Dozal. She soon ran past Gauthier and Xavier, wiping perspiration from her forehead as she ran. The two men were too busy firing their laser rifles at the Dozal to ask her what was going on. Haddad passed Cobb and Juanito and kept running past them until she reached the area where the satchel charges were lying on the ground.

She grabbed the first charge and saw that Serpas and Jose were giving cover fire toward the Dozal. Only Truang and Haake were paying attention to her. Haddad threw the first satchel charge to Haake who caught it in midair. She threw the second to Truang who missed it and it bounced on the upper hull of the ship and fell back toward the side of the ship where

Blomquist and Eklund were at. Haddad found the back pack full of grenades and decided against throwing them upward and risking Truang being unable to hold on to them as well.

Haddad grasped the right arm of Raklitz and helped her to her feet. She glanced at the injured Verburgt was a mere fifteen feet away from them. It was screaming in agony and not paying attention to either woman.

"Come on," Haddad urged Raklitz urgently.

She held Raklitz upright as they ran back the way she had first come. Haddad only two thoughts in mind. The first was to get Raklitz back inside the ship. The second was to get back on the roof with the grenades as the Verburgt only seemed to be harmed by heavy explosives.

The Dozal were now closing in rapidly. An orange colored Dozal leaped in the air at Pepito. He picked up one of the metal spears that held it firmly in both hands. He pointed the tip at the Dozal and impaled the furry creature through the mouth. The tip of the blade ripped out the back of the Dozal's skull. It fell to the ground and Pepito pulled his spear free just in time to stab a second charging Dozal in the chest. A third stopped a mere three feet away from Pepito and was crouched down hissing at him, baring its' sharp fangs in a menacing manner. Pepito thrust the spear at the creature only to miss as it dodged out of the way. It tried to circle Pepito who spun forward and was able to stab the Dozal in the back, just below the neck. The Dozal made a sad death cry that caused Pepito to feel guilty about killing it. The remorse he felt momentary as two more Dozal were closing in on him. He stood to face them.

Manuel noticed that his brother was making a valiant stand as the creatures began to circle them, looking for a weakness. He kept firing his laser rifle at the creatures as he concluded that Pepito was demonstrating that he was able to handle himself. Most of the time he hit his target, but due to their fast speed, he would miss his target occasionally. Blomquist and Eklund were kneeling behind their metal tool kits, firing their laser pistols at the large cat like creatures. Blomquist felt bad about killing them, thinking that the Dozal were pretty animals with their color patterns and faces.

Haddad arrived at the side of Gauthier and Xavier. Cobb and Juanito were there also, forming a half circle together as they fired their laser rifles at the Dozal. Cobb was panicking from the sheer numbers of the creatures. Haddad could hear him screaming obscenities at the creatures as he fired at them.

Gauthier was undeterred, firing his laser rifle with the butt in his shoulder. He was carefully aiming and seemed to never miss. Juanito was keeping a cool disposition, aiming at a selected Dozal, squeezing the trigger and then finding another in his sighting scope and repeating the process.

"There's too many!" Cobb was screaming as he fired in

the direction of a cluster of them.

"Calm down and keep firing!" Gauthier barked at him.

Haddad released Raklitz and allowed her to fall to the ground. She pulled a thermite grenade from the back pack, pressed the red detonator button and threw it into the group of Dozal that Cobb was firing at. The explosion sent several Dozal body parts and purple sand flying into the air and many of the feline predators were rolling on the ground, burning alive. Haddad spied another cluster of them and threw another thermite grenade toward them with similar results. The Dozal scattered backwards due to their mutual shock of the fire bombs taking out so many at once.

Knowing full well that the other Verburgt would soon be on them, Haddad ran for the rear ramp of the ship and left Raklitz behind. She was slowing her down too much and the cadets on the top of the Raumschiff would need the explosives. Haddad found the second satchel charge and it was lying thirty feet from the ship. With the Dozal circling so close, she dared not go after it. She ran behind Manuel and Pepito on the way to the rear ramp. She sprinted as fast as she could back to the roof.

Raklitz pushed herself and used her hands to steady herself on the side of the ship. She walked sideways to get back inside. Little did she know that Haddad had sealed the rear entrance of the space craft. Raklitz made it to the area where

Blomquist, Eklund, Manuel and Pepito were firing madly at the raging Dozal. Raklitz wondered what would make a pack of animals ignore all logic and charge to their deaths. Their attack made no sense. The Dozal were dying left and right, yet they lacked the common sense to give up the fight against superior firepower. Raklitz found one of the metal spears and picked it up. Better to go down fighting, she thought to herself as she braced herself for any random Dozal that would get near her.

At that moment, Jose was positioned on the top of the Raumschiff, firing his laser rifle in the direction of the approaching Verburgt. The four giants were getting too close for comfort. He observed them hitting their torsos and bodies together as they ran toward the Raumschiff. Haake, Truang and Serpas were also firing at the sixty foot giants. Haake saw Haddad climbing up on the roof out of the corner of her eyes. She was grateful to see that she had the pack full of grenades in her hand.

"They are getting close!" Haake yelled to Haddad.

Haddad gave each of them a grenade. "Let's give them hell!"

Serpas pressed the detonator button on her grenade knowing that she had ten seconds to get rid of it. She threw the explosive as hard as she could with her right hand. It sailed toward the Verburgt and landed a few feet in front of them. Jose waited a few seconds before throwing his. Truang, Haake and

Haddad each threw a grenade shortly after Jose did. The five grenade explosions went off. The first, which was the grenade thrown by Serpas, did little to no damage at all to the four giant creatures. The other four grenades exploded one after another.

The closest Verburgt took most of the damage. It lost most of its' right leg and right side from the shrapnel. The giant collapsed to the ground and caused the Verburgt directly behind it to trip over it. The other two Verburgt were hurt by the shrapnel but not as serious. They kept charging forward.

Jose extended his free hand to Haake. "Maria! Give me the last satchel charge!"

Haake handed it over and watched him pull the cord on it. He threw it in the direction of the last two Verburgt as the women kept firing their laser rifles, hoping that his aim was true. The charge detonated in midair, causing the heads of the two Verburgt to be vaporized in the brilliant explosion. Their headless corpses slid to the ground and impacted the side of the ship with a thud.

Their celebration was short lived as the last of the four Verburgt had regained its footing and was now leaping into the air. The cadets were in awe as to how high it could jump given it must weigh close to a ton. It was coming down hard onto the ground, a mere five feet from the space craft. It brought down the large spiked tail and smashed it on the hull of the ship. The craft twisted in circles from the impact. All the cadets on the roof stumbled and grasped for anything to keep their balance. The Verburgt shot out its' long tongue and tried to ensnare Haddad who was able to narrowly roll out of the way. The tongue continued whipping around until it latched onto one of the cadets.

Haake had been on her hands and knees when she felt something warm and wet wrap around her legs. She screamed in horror as it pulled her. She hit the hull of the ship face first and lost her grip on her laser pistol. She felt herself being pulled across the metal hull toward the Verburgt. She screamed to the others for help.

Haake saw that Truang was struggling to stand. Jose was running toward her, trying to grab her outstretched hands. Serpas and Haddad were too far away from her to help, but were firing their lasers at the monster's eyes. Jose made one last ditch effort to fire at the tongue of the Verburgt. He missed by inches. Her fingernails split as she struggled in vain to grab hold of anything on the hull of the ship.

"Help me! Help me!" Haake screamed at the others. The terror in her eyes was evident to all of them.

Maria Haake felt the jaws to the Verburgt close around her. Her ribs were crushed along with her lungs on the first bite. The other cadets heard the sickening sound of the bones being crushed. Her blood spattered all over the inside and outside of the large jaws of the Verburgt. Blood was running down the chin and neck of the creature and dripping onto the hull of the ship. On the second chew, it crushed her legs and mid-section. She felt herself being swallowed as she was still alive. Death soon followed for her. Her screams ended as the Verburgt licked the dripping blood from the massive jaws. Other than the fresh blood on the hull of the ship, it was as if Maria Haake had never even existed.

The Verburgt was encouraged by the tasty flavor of Haake and wanted more. It lashed its' tongue out at the others, the blood and some intestines of Haake dripping from it. It came close to ensnaring Truang as she rolled away at the last second. Jose used his machete to slash at the long tongue. The Verburgt roared in pain as half of the tongue was severed by the blade.

It was about to retaliate by smashing the hull with the tail again when an explosion occurred behind it. The mid-section of the monster was vaporized by a satchel charge. The two halves of the Verburgt collapsed to the ground, purple sand billowing around it. The cadets were stunned and wondered who had come to their aid.

Haddad looked over the side of the ship to see fifteen-year-old Jorge saluting her. He had chased after the other satchel charge that Haddad had given up on. He held one of the metal bed frame spears in his right hand. It was covered with the color of Dozal blood, as was his clothing. Around him were the corpses of seven Dozal that he must have killed in order to retrieve the satchel charge. He quickly ran back toward the other side of the ship to help the others in the continued fight against the Dozal.

Although it seemed hours later, the remaining Dozal withdrew their attack after another few minutes. There was silence all around them for the first time in what seemed like an eternity. The entire battle with the spiders, Dozal and the Verburgt took forty-five minutes. But for each of the cadets it felt like a lifetime. The piles of dead Dozal could be seen for quite some distance. The large chunks of body parts from the dead Verburgt were lying next to the space craft. The smell of the burnt flesh and scales stung Truang's nose. She was coughing from the stench and covering her mouth.

"Get back to work!" Gauthier urged them on. He had no idea that there had been a casualty. He had been personally injured when a Dozal got close enough to slash his back with some claws. It was painful, but not fatal. He hoped that their show of deadly force would cause the other creatures in the jungle to think twice about attacking them.

"You okay, John?" Xavier asked. He had a bloody spear in his right hand and his laser rifle in the left. "Things got too close for comfort there. I thought that Dozal had you. That was a great spin move you made to get away from it."

Gauthier grunted and reached the gashes in his back with his left hand. They weren't too deep. "I just got lucky."

Cobb, with his eyes wide with excitement, was shaking his head and laughing. "We did it, John! We pushed them back! The Gorski's would never do it this good! Man! What a rush! We should have filmed this! We would have been on the news man! Every woman out there would throw themselves at us! John! We are heroes, man! Heroes!"

"James, shut up." Gauthier glared at him as he spoke. "Keep your head in the game."

Inside the ship, things were more solemn. Villandiego was lying on the floor suffering from a head injury. Raklitz checked herself by using the medical facility computer x-ray machine and found she was bruised badly and had three broken ribs. She joined Jorge in the computer station to assist in scanning for any more hostile creatures. Haddad and Truang had taken their places back in the pilot section. None of them talked about Haake. The way she died weighed heavily on each of them since it could have easily been them and not her that were eaten alive.

"Hey, Jorge!" Truang finally said for all to hear. "That was really brave of you going after that satchel charge. How many Dozal did you have to kill to get to it?"

Jorge closed his eyes since all his brothers heard the

question. He knew Manuel would give him a tongue lashing for venturing out on his own as he had. "I think I killed six or seven, using a spear. Just like my father taught me."

"Kid, you did great!" Jose said so that Manuel would go easy on his brother.

"I am picking up more movement from the forest," Raklitz announced. Her voice sounded tired.

"What is it?" Serpas asked even though she did not want to know the answer.

"Looks like three more Verburgt." Raklitz sighed as she judged the large size of the creatures in the scans.

Jose looked at Serpas and shook his head. "We are out of satchel charges and only have a few grenades left. Pray they don't come this way."

Serpas shook her head from side to side. "They will smell the corpses, Jose. You know that they will come for us."

"At least we gave them hell," Jose knelt on the hull of the ship and looked over the spatters of Haake's blood. He decided that he would shoot himself in the head before dying that way. Her screams as she was being dragged into the mouth of that monster would haunt him for the rest of his life.

"It gets worse," Serpas reported. "I see a cloud approaching us at rapid speed. Looks like Cawlers. It would seem that Mother Nature is not happy with us."

"The Cawlers heard the screams of the dying. They are

coming to feast on the carcasses." Jose looked up into the sky and saw the large force of winged predators soaring in their direction. "Of all the creatures of New Edinburgh, they have the best sense of hearing. It was inevitable that they would come."

All of the remaining fifteen cadets were now overcome with a feeling of hopelessness. They had fought off sand spiders, two hundred Dozal and several Verburgt. Their leader, Gauthier, hated to ask the question, but he knew that he must do so.

"Nikki, Nina? How much longer until the repairs are done?"

There was a pause. Blomquist finally responded to him. "We could use about forty-five more minutes if you could buy us that much time."

"The Cawlers will be on us in ten minutes," Raklitz reported.

"Everyone get back inside the ship," Gauthier ordered softly. "We will lock ourselves inside until the Cawlers clean out the corpses of the dead Dozal and Verburgt. It may be several days, but now we have no choice."

"And if those other Verburgt come they will damage the ship more?" Manuel asked in a worried tone of voice. "Maybe we should stand our ground now."

"No. Everyone inside. Now." Gauthier was resolute in his decision. He had seen the Cawlers in action once. He feared their speed and ferocity. Fifteen cadets against an entire colony of Cawlers on a raid was suicide. They would have to wait for their next opportunity to finish the repairs and pray that the Verburgt ignored them. He saw that his friend, James Cobb, was using a machete to severe the head from one of the dead Dozal.

Cobb smiled as he was hacking through the bone. He looked over at Gauthier. "No one will ever believe us, man. This souvenir will be our proof."

Gauthier shook his head in disgust. He pointed the barrel of his laser rifle in the direction of the rear ramp of the Raumschiff. "Get back in the ship, James."

Blomquist and Eklund readily accepted Gauthier's assistance in packing up their tool kits. They had affected many positive repairs on the rear propulsion system, but the work was incomplete. Neither of the engineering cadets said a word as they packed their instruments into their boxes. Eklund continually looked up into the sky, her eyes filled with dread.

CHAPTER TEN

Basil Varek had his stolen MI Raumschiff flying at the swiftness of one hundred thousand kilometers an hour. Colan had located a second possible crash site near Lynott's Land and he was determined to be there before sundown. Wanda Essex was sitting next to him in the pilot section typing on her computer console before her, hoping to find some scans for proof of life below.

"There is a large flight of Cawlers descending on the wreckage site," she reported to Varek. "I am scanning several Verburgt to the west of it. Basil, I am picking up signs of a battle. There are dead Verburgt, Dozal and sand spiders all around that ship. Someone down there really took it to them."

"That's got to be them," Varek felt his mood lighten. "I just hope we are not too late."

Essex regarded Varek for a moment in silence. "You know, you are not what I thought you would be. I mean, from your reputation. Not just you. You and your friends on campus. You are not a bad person after all."

Varek looked at her as he steered the ship. "I don't follow what you mean."

Essex sighed, "People around campus say bad things about you and your friends. They say you stick people's heads in toilets and flush them to give them swirlees, whatever the hell a swirlee is. Others claim that you hung them from power line poles by their underwear. Other cadets say they were forced by you to eat poggie feces. And then there are those bar fights that everyone talks about in the dorms. I hear your name mentioned in connection with some of those. You are not that guy, are you?"

Varek swallowed and looked at her lovely face. She was a beautiful girl and from a fine upstanding family. Her grandfather had been a popular politician; her father and mother were well known in the community as successful business people and were very charitable. Her cousins, which included the Kander family, had a similar reputation. Varek had considered the possibility of a romantic relationship with the woman. His belief was that a relationship with Essex was a sad fantasy on his part. She was a woman that deserved a better man than he was. For the first time in his life, Basil Varek felt ashamed and guilty for the past three years of hazing other cadets.

"I am sorry to disappoint you, Wanda. Everything that has been said about me is true. I am a bad guy. I did all of those things."

"I don't believe it."

"A swirlee is when we stick someone head first into a

toilet, flush it, and watch their hair swirl around the toilet bowl." Varek told her. "We prefer to find a toilet that was recently used and unflushed. That raises the decibels of the screams from the cadet that we are victimizing at the time. I am a very bad person, Wanda."

"I think that calling yourself a bad person is going too far." She glared at him for a moment. "I mean, here you are, in this ship that you stole at a risk of criminal prosecution to do one thing. You are single minded in purpose to rescue your friends. At this precise moment in time, you are displaying friendship, loyalty, a willingness to sacrifice and committing treason to help others in need. Bad men do not do those things, Basil. Bad men have no loyalty. They have no true friends. I think that there is more to you than you give yourself credit for. You want to know what a bad man does to other people? Those men that were trying to rape me were bad men. They were going to violate me in the worst way. If you and your friends hadn't shown up, they would have." She had tears forming in her eyes as she recounted the horrific memory. "They would have, Basil. Thank you for being there and saving me."

Varek had a good view of the cluster of Cawlers in the distance. He estimated that there were about a hundred of them. "Get down below and tell all of the others to get ready. There are over one hundred Cawlers that we must fight off. Find June and have her try contacting that crashed ship. I think we have found them."

Essex stood up, disappointed in the abrupt manner in which he had terminated their conversation. "You really should learn to take a compliment better."

She left him to do as he requested. When she climbed down the ladder she saw many the Ward family in the hexagon shaped command room and adjacent computer and weapons rooms. They were drinking coffee and mourning those that did not survive. Essex approached Jason Ward and one of his daughters that was an astro-physics student at the Academy named Jessica. "We found another crashed ship. There are over one hundred Cawlers diving on it. Get your weapons and get ready for a fight."

"Where are you going?" Jessica Ward called after her as Essex moved toward the ramp.

"Looking for June. Anyone see her?"

"She was in the lower level in the kitchen," Klara Ward called out to her. Klara was in her mid-twenties and had avoided the Academy to study law. She had worked as a defense attorney before the purge came and she had been forced to flee with her father. She had a bandage on her forehead and her left arm in a sling due to injuries she suffered in the crash landing of the Ward transport ship.

Essex ran down below and saw Marble, Vezpucci and

Kazembe with some of the other Ward family members organizing weapons. Essex moved past them and jogged down the left hallway to the kitchen. She found Colan sitting at a small table by herself, humming a nursery rhyme, drinking a glass of grape juice and sucking on a lolly-pop. She was curling her hair through her right index finger and staring at the ceiling as if she no cares in the world.

"June! Basil needs you. Come on."

The idea that Varek would send the Essex slut down to order her around filled Colan full of rage. Essex had been dominating all of Varek's time which meant Colan was unable to bond with him. Colan stood up and smiled when she realized that they were alone. She had a laser pistol hidden under her dark, torn sweater. Colan calmly walked up next to Essex and pulled out the laser pistol, sticking it in her ribs. Essex was stunned by the unexpected move. Colan grabbed her right arm and dug her fingernails into her flesh just enough to cause discomfort but not break the skin.

"What the hell are you doing?"

"Shut up, bitch!" Colan hissed. "Do exactly as I say or I will burn you down."

"What is this about?" Essex was trembling as she questioned her actions. She could see in Colan's eyes that she was not emotionally stable.

"Shut up and walk." Colan stabbed the barrel of the pistol into her back. Essex winced with pain. "This is about you stealing a man away from me. We women are outnumbered over eight to one. Finding a man is hard enough without tramps like you fucking things up for the rest of us. Move. To the cryo-sleep chamber room. If you cry out I will blast a hole through your chest. Don't try me."

Essex complied moving slowly out of the kitchen and into the hallway. She hoped that a random passenger would look their way and see that she was in distress, but no one did. Marble was in eye sight of Essex, but she did not look their way.

"June, if I did anything to offend you, I am sorry."

"We women are supposed to stick together, bitch. You messed with the wrong person. I see it all the time at the Academy. A girl like you comes along and shows off some cleavage and gives an alluring smile to another girl's man and goes off and fucks him. I know that is your plan. I see the way you look at Basil. You probably already sucked on his Standing Hampton in the pilot's section so that he wouldn't keep thinking about me. I know you are already moving in on him. Hell, you are probably already sleeping with him. For that you need to be punished."

"June, if there has been some sort of misunderstanding between us, I am certain we could work it out." Essex found herself at the cryo-sleep chambers doors. They were closed, which was odd in that protocol was to keep all doors opened except for the sleeping quarters. That rule had been in place to ensure easier access to the sections of the space craft. Essex looked inside through the looking glass in the center of the right side of the sliding door. The tubes all seemed in order and there were no passengers in the chamber. She wondered why Colan would want to take her there. The best way to eliminate an enemy on a space ship would be to jettison them from one of the air locks.

Colan ordered the computer to unlock the door. The entrance slid open and Colan shoved Essex inside. "It will all be worked out when you are dead. You are in deep shit now, honey. You will never be able to fuck with another woman's man again. Computer, seal the door."

Essex turned around to see the door slide shut behind her. Essex watched through the looking glass as Colan was laughing hysterically. Before Essex could try and determine why Colan held such animosity toward her, she heard a half growl from behind her. Essex knew that she was most likely in deep shit as Colan had said. She slowly turned her head to see the Dozal lying on the floor. It was still not fully awake but her eyes were open and staring at Essex. The creature was most likely confused as to how it ended up in the metal room surrounded by all of the long metal cryo-sleep tubes. Certainly, the movement of the craft in flight was disconcerting to the animal. Essex feared that the confusion the animal was experiencing would soon be replaced by the instinct of hunger. Essex saw out of the corner of her eye that Colan was still watching through the glass, laughing. Essex pulled out her Holographic-communication device and tried to contact Varek. She found that her device was being blocked in some manner. She concluded that Colan must have written a program on the ship computer to block out all interior communications. The Dozal was sitting up now and watching Essex.

Essex knew she had only one chance to survive. She slowly moved toward the closest cryo-sleep tube and began to lift her left leg into the opening. The Dozal suddenly growled and leaped up to its' feet and began to charge at her, hissing. Her sharp fangs were ready to tear into her flesh and feast on her carcass. Essex slid into the tube and sealed the transparent metal covering over her. The Dozal crashed into the tube and growled with anger. It was scratching the tube frantically while Essex watched, feeling threatened by how close the predator was to her. Fortunately, the Dozal was not able to deduce the proper method of opening the tube. It scratched at the metal casing, growling with rage and hunger due to the inability to secure its meal.

Colan watched the events unfold from the other side of the doorway. She cursed Essex for outsmarting her plan and began walking in circles, holding her ears with both hands. Essex had been mere seconds away from a horrific demise. She kept mumbling to herself. "What to do? What to do?"

She decided that she would go in and open the tube and force Essex out at laser point so that the Dozal could feast on her. Colan ordered that the computer open the doors. She heard Varek beckoning for her to join him in the pilot section immediately. She ignored the pleas from her potential lover and walked into the cryo-sleep chamber with her laser pointing at the tube Essex locked herself into. In her psychosis, Colan forgot one thing. The Dozal was standing on top of another cryo-sleep tubes, watching her with great interest. After a few seconds of observing the new prey, the Dozal forgot Essex and pounced on the human that had seemingly ignored her. Colan cried out as the furry creature knocked her to the floor. She lost her grip on the laser pistol and it went sliding across the metal floor. Colan learned firsthand about the jaw strength of the Dozal as it bit into her left shoulder and ripped flesh and muscle out with little effort.

Colan screamed loud enough for the others to hear so that they might rescue her.

The screams could be heard down the hallway. Vezpucci, Marble and Kazembe dropped what they were doing and ran in the direction of the yells. The Dozal trapped Colan on her back and used the claws from the front right paw to slice open her stomach. Colan struggled as the Dozal opened the abdominal wound further with its' powerful jaws and pulled out a mouthful of intestines. It ripped out her stomach as she screamed from the intensity of the pain.

Vezpucci was the first in the doorway and saw the Dozal bite down on Colan's throat and crush it. Colan was spitting blood and the floor was filling with red for her severed jugular vein. Her legs and arms were twitching as the Dozal was chewing on her flesh. Vezpucci cursed, pulled his laser pistol from his holster, set it to kill and fired. He hit the Dozal in the head, blasting a hole in the skull of the creature. The corpse of the Dozal fell to the side. Vezpucci ran to Colan's side and found that her eyes were staring at the ceiling. She was gone.

Marble could hear the banging in the direction of one of the dozens of cryo-sleep tubes. She ran to the noise and looked in to see Essex inside hitting her palms on the tube. Marble opened it and helped pull the woman out.

"Colan is crazy!" Essex said breathlessly. "She tried to kill me!"

Kazembe pointed to the ground at Colan's mangled corpse. "Her killing days are over. You better get topside. Varek says we are almost there."

Essex stood and was still shaking with fear. She stared at the growing pool of blood on the floor and the mangled remains of June Colan. "Okay. Yes. I am on it."

Essex quickly departed the cryo-sleep chamber, unsure what could have driven Colan to the point that she would want her dead. But that mystery would have to wait until after the conclusion of the current rescue operation. People were in danger and she needed to assist.

The purple spider with the burned marks on her body returned to the scene of the massacre with another large number of brown spiders to exact her revenge on the humans. She observed that the humans were all rushing back to the safety of the metal shelled object. She screeched a command to urge the other spiders on faster.

The Cawlers were now circling the carcasses of the deceased Verburgt and Dozal. They would swoop down and take a chunk of meat and fly back upwards. It was not as satisfying as looking their prey in the eyes as they killed it, but food was food.

The three giant Verburgt in the distance observed the Cawlers diving for food. All three of them came to the same conclusion: that was there could be the possibility of food for them. The three creatures began moving in the direction of the Cawlers.

The long table in the command station of Raumschiff *Clovis 21* was almost full. The seat that had been used by Haake in previous gatherings was empty. Villandiego was present with a bandage around her head with a spot of blood on her forehead due to the bad fall she had suffered. She was not suffering from any lingering issues due to her injury and wanted to participate.

Gauthier had some medical gauze that had been wrapped around his torso to cover the slashes on his back. He faced his classmates for what he believed to be the last time. He looked at Raklitz first. She had a similar wrap around her body due to her own injuries.

"Give us the bad news," Gauthier directed her.

Raklits sighed and looked at the other cadets for z second before responding. "The Cawlers are all around the ship. I scanned about sixty new spiders surrounding the ship and there are three new Verburgt marching in our direction."

"Fuck me," Cobb mumbled.

"Shit gets better," Raklitz added with a song in her voice. "An MI Raumschiff is flying right toward us. I guess that shooting us down wasn't good enough. They are coming back for the kill."

Haddad was sitting next to Gauthier and held his hand under the table. She could see in his eyes that he was filled with despair. He was doing his best to put up a good act for the others by making the tone of his voice sound positive.

"Let's just blow ourselves up," Cobb blurted out as he stood pounding his right fist on the table. "Why give those MI bastards the pleasure? They will probably just arrest us, break our legs and then dump us on the planet surface to become food for the Cawlers. We are dead anyway. I don't want to be eaten like Maria. Not me. We can wire the ship to blow. We are gone in a split second. No fangs ripping us to pieces. Let's do it. Nikki, Nina, you two know how to rig the nuclear power cells to blow. Come on. Let's do it."

"Sit down James," Gauthier told him.

"But we should make it easier for us!" Cobb yelled at him.

"I said sit down!" Gauthier stood and glared at his friend.

Gauthier was glad that Manuel and Pepito intervened and stood on either side of Cobb. They took hold of his arms. Manuel whispered into Cobb's ear. "James, you are my friend. But I will personally throw your ass outside with those spiders and Cawlers if you don't sit down and shut up. You feeling me, old buddy?

Cobb did not respond. He stared into Manuel's eyes and slowly sat down. Cobb knew better than to challenge him. The Calderon's knew how to fight dirty and often times their opponents got hurt.

"Thank you," Gauthier smiled at the brothers. "This is our only shot as I see it. We have six motorcycles and six drivers. How fast can those things go?"

"Over one hundred fifty kilometers an hour. But that is on flat surfaces. Out here, it is a guess. Going over hills, deep sand, grass and having to maneuver through forests will slow us down considerably. We can go plenty fast if we need be," Manuel told them.

"Cobb gave me an idea. Six motorcycles driven by the Calderon brothers, each taking one passenger. That is twelve. Lynott's Land is fifty kilometers due North West. Even in this rough terrain, you should be able to make it before nightfall. Three of us will stay behind to fight the MI soldiers to buy you time. We will blow the ship when we get over run as a signal to you that you are on your own." Gauthier rubbed his hands together as he spoke. "Naturally I will stay. I need two of you to volunteer for a suicide pact. Whoever stays is assured of dying."

"I am staying," Haddad told them. "I cannot leave here without you, John."

"I will too," Cobb added. "My idea to blow the ship, I should get to be a part of the fireworks. I will stay. Just think, they will write songs about our sacrifice. No, not just songs but plays. Movies. Even operas. We will be made immortal! Think of it John! This is the most epic way to go out, man! Little kids will grow up learning about us in grade school. They will wonder, what were their last thoughts? Who came up with the idea? Man, John! I am honored to die with you, man. We will be bigger than the Alamo or the three hundred Spartans! Epic, man.

I am telling you! Epic!"

Cobb's rant ended when Manuel fired his laser pistol and stunned him. Cobb fell face first onto the table. Manuel shrugged to the others. Blomquist and Eklund clapped their hands to show their approval of shutting Cobb up. Manuel holstered his laser pistol and sat back down without comment.

"Thank you for that. He was giving me a headache," Truang stated while rubbing the sides of her head.

"Guys," Raklitz interrupted them from the computer room. "We are being contacted by the MI space ship. They are asking for James and John by name. Somebody named Basil, says he knows you."

The Calderon brothers stared at each other in stunned silence. Gauthier stood up slowly and smiled. "He is on that MI ship? Is he a prisoner?"

"No. He says he stole the ship to come find us."

"Yeah!" Juanito hugged his brother Jorge.

The other Calderon brothers were embracing and shouting with joy. Gauthier pulled Haddad close to him and kissed her.

"This is good news; I take it?" Eklund wanted to know.

"The best," Gauthier responded and motioned to Raklitz. "Put him on ship wide communication so everyone can hear."

"John!" It was the voice of fellow Bragg Gang Member

Basil Varek. "Are you okay?"

"I am fine my friend! I could French kiss you right now! How did you find us?" Gauthier held Haddad as he spoke.

"We will have time for that later," Varek responded. "Listen. Your ship is covered with those damn spiders. You are surrounded by Cawlers and there are Verburgt that will be here any second. So, my partners in crime proposed that I lower a towing cable and attach it to the ship, lift you off the ground and we all fly to Lynott's Land together. Is there any problem with the structural integrity of the ship?"

"No. She can take it." Blomquist answered for Gauthier.

Eklund wept with joy as she listened. She had not been ready to die, especially not out in the Forbidden Region as a part of the food chain. She covered her eyes with her hands as she sobbed. Blomquist put her arms around her friend and held her close.

"Good," Varek paused as he steered his ship into position. "We will have to take care of those Verburgt first. So don't you folks go anywhere?"

"Basil, this is Manuel. How are you going to take care of the Verburgt?"

"I stole a MI Raumschiff. This is a fully loaded war machine. I am going to turn those Verburgt into giant sized fried frog legs. Keep your heads down." Varek laughed as he spoke.

Varek nodded at Marble and Essex who had joined him

on the pilot section of the space craft. Essex gave the verbal order to Vezpucci and Jessica Ward who were waiting in the weapons section. The two fired armor piercing rockets at the giant creatures with deadly accuracy. The poor Verburgt never knew what hit them. All three of them were struck by a rocket in the chest. The explosions left only their giant legs while the rest of their bodies were obliterated into tiny chunks. The explosions caused the Cawlers to flee in a panic. The spiders held their ground as they continued to cover the hull of the space ship, probing for a weakness to sneak inside.

Kazembe lowered the tow cable and waited until it hit the hull of *Clovis 21* and attached. "We have them!"

Varek smiled and began to lift the damaged ship off of the ground. The female purple spider was hissing and ran to the cable. She began to gnaw on it with her fangs in an attempt to keep those that had killed so many of her offspring on the ground.

Gauthier and his fellow cadets buckled themselves in as the ship was being lifted up. There was still hugging and laughter as to their good fortune. They were on their way to safe harbor, or so they hoped.

Gauthier held Haddad's hand. "I love you."

She smiled at him. "You sure about that?"

"Never been surer of anything in my life."

"Then I love you, John. And I am very sure."

Eklund was smiling and had to wipe tears of joy from her cheeks. "We are not going to die. Thank the Stars."

Varek steered his ship carefully as he recalled from training that the cables could not handle too much speed. He did not want to lose his friends after all that he had to go through to find them.

"You did a good thing here, Basil." Essex said with admiration in her voice. "You are not a bad man. You are a hero."

Varek smiled back at her. "I will be if we get safely on Lynott's Land."

"We'll make it," Marble told them. "These cables are the newest models. We could tow a Battle Cruiser with them. We will make it."

Varek took that news well and sped his ship along. As he flew them all toward Lynott's Land, the purple sand spider and several dozen brown ones were chewing on the cable that linked the two ships together. His main fear was not whether or not the cable would hold, but rather whether the Planetary Defense would catch them on a satellite scan and launch an attack against them. As long as they were towing the damaged ship, Varek would not be able to engage any potential enemy. He hoped that the Gods would be merciful and allow them to travel undetected until they could land on some safe landing strip in the next province.

CHAPTER ELEVEN

New Edinburgh UN Representative Jason Ward began to formulate plans to capitalize on his new found luck. With most of the politicians that seemed aligned together to serve the best interests of the people eliminated by the new regime, Ward found that he was one of the few survivors. While the people that rescued him were concentrating on locating and rescuing the cadets on board Clovis 21, Ward was planning and scheming. He began searching news reports and learned that the influential Hsu family was extinct. The lawyer named Goldsmith that had indicated he may run for elected office was now worm food. A former political ally of Ward named Wyclyffe had been decapitated before thousands of cheering citizens. Representative Rice and her family met a similar fate in one of the other territories. Ward's plan was simple. He would embrace the cadets that had rescued him and the surviving members of his family. He would be a champion to the people in ousting the cruel military leaders and the Rosenburg family. And when the smoke cleared, he would be the one to rise up and become Secretary General. The people would have no choice but to follow him as all the other leaders would be dead.

To begin his slow campaign to aggrandize power to himself, Ward advised Basil Varek and his small band of pilots to contact a man named Patrick Doyle Lynott. Ward waited patiently for the cadets to complete the task. Lynott was a very difficult man to find. He was the self-appointed Protective Governor of the region known as Lynott's Land. Ward had been on friendly terms with Lynott for the past decade. They had similar political views. Ward counted him as a friend and hoped that would guarantee a grant of asylum in Lynott's Land.

The Lynott family had been one of the first to contract with the Glorious Leader to purchase large parcel of land for colonization. They were granted one hundred twenty-seven kilometers of land mass on the Northern Continent. The Marines and Army spilled their blood fighting and killing the indigenous life forms in that area so that humans could replace them. The Lynott family accomplished amazing milestones in the fifteen years that they first began building their colony. Lynott's Land was surrounded by a Protective Great Wall, similar to the one around Clovis City, and had many housing districts, industry areas, governmental offices, high rise business buildings that went from a few floors to as high as two hundred fifty floors high. There were over fifteen thousand MI soldiers under the command of General Leta Tan located on the colony. Tan and the Lynott family had a very good working agreement, which was to stay out of one another's business.

There were four landing strips in the region. One was for private transports, the second was a military strip for the two Space Command Squadrons assigned there, the third was located on the massive MI Brigades facilities under the command of General Tan and the fourth was the private landing areas for the Lynott family and their closest friends. The fourth strip was the destination the Ward desired. The first three would assure immediate arrest for the remaining Ward family members as well as the cadets on the ship. All three had a presence from Tan's soldiers and therefore would not be an optimal selection to land at either location. Lynott's private landing areas had no soldiers and would therefore be the preferred place to land, rest and begin to gather allies for the fight for Clovis City.

"Are you certain this Lynott character can be trusted?" Marble asked from her co-pilot seat in the upper level of the ship.

Ward smiled at her and at Varek who was in the main pilot seat. Ward found an empty seat in the tactical weapons section so that he could guide them to their destination. Ward could sense the tension from Marble. He could not blame her. He had killed her friend without question. It had been an unfortunate event that Ward hoped would not stain his future political aspirations.

"I have known Doyle for a very long time," Ward told

them. "He will hide us, at least for a little while. It will buy us time to find other allies. Do not worry. We will be safe there."

Varek said nothing. He was worried about the safety of his friends in the belly of the space craft that was attached to the tow cable. He was equally concerned about his new-found friends that were on board the craft he was flying. They had all been through much excitement and were fortunate to be alive. Varek was willing to take his chances with the Lynott's over facing more of the hungry Cawlers and Dozal any day of the week.

Essex was monitored the communications from Lynott's Land on the computer section of the ship located on the second level. Her mind was still wrapped around her near-death experience engineered by Colan. Essex concluded that Colan had somehow fooled the psychiatric doctors that had to examine her for clearance to attend the Academy. Based on the behavior she observed, Colan had not been mentally well. She had hallucinations and made statements of things that she believed to be factual that were actually fantasy. Sitting in chairs around the computer station were Jessica and Klara Ward, two of Jason Ward's daughters.

Essex had recalled her father and grandfather speaking of Patrick Doyle Lynott over a family dinner. Essex had been about fifteen years old when that conversation occurred. She remembered that they claimed Lynott had become a recluse and preferred to remain in doors. Lynott was allegedly more machine than man, having most of his internal organs and bones replaced by advanced medical organ replicas. The seven-kilometer radius in which the Lynott family lived was surrounded by a large metal fence, armed guards, trained attack dogs, booby traps and computer activated laser weapons. Lynott had dozens of wives, hundreds of children and almost a thousand grandchildren. He had a reputation for screening male visitors to his secret hideaway to determine whether they would be suitable to marry one of his granddaughters. His grandsons seemed to venture out to find their own way in life while the female offspring remained behind to be used by the patriarch of the family to garner favor with another family or group.

They soon received a response from the mystery man named Patrick Doyle Lynott. He demanded to learn the identity of who would dare disrupt his day.

Essex contacted Ward and let him know that Lynott was on their communication frequency. Ward told her he would handle things from there.

"My old friend. This is Jason Ward."

There was a pause that grew uncomfortable. Marble and Varek exchanged glances, wondering whether or not Ward really knew this man after all. Their fears were ended when they heard the sound of laughter on the ships speakers.

"Jason! It has been far too long! Please tell me that you are on your way to land! I have missed our games of chess together!"

"As have I, Doyle." Ward was smiling as he listened to the sound of the voice of his old friend. "Do we have permission to land?"

"Of course, of course! Please!"

"Doyle, we have a problem. We are towing a damaged ship with us. It needs many repairs. It also has many sand spiders clinging to it. Can you have some staff meet us at the landing area to burn those creatures off?"

Lynott was laughing again, finding humor in the situation. "Yes, my friend! I would love to hear the story of how you were able to attract sand spiders to your ship! My guards will handle them. Land and we will dine on beef ribs, fried Jumper Tails and Cawler egg soup. Those bastards ate so many humans that is poetic justice that we would eat them!"

Ward understood from firsthand experience what he meant by that. "I agree my friend. Do I have a story to tell you?"

"Wait until we dine together! I love to hear stories while I eat. I will make certain that we will have plenty scotch waiting for you."

"Until dinner then." Ward signed off the communication.

The purple spider had tried in vain to cut through the

tow cable that connected the two metal shells. The cable was too strong. She sensed that the ship was slowing and was approaching a strange facility. She could see a paved area with other metal ships surrounded by men and women with similar weapons that were used to repel her attack. Her spiders were being taken to be exterminated. She could see the tree lines below growing closer as the ship descended. She shrieked at the remaining brown spiders that had not been blown off the hull of the ship during the flight. The purple spider leaped from the cable and down toward the tree line. She spun a web and connected with a tall tree. She spun in circles until she came to a soft landing on the grass below.   She was elated when about twenty of the brown spiders were able to replicate her actions and land safely on the ground. Many other spiders fell to their deaths or failed to jump off at all. The spiders waited behind the trees and watched the remaining brown spider being burned to death by the men and women wearing camouflage fatigues on the paved area. The large spiders squealed in pain as the flames from the weapons engulfed them.

The purple spider mourned their deaths. She waited with the other brown spiders to see the humans that departed the metal shell. She wanted to see them and obtain their scent. Then she would hunt them down, one at a time if need be, and plant her eggs inside of them.

Gauthier and the survivors of the *Clovis 21* had been celebrating for the past half hour as their damaged ship was being towed. In the food storage area, Juanito and Pepito Calderon had found some ales and whiskey for them to share. Most of the cadets and the young Jorge Calderon began to drink. Gauthier took Haddad to the pilot section and the two shared a large twenty-four-ounce bottle of cold ale, each passing the bottle back to the other after taking a drink.

"So what is our next step?" Haddad asked him.

"Your family is on Ferro's Province?" Gauthier asked after taking a sip of the ale.

"Yes."

"After we get in a night's rest, perhaps we should find a way to make it to them and hide out for a while."

Haddad shook her head in the negative. "No, that is not a good idea. If they find out that I have been sleeping with you they will kill us both. The religion that my family practices views a man like you as an infidel. My own family will have to kill me."

Gauthier laughed and soon realized that she was not joining him. "You aren't joking. They would really kill us?"

Haddad nodded, "Yes they would. You knew Nour and his family. They were as rigid in their beliefs as my family."

Gauthier took another sip of ale as he recalled Azeem Nour and his siblings. They were not very tolerant of opposing viewpoints on the issue of religious beliefs. "I see what you mean. Fine, we avoid Ferro's Province. We will have to find another place."

Serpas cuddled up in the lap of Manuel on a leather couch that folded out of the wall in the command section. They each had poured themselves some whiskey and were enjoying the ride.

Pepito left the gathering with Villandiego in his arms. They found a sleeping quarter's room and immediately began to remove each other's clothing.

Fifteen-year-old Jorge seemed to have developed a crush on Blomquist and followed her everywhere she went. Blomquist spoke with him and would laugh when he would tell her how beautiful she was. Blomquist found that she enjoyed the attention and the company. But she could not forget the fact that he was underage.

Juanito took an ale bottle back to his room and sat on his bed. He took a few sips and ran his left hand over the covers. He recalled making love to Haake on the bed. He closed his eyes and mourned her. He wondered what might have been had she survived.

Cobb missed out on the libations as he was still unconscious due to the stun blast he received from Manuel.

Truang, Eklund and Xavier sat together in the corner of

the main table. They spent the flight talking about ships, engines, which tool manufacturer was the best and the girls showed an interest in the design specifications for the motorcycles. Xavier was elated to explain to them all the specifications, materials and engine work that went into building one of them. He rarely had the chance to entertain a woman and now he had two that were hanging on his every word.

They felt their ship being lowered to the ground. Varek proved his worth as a pilot when he guided the towed space craft to the paved landing area and placed it back on the ground without a sound. Kazembe disconnected the cable and they all watched as the Lynott family guards began burning the spiders off the hull.

"I guess we are safe for now," Gauthier whispered into Haddad's ear.

She watched the spiders burning from the observation window. "Why did they hold on through the entire flight?"

"Remember, Tara, those creatures think differently than us. It is just like the Dozal refusing to end their attack even though we killed ninety percent of them. They think differently than we do. Maybe they were angry that we disturbed their territory."

"Hey!" Manuel screamed up at them. "We are clear to exit the ship!"

The survivors all met out on the concrete landing area.

When Varek joined them he was greeted by many hugs and kisses on the cheek from the women survivors.

"I am so glad to see you in the flesh!" Gauthier told Varek as they hugged. "We thought we were dead for sure!"

The guards for the Lynott family stood back and watched without emotion as the cadets and the Ward family shook hands and exchanged hugs. Haddad noted that the majority of the guards were clad in camouflage fatigues with knee high black boots. There was thirteen of them dressed in black tuxedos with white ruffle shirts, black bow ties and black formal shoes. She estimated that about eighty percent of them were female. All of the guards were Asian and many of them seemed to be exact twins. Each of them wielded laser rifles and laser pistols.

Essex watched as Varek was greeted by the survivors. She smiled for him due to how relieved he was that he had found his lost friends. As the survivors continued to hug each other, Essex observed a man that seemed to be close to seven feet tall approaching them. He was in a black tuxedo, with a bow tie and white ruffled shirt. His short dark hair seemed to be perfect, not a strand out of place. Walking behind him were thirty-six beautiful young women that were wearing conservative white and pink dresses with black high heeled shoes. There were blondes, brunettes and red heads. Essex noted that most of the women were white but there were two that were black, three Latin women, two Asian, one Indian and one Harcourt. Essex wondered if they were the wives of the man in the tuxedo.

Jason Ward noticed that his old friend Patrick Doyle Lynott was approaching him. Ward ran toward him and the men hugged. Lynott was the man that Essex had seen in the tuxedo. The men were talking as the women stood a few feet back. Finally, Ward began to clamor for everyone's attention. The two groups that were now united looked to Ward. The casual observer would not be able to detect that the majority of Lynott's body consisted of surgically enhanced limbs. His legs were completely metal with fake skin wrapped around them. His arms were also fake, as was the left half of his face. But the fake skin wrapped around the metal was from advanced science so that it looked and felt as if it were real human skin. Lynott had suffered several injuries as a young man and had required many surgeries to recover. The robotic and prosthetic limbs were the result of the surgeries. Lynott loved the fact that he had received the new limbs as he was ten times faster than the average human and could lift triple the weight of an average man.

"My friends and family. This is Patrick Doyle Lynott, patriarch of this fine row of mansions and manicured lawns." Ward was beaming at Lynott as he spoke. "He has indicated that we will all have our own rooms in his mansions to stay as long as we wish. He is an amazing host and a dear friend."

"Welcome to my hacienda," Lynott bellowed in a bass baritone voice. "You are my guests and I want each of you to enjoy my hospitality while you are here. I have seven mansions that are each twelve floors high and have approximately two hundred fifty rooms in each. I have gymnasiums, kitchens, a large theater, medical staff, security, golf courses, soccer fields, tennis courts, swimming pools, a zoo, a ski lift to the mountain side, hiking trails, a fully stocked lake for fishing, a vast library, the most advanced computers, horse stables and just about any luxury you can imagine. You may enjoy all of them as my guests. Treat my home as yours. My granddaughters here will escort each of you to the Far East mansion and to your rooms. The second floor of the mansion has an exquisite dining room that will seat seventy-five comfortably. I suggest that each of you shower and my granddaughters will have fresh clothing delivered to your rooms so that you may dine in comfort and dignity. Dinner will be served in ninety minutes." As Lynott spoke, he moved around with grace and maintained eye contact with each of the guests.

Xavier began to clap for Lynott and soon the other cadets did the same. The granddaughters began to choose the males and take them by their arms to lead them to the east mansion.

Haddad stepped in front of a lovely blonde as she

approached Gauthier. "He's with me, sister. Sorry."

The blonde smiled at Haddad. "Do not apologize, miss. He is your man; it is your duty to defend what is yours."

Haddad nodded as the woman left to find someone else to take to the mansion. "That was odd."

"Let's follow them. I am starving," Gauthier told her. They walked together, holding hands and took in the view of the massive mansions in the distance. Some were constructed from types of stones that had to be imported across solar systems. "Each mansion had to cost a fortune. How come we never met a Lynott before?"

"I doubt that any of the Lynott's would have an interest in joining a military academy or doing tequila shots at O'Malley's." Haddad observed. "This is without a doubt what it means to be rich. I saw this when my family moved here years back. We stayed with the Nour family. They had money and lots of land. We were told to leave when my sister rejected an arranged marriage. It was quite intimidating."

"You know that the Nour family control an awful lot of the precious gemstone mines on the planet?"

"I know. My older sister was not impressed. The one she was supposed to marry was named Azeem. She told me he was a pig."

Gauthier shrugged at that comment and followed the crowds in thought. He had met the Nour family one time and recalled interacting for a short time with Azeem. He had been a Bragg Gang member the year before Gauthier joined. There were many stories that painted a bad picture of Azeem Nour. "Would your sister say I was a pig?"

Haddad laughed. "My sister would try and steal you away from me."

"She would fail."

"My sister is much more attractive than me."

"I highly doubt that. Besides, it doesn't matter."

"She is smoking hot."

"Doesn't matter."

"She was prom queen at her high school and she competed in beauty pageants."

Gauthier stopped and kissed her. "You trying to get rid of me?"

"Just testing you."

The group looked upon the eastern mansion in awe. The steps leading up to the front Doric columns were made from granite imported from old Earth. The large double doors were ten feet high and opened by voice command. The building was shaped in the form of a hexagon, of six wings bearing the exact same length, width and height. The center of the building was open to the elements and had a large swimming pool, gymnasium, several grills and a fully stocked bar.

The cadets and Ward family members were led inside, save Jason Ward who walked toward the northern mansion with Lynott for a private dinner. Kia Marble glared at the backside of Jason Ward as he went in a different direction. She wanted to kill him for what he did to Meelia. She worried about the reaction of her hosts if she did so on the Lynott property. Marble followed the cadets. She needed a shower and a good meal would do her some good. Juanito and Jorge carried Cobb over their shoulders, dragging his feet on the ground as they moved.

The thirty-six women were their tour guides, showing them the large lobby style entrance and motioning to the long and wide staircases to the left and the right that led to the dining room and the upstairs bedrooms. The ten-foot-tall and five-foot-wide one way windows were sectioned every ten feet, giving them a nice view of the gardens that surrounded the outside of the mansion. The floors of the first floor were covered with black tile and an occasional white or red carpet underneath a table or computer terminal. The high ceiling had many crystal chandeliers and some mural paintings of major events from the major religions. The cadets and the Ward family members were staring upward in awe.

"Look, kitties!" Eklund knelt next to several kittens and larger cats to pet a group of black and white cats that were meowing and rubbing against her legs.

There were several men in tuxedos and women in formal

gowns waiting inside the mansion for them. They were a mixture of skin colors and ages. They each had hand held scanners and began to use them on each of the cadets and Ward family members.

"What are you doing?" Truang asked one of the men.

"Scanning for your measurements so that we can provide for you proper fitting clothing," the man in the tuxedo responded.   His voice sounded flat and lacked emotion.

"Thank you," Truang told him. She was so grateful to be alive that any sense of normalcy escaped her.

He did not respond as he scanned her arm length and leg length. When he was done, he moved on to Raklitz who was standing behind her.

Raklitz waited for the hosts to complete their scan of her friend Villandiego. Both women were told by a well-armed Asian woman in fatigues to report to the second floor of the mansion for medical attention.

Raklitz moved next to Villandiego and whispered into her left ear: "I scanned the entire population of the mansions before we left our ship. About half of the occupants here are related to Mr. Lynott. The other half are of Asian ancestry."

Villandiego shrugged, "So?"

"So, the Asian security guards here are all related. They share DNA traits. Don't you find it odd that the entire set of people living in each of these mansions come from just two families?"

Villandiego smiled politely at another Asian woman in uniform that motioned for them to move up the staircase. As she walked up the long, winding staircase she responded to Raklitz in a hushed tone of voice. "But there are many mixed races here. You are saying to me that they are all related to one another? So are you insinuating that these people interbreed with one another?"

"I don't know what I am suggesting," Raklitz whispered. "I just find it odd that none of the adults here have spouses around that have different DNA strands. Just very strange."

"But I saw many people of different races here. How can that be? They cannot all be descended from the same family. Right?"

Raklitz put her arm around her and looked around as if she were concerned they were being spied on. "I think that they are interbreeding with one another. They might have had much diversity a few generations back, but they are procreating with each other."

"Let's worry about this later," Villandiego urged her. "I want to get examined and then eat. I am starving."

The Harcourt woman stood before the mass group of cadets and Ward's to address them. "Before each of you retire to your individual suites, we need for you to speak your names into the intercom near the staircases. The entire mansion is secured by a voice activation system. You may come and go with a simple voice command. Anything that you desire will be there for the asking. Mister Lynott wishes each of you to have a wonderful vacation. If you have any complaints as to the facilities, please do not hesitate to bring them to our attention. We are here to serve you. Our chief of security is Yung Tao. He is watching everything from his basement offices. So, don't make any attempts to steal any of the expensive paintings or dinette sets. His guards will set upon you and then you will be thrown over the protective walls into the Forbidden Region."

"What are your names?" Jorge asked them. "I mean how do we call you?"

An attractive blonde woman smiled at him. She was wearing a skin tight, silver gown with dark blue trim and silver slippers. "We are the granddaughters of Mister Lynott. We will meet each of you individually over the course of your stay. My name is Lesa. I am the manager of this mansion. Please speak your names into the intercom and then proceed upstairs, select a room to your liking and shower. Towels, soap, shampoo, bathrobes, perfumes and colognes are waiting for you. When you exit the showers we will have appropriate attire for you on your beds and your desk drawers."

Lesa Lynott motioned to the stairs with both hands

outstretched.

One by one, the guests spoke their names into the wall speakers as directed. The thirty-six single females watched with keen interest as the gathering made their way upstairs. From their observation, it seemed as if Gauthier and Manuel Calderon were involved. The rest of the men were fair game.

Jason Ward was escorted to the central mansion by Patrick Doyle Lynott. The two men conversed about chess, soccer, and tennis as they walked. After entering the mansion, they were assured of being out of listening distance of the others and they changed the subject of their conversation to politics.

"They killed Wyclyffe," Lynott said softly. "One of my daughters was married to him. They cut off her head in the courtyard of the U.N. Building while the fickle crowds cheered her death. I am tired of the Rosenburg's. They have finally gone too far."

"I agree, Doyle. The cadets that rescued me and my family are trying to mount an offensive against the Rosenburg faction. If they are to succeed, they will need allies." Ward followed Lynott up the long, winding stairs to the right of the hallway after they had entered the mansion. "All of my wives were killed in Clovis City and in the Forbidden Region. Those of us that are alive barely escaped."

Ward went on to relate how the MI soldiers were sent to arrest him and all of his family. Ward and his wives fought back.

So did his sons and daughters. They wiped out an entire platoon of the soldiers and five Babbcottiatta in the battle. Several of Ward's wives and children perished in the fight. Ward led his surviving family members on a mad dash to their private transport ship to escape the crackdown of Clovis City. They would have made it had the ship engine not failed. They crashed in the Forbidden Region and lost thirteen more family members until the cadets arrived.

"It would seem that these young kids know how to fight. They will make good soldiers for us," Lynott concluded as he stopped at the fifth floor of the mansion where a large marble chess board was waiting with silver Viking and gold Roman pieces were placed in their proper locations. Lynott sat down behind the side of the board with the Romans.

"Yes, they can fight and they are resilient." Ward sat down behind the Viking side of the board. "You have protected the excesses of General Tan for years. Will she follow your orders? I mean, if you were willing to send her troops in against the Rosenburg's?"

"No, she would refuse such a request and most likely would turn on me," Lynott moved the pawn that was in front of his Queen. "She benefits too much from this raid by the Glorious Leader. We must be patient, Jason. We must wait. A solution will present itself to us soon, it always does."

"And in the meantime?"

"We enjoy each other's company, we play some chess and perhaps some tennis matches as we have done in the past. My granddaughters will satisfy their urge to breed with the males that have arrived, including your sons and grandsons. You are fine with that, are you not?"

Ward laughed, "I would be proud to have my sons breed with your granddaughters. Plus, I am now a widower as all of my wives are dead. I need a few new wives and would love to marry a few of them for myself."

"They are very young and full of sexual energy." Lynott warned him. "You might find them too much to handle."

"I would love to find that out for myself."

Lynott lifted up his queen chess piece and inspected it for a moment, deep in thought. "You will become the Secretary General of this planet, Jason. It will happen. I believe that if we have the proper ground attack and superior firepower in the skies, we can prevail. We just need to move some chess pieces into the right positions to get you there."

"When the cadets rescued me, I accidentally killed one of them. I thought they were MI and fired on them," Ward said with no evidence of regret in his voice. "If I do start to rise to power, the cadets might speak of the incident. It could harm my popularity and damage me if we end up with free elections."

Lynott set the chess piece back on the board. "They are

all pawns, Jason. All of those cadets are pawns. Pawns normally get sacrificed for the greater good. Which cadets saw what happened? And of those, which ones can be trusted to keep their mouths shut with the proper, shall we say motivation?"

Ward stood up and paced across the marble floor. "I had a long conversation with the cadet named Vezpucci. I brought up the subject with him. He told me had he been in my shoes he would have done the same thing. He is also sweet on my daughter, Jessica. I have spoken to her and encouraged them to begin seeing each other. If they become lovers, and they will, Vezpucci would not betray me at that point. But I am concerned that using Jessica in such a manner might prohibit my ability to one-day trade her for political favors in the future. I have instructed her to get close to Vezpucci, but not too close. Cadet Kazembe also told me she would have acted as I did. They understand it was a stressful event. The only one that I am worried about is Ensign Marble. She glares at me and seems to have bad intentions toward me. She may have to be removed. I never had the opportunity to speak of the issue with Varek or Essex."

"Essex? There was an Essex with you?"

"Yes. She is the granddaughter of the first mayor of Clovis City."

"We cannot harm her, Jason. Her family is as powerful

as mine. We need them if you are to elevate to power. But the Marble woman? I will have my Harcourt wife read her mind and see what she is thinking. If she is wanting some retribution, we will have to arrange an accident. Even with all of our technology and safety measures, humans still drown in pools, fall from buildings or fall off the Great Wall into the Forbidden Region. Things happen."

Jason Ward smiled at his friend and sat back down at the chess board table. "Yes, they do. And Varek? What do we do about him?"

Lynott leaned back in his chair and ran his fingers through his hair. "We watch him. We can make offers to him. He might find one of our women desirable enough to do whatever we ask of him. Besides, if he is as heroic as everyone seems to think, it would be a shame to kill such a man. A hero could be useful to help us advance our political agenda. I take it he is a commoner?"

Ward nodded. "I had Klara check him out on the computer memory banks. Varek has a good grade point average and a sketchy past. His family is gone except for a brother and sister that are much younger. If we kill him, few would care. But I agree with you. I like him. He is a good pilot and he is loyal. If we can get such a man on our side, he would be an asset."

Lynott smiled and nodded as he contemplated his next move. He gladly accepted a tall glass of whiskey on the rocks from an attractive, young Asian woman. She smiled at Ward and handed him a similar drink. Without a word she departed to leave the two men to their game of chess.

"Is she one of Tao's children?" Ward asked.

"One of his grandchildren," Lynott informed him. He took a sip of his whiskey and nodded his approval. "This comes from my personal brewery, Jason. Enjoy it."

"How many generations does your family go back with Tao's?"

Lynott smiled at his friend and gingerly placed the glass on the table, just next to the chess board. "Our families have been united for over five generations. Nothing can separate our families. Tao is in with anything I decide to undertake."

Ward nodded, "I am not questioning Tao's resolve. I have always liked him and the few children of his that I have met. How many Tao's are there living on your compound?"

"Five hundred ninety-three."

"That many? Where are they all hidden?"

"They all live in the southern mansion," Lynott responded. "At one time, there was over nine hundred of them. Some left to pursue an education elsewhere; others went to work on other planets. Many of them were married off to secure favors or business deals. The Tao's know how to play the game politic. He has several grandchildren that need spouses. Any of your children ready to be a part of an arranged engagement?"

Ward sipped from his drink and leaned back in his chair. "All of my children understand power and their duty. What would be the advantage to me marrying off some of my children to Yung Tao's?"

Lynott shrugged as he studied the chess board. "Each of his offspring are extremely intelligent, talented and loyal. Also, as you are aware, Tao's children were all genetically altered in the womb to be faster and smarter than the average. The advancement we noticed with Tao's offspring has continued with his grandchildren. They are all quite amazing. Your children would be lucky to have those qualities in a spouse. I will have Tao speak with you later tonight and he can fill you in on which of his seed are ready."

The sand spiders began to surround the eastern mansion to search for an entrance to get at the humans inside. One of the brown spiders alerted the others that danger was approaching. All of the spiders scurried across the concrete pavement back toward the trees began to dig under the grass as three German Shepherd guard dogs were running in their direction, sniffing and looking around before they put their noses to the ground and sniffed some more. The dogs detected a scent they had never been exposed to before. They followed the smell into the trees. The spiders ambushed the dogs and impaled them with their stingers. The dogs were taken by complete surprise and didn't even get a chance to bark. For the spiders, they had just killed their meal of the day.

CHAPTER THIRTEEN

She struggled to keep herself from passing out from the pain and the loss of blood. Cara Perez Guerrero had been hit by several shrapnel pieces while relaxing at her home during the early morning hours. Her neighbors, the Collins family, were attacked by soldiers and aliens transported in a large Raumschiff just after dawn. But the Collins clan had been prepared and shot the ship out of the sky. Guerrero's home suffered some outer damage in the resulting explosion and her injuries were caused at that moment. She screamed for help to her mother and younger siblings.

Her mother was by her side in seconds as one of her sisters used her Holo-com device to demand immediate emergency transport to the hospital. She was crying has she held the wound on her side. But her tears were not from pain, they were from fear of losing her two unborn children in her womb.

Cara was studying to become a pilot with aspirations at becoming an officer in the Space Command. Upon arriving at the military training academy, she discovered that the student body was divided up into several factions. There was the Bragg

Gang that boasted the largest membership of just under one hundred cadets. The Gorski Gang was normally about twenty members. Some semesters the Gorski Gang would have more or less. There were other groups known as the Collins Faction, the Medical Student Union, the Asian Pilots Association, the Future MI Cadets and many others. The group that Cara had aligned herself with was the group known as the Ladies Pilot Club. Her first leader of that group during her initial year had graduated and moved on to her career. Cara found that she had little patience for the gangs, so she began to ease away from the Ladies Pilot Club and did her own thing.

And the thing she enjoyed the most was sex. She had only two lovers before signing up at Clovis Academy. Cara was an attractive woman and had no difficulty finding men that lusted for her. During her first year, she had slept with over twenty different men. In her second year, she tried threesomes and other wild sexual escapades. She began to believe that no one man could captivate her.

Then she met Pierre Zerbe. Like Cara, Zerbe had been a loner after he rejected his membership with the Bragg Gang. And they both liked wild sex. Zerbe was willing to try anything for erotic pleasure. When he and Cara finally tested one another, they found that they were a good match. Not only in the bedroom, but they shared similar interests. They were both cadet pilots and had the same goals for their future. Before they knew what had happened to them, they were in love. And soon Cara was pregnant with Zerbe's children. They had planned on marrying and sharing their lives together.

But, alas, it was not meant to be. Pierre Zerbe died on the Blood Moon.

Cara found some solace in her friends. Doctor Freya Doernitz had become her closest confidant and the two women used the services of a local law firm to sue the evil individuals that had caused the deaths of Zerbe and Freya's husband. The Rosenburg Corporation was willing to settle in return for avoiding a public trial and the probing discovery requests that had been filed by the lawyers representing Cara and Freya. The two women were made very wealthy.

Cara used her settlement money to purchase many stock options in some growing corporations so that she could provide for her children. She wanted to make sure her widowed mother, her siblings and some cousins were cared for so she bought her current home in one of the prestigious housing developments in Clovis City. She had her family move into the three floor, twenty-seven room mansion. She continued her education, kept her scheduled medical appointments to ensure that her twins would be born healthy. Her friendship with Freya grew as did her association with her neighbors, the Collins family. She also grew closer to the other cadet pilots that had been impacted by the Blood Moon Incident.

She cried at the thought of losing her precious children. Her breathing was labored and she felt herself go in and out of consciousness. Her mother and siblings encouraged her to hold on. Fortunately, the emergency crew from the hospital arrived at her home in under two minutes. The nurses and the lone doctor that arrived quickly stabilized her by administering some drugs and stopping the loss of blood. Cara was carried out of her home on a white stretcher and placed in the back of an emergency hover craft. The flight to the hospital took under two minutes.

Cara felt herself slip from intense pain to ecstasy. She was not sure what drugs the emergency crew gave to her, but she had never felt better in her life. She smiled as she saw the lights on the ceiling above her pass while her stretcher was placed on a wheeled cart. She was pushed rapidly down the hallway and could hear people speaking to her. All she could do was smile.

When she came to a stop she heard the voice of her friend speaking to her.

"Cara. Cara, look at me." Doctor Freya urged her. "We are going to put you under and operate. We believe your babies were not harmed. I will be there for you when you wake up."

Cara smiled weakly at her friend. "Thank you. Save my babies. Please."

Freya nodded to a nurse who injected something into Cara's arm. The cadet pilot felt herself floating and her body tingled for a few seconds before she passed out.

Klaus Rhinehard had not been ready for the moment that his wife would go into labor. He had believed he had everything planned out. He had two suitcases packed with clothing for the mother and the soon to be born twins, diapers, wipes, toiletries, and towels for cleaning. He had gone over how he would get his lovely wife, April Mejia to the hospital when she alerted him that it was time. She had been experiencing contractions throughout the day, but that had been something that was occurring with her for the last week.

While he was sitting in his rocking chair at his home that was supplied by Clovis Academy he drank a glass of sekt wine and smiled at his wife. The married cadets were always given a home to live in as opposed to being in the dormitories. He watched April as she laid back on one of the white couches in the living area. The house was decorated with statues of old style Viking warriors and paintings of battle scenes. Klaus had been given the majority of the works of art by a probate distribution of his great grandfather's estate several years ago. Klaus had been favored in such a manner since he was one of the few Rhinehard's that believed in the Norse Gods and paid homage to them. His wife did not comprehend his fascination with the old religion. She enjoyed listening to her husband when he would tell her if the promise that all brave warriors would be taken to

Valhalla. He spoke about it with great passion. She never believed in the Norse religion as her husband did, even though he tried many times to convince her that the Norse gods were the true deities in the universe.

"What are you watching?" She asked him as she softly ran her hands over her extended stomach. She had enjoyed her pregnancy but was ready for it to end. She wanted to hold her unborn twins in her arms and give them all the love she felt for them. She knew that Klaus felt the same. She had no doubt that he would be an amazing father.

"The news," Klaus told her. He had a large seventy by eighty-inch view of a reporter interviewing Rebecca Rosenburg, the new UN Secretary General. She was thanking her predecessor, Alexander Lyss, for all of his service to the people of New Edinburgh and wished him well.

"I bet they forced his ass out," April remarked. "Any news about our friends?"

Klaus shook his head. The soldiers under the command of Reynita Calderon had refused to allow Klaus or April to participate in their plans to fight back against the Sikorsky forces. Although both were disappointed, they realized that was the correct decision. April was due to deliver the twins in her womb any day now.

"We could have helped them," Klaus lamented as his wife gritted her teeth due to another contraction.

April nodded and listened as Rebecca Rosenburg revealed that Colonel Nikolai Gorski had escaped. She announced that anyone that could supply information that would lead to the apprehension or death of Nikolai Gorski would be awarded one million dollars. She continued by offering monetary rewards for the heads of Piotr Gorski, the Evart women, some of the Goldsmith family and others.

While the list of names that were wanted were being called out by Rebecca Rosenburg, April felt another contraction.

"Amor, they are too close together," she informed him as another contraction hit her. She groaned out loud.

Klaus stood up as he saw the look on her face. "April, was ist los? Are you okay?"

She looked over at her husband with desperation in her eyes. "It's time! We need to go!"

"Jetzt? Now?" He reached to take her hands in his.

"Yes! Now cabron! Now!"

At that moment, all of the careful hours of planning by Klaus went out the window. He reached for his hand held communication device and contacted the hospital with panic in his voice. The receptionist that responded to his call tried to calm him down and informed him that a medical transport would be on its way.

Klaus helped his wife toward the doorway as the

medical transport ships had a reputation for responding in sixty seconds to their housing village. She was groaning and holding her stomach as he led her. She leaned against the wall as he pushed the two suitcases toward the door. The time had come.

They were about to become parents.

As they moved out of their home, they could see the white with red trim transport ship flying toward them. It was about fifty feet off the ground and quickly landed on the transparent concrete street in front of them. Before it landed a female in a one-piece white medical outfit was leaping from the side entrance of the ship and landed with both feet on the concrete. She was running toward them as fast as she could. April and Klaus were happy it was someone that they knew.

Nurse Shaila Patel took April by the arm. She began asking her questions about the frequency of the contractions as she moved her toward the ship. A few other medical nurses joined her and moved Klaus aside as they took over escorting his wife onto a rolling bed that they had pushed toward them.

The flight to the hospital from their home was approximately five minutes long. Klaus held April's hand as she groaned in pain. She had rejected the offer of a C-section from her doctor as she wanted to experience a normal birth. Based on the new pain she was experiencing, April wondered if she could get the pain medication that her physician had once counseled her on. She let out a scream as her concerned husband tried in vain to encourage her.

Doctor Priya Patel had assisted Freya in saving Cara's life. Patel was a board-certified doctor that had become the hospital expert on child birth. She was elated that Cara had survived her wounds. Her twins were a different matter. The girl had to be placed in the Intensive Care Unit and might die due to the wounds she suffered in the explosion. The boy was safe and receiving oxygen treatments. Patel was waiting for the mother to wake up so that she could inform her of the news.

After Patel had completed her operation on Cara, she returned to her small five by ten-foot-wide office to rest. She had been working for over twenty-four officers on patients being flown in on emergency following emergency. The military crackdown on the city had caused many casualties and injuries. Patel and the medical staff had been working to save lives of soldier and civilian alike as the patients poured into the ER like a sea with no end. She wanted to simply rest, if even for only a minute, to catch her wits and close her eyes. As she sat down at her desk and put her head back, she rubbed her head with both hands. Her medical uniform was stained with blood from a patient she had just finished operating on.

"Doctor Patel, please help us."

The voice from the corner of her office startled Patel and she sat up quickly. She looked in the direction where she heard the person speaking and narrowed her eyes. She saw medical student Lynn Goldsmith huddled in the corner with two children, a boy and a girl.

"Lynn?" Patel whispered. She had heard about the murder of the Goldsmith family. The rumors were that all of them had been killed. Clearly the rumors were wrong. "Is that you?"

Goldsmith nodded her head in the affirmative. Her blue eyes had the look of a hunted animal in them. Her bright silver hair was matted from soot and perspiration. Her clothing was covered in mud and stains. She smelled as if she had been hiding in some of the underground sewage processing tunnels below the city. "Yes, it's me. I am sorry to sneak in to your office, but I didn't know where else to go. They killed our family, Doctor Patel. There are orders to kill the rest of us on sight. We have nowhere else to go. Please help us."

Patel stood up and felt a rush of energy come over her. She had always liked Lynn Goldsmith. She had been a good student and did well in all of her student internship shifts at the hospital. She had the potential to become an excellent physician. "I heard about your family, Lynn. I am so sorry for your losses. Who do you have with you, Lynn?"

"My little sisters, Bobbi and Evianna. They were the only ones I could rescue from the soldiers. They were spending the night with some neighbors when the attack happened."

Goldsmith's voice was shaking from both fear and fatigue. She had been on the run for quite some time and fending for two young siblings as she had must have drained her strength.

"You three can stay here. Keep out of sight. There are Militzia all over the hospital and they will not hesitate to follow their orders to kill you. I will sneak in some food, fresh clothes and wash wipes so you can clean up."

Lynn began to weep openly. After finding her sisters she took them to the underground sewage system and never stopped running. She could have used her cash cards to obtain food or a hotel room, but Lynn had deduced that the soldiers would have been scanning the computer activity for such a move. So she decided that she had to turn to someone that would help her. Most of her father's friends were being hunted or were dead. She had to find a person that she knew to turn to. After hours in the raw sewage she pushed her sisters to make the journey to the center of the city where the hospital was located. She knew that the Patel family had been her only hope to save her nine-year-old sisters. She was relieved that she had made the correct decision in who to trust.

Patel received a message from her sister, Shaila, that another pregnant woman was on the way. Patel notified her nursing staff to scrub up and prepare for another birth. She asked the hospital computer to download the files on April for her inspection. After the medical emergency with Cara, Patel was ready for a routine birth.

"Lynn, I have to go. Stay here and wait for me. Do not leave this room for any reason."

"Yes, Doctor." She nodded.

"Thank you," the twins Evianna and Bobbi said in unison.

Patel smiled at the children and left the room.

CHAPTER FOURTEEN

From his large tower building, Alfred Rosenburg observed the fires in the distance. He knew exactly what was occurring. His family was purging Clovis City of those that had been deemed as traitors. That would mean Sean Collins and his family would be arrested or killed. The Li and the Goldsmith families would be targeted. He crossed his arms over his chest as he looked over the city that he had called home. This was not what he wanted. Although Collins and Goldsmith prosecuted him, Alfred understood their actions. They were honorable men that Alfred would have liked to call friends. But due to his family name and the actions of his father and siblings, he would never be able to enjoy a positive relationship with men like Collins. They would always be adversaries.

Ellis Ragnarsson stood next to him and watched the fires. His muscular arms were crossed over his chest. He was wearing a blue, long sleeved shirt with silver pants. His hair was perfectly groomed and his piercing eyes seemed to catch everything. "That one to the left looked like a Raumschiff exploding."

"Yes. It is nearby the subdivision where Collins and

Doctor Cardenas live," Alfred noted. "Ellis, I really do not like the tenor of this. It is wrong. These people only enforced the rule of law. I know that you and I were going to do some jail time, but we deserved it."

"Speak for yourself."

"Hear me out. Our families committed some horrendous acts. You and I helped them do it. We got caught and should be punished." Alfred paused and pointed out the large windows. "But this? This is wrong. If the people find some leaders, get organized, find some weapons and fight back, you and I will be hunted as mere criminals at best or as war crimes defendants at worse. Our families are wrong to take this action. They should have left it all alone."

"What is done is done, Al. I am happy to be free. Sitting in that ten by ten jail cell waiting for a potential gang rape to come my way was more than I care to put up with. Besides, what the hell can we do about it now?"

"Nothing, my friend. Nothing. We are two men with means, but we cannot fight an army of MI soldiers and hundreds of Saharakaree. We cannot do a thing. But we can save ourselves. The people will fight back. They may even resort to guerrilla warfare. When that happens, you and I, as Rosenburg's and Ragnarsson's, will be hunted down."

"So then, what are you suggesting?"

"That we leave. Now. Give the law firm to our associate

lawyers and let us go somewhere that will be safe. Jada Ying can run the firm. She knows the business end of things quite well. We have money, gold, silver, platinum, diamonds, weapons and two Super-Raumschiffs filled with enough provisions to last five life times. Let us leave this planet behind and start a new life elsewhere. We can get a fresh start."

"A fresh start would be good," Ellis agreed. "I don't mind leaving. None of my bitch wives came to visit me while I was in jail, so fuck them. I can leave them behind to die here with a clear conscience. My children, too. Those little shits didn't even send me a postcard while we were in jail. Yes, Al, I agree. We should leave. But where would we go?"

Alfred pursed his lips and faced his friend. "We go out past planet New Berlin. There are some lunar bodies on the edge of that solar system that are reportedly able to sustain life. Rumors are that they are sparsely populated and full of opportunity for men and women that are willing to take risks. We can start over and be whoever we want to be. We can change our names and start over."

"What are we waiting for?"

"We need to contact some of our old pilots and perhaps get a few slave girls to keep our beds warm at night. Once we round up those few loose ends, we leave this place forever. All of my wives and children were either arrested or killed. With my father dead and Cush, Darryl, Caine and David gone, there is not much left of the brains of my family. Matthew and Penelope were the smart ones and I have learned that they have gone missing. Nicolette and Kristin are also gone and that leaves the others that have very little in the way of intelligent thought. We can start a new life, my friend. I just wish that I knew where Matthew and Nicolette ended up. They had the human DNA replication technology down to perfection. I would love to have had them go along with us."

"No idea where they are?"

"None. We should leave. The real estate managers will make sure the building rental profits make it to my banks. We will have money and new identities. This planet will have new leadership and direction and I do not want to be any part of it.

"Good. It will never be the same again anyway."

Doctor Matthew Rosenburg had been monitoring the current events from the medical laboratory given to him by General Tan. He was aware of the Royal Family purge that was inflicting heavy casualties in Clovis City as well as the lunar base. He had learned of the martial law that had been imposed on all the eleven provinces of the northern continent of New Edinburgh. He was cognizant that the best chance for him to save his remaining children was to keep up to date on the news reports.

The lab was about twenty-four hundred square feet and

had high ceilings with metal beams on the top. The floors were covered with light blue tile and the walls were painted light grey. There were large florescent lights that illuminated the large room so that all of the blue colored medicine cabinets, grey computers and red desks with surgical instruments were visible to any staff. There were only three that had worked on the fifty Ragnarsson clones. That was Matthew Rosenburg and his two daughters.

Matthew had forbidden Tan to send in any of her own people as he did not wish to share the secrets of the cloning techniques. It had been a Rosenburg family secret and he wished for it to remain so. Plus, the ability to make a duplicate was his main ticket to safety. He was aware that Tan would kill him and all of his children if she were to somehow acquire the technology.   To remain relevant and alive, Matthew had no choice but to guard what he knew at all costs.

All forty-nine of the clones were lying on rolling beds with their skull incisions healing. One was the color of an Anglo male while the other forty-eight were still green. Matthew had begged for and received permission to send two of his spouses to his mansion at the Rosenburg Ranch Territory to obtain the necessary microchips and equipment to correct the errors in the clones. He worked day and night with his daughters as they eliminated all the possibilities, one by one, until they determined that the Ragnarsson Replicants had defective computer chips in their brains.

Matthew had been overjoyed that the young Lieutenant named Calderon had been able to have all of his children, save one, returned to him. He would be forever grateful to the young officer for her efforts on his behalf. He was certain that he would never be able to repay her for how she found his missing wives and children. He would have time to later mourn his son, but now was the time to prepare to save his other children.

He had dissected one of the fifty green skinned clones of Dell Ragnarsson, Junior. He could conclude that the reason the Ragnarsson Replicants failed to activate was from a design defect in the memory receiving microchips that had been hastily installed in the brains of the non-living bodies. Matthew and his two daughters, Maggie and Jaime, had worked well together in unraveling the mystery of the imperfections. He was proud of the two girls and hoped that his actions would get them safely away from the cruel Leta Tan and her army of women.

His plan had risks. He had gone over his chances of succeeding in his mind. He believed he had about a fifty percent chance of getting his daughters and wives off Lynott's Land alive if he followed through with his hidden agenda.

Matthew had done as Tan demanded. He used the skin of the several female prisoners to replace the green skin of one of the Ragnarsson duplicates. His daughters had skillfully assisted in grafting the new skin to the seemingly lifeless clone. It was now ready to receive the mental patterns and memories of Leta Tan. Matthew would do as the General had demanded and place her brain patterns inside the newly refitted clone. But at the same time, he was going to have his own brain scanned into the remaining forty-seven green-skinned clones. In addition, the Ragnarsson Duplicates would receive downloads of information on military tactics, self-defense information and weaponry proficiency.

Matthew was aware that Tan was far too vain to allow her own memories to be used in the ugly looking green skinned clones. While she would spend hours, hopefully days, reveling in her second life as a muscular and handsome male, he would plan his escape. Matthew hoped that she would be so caught up in the circumstances that he would not be asked to reveal the fate of the other duplicates.

"Daddy? The clone is ready to receive General Tan's brain patterns," Maggie said as she was scanning the white skinned duplicate body of Junior Ragnarsson. "When do we inform her of our success?"

"Right away," he told his daughter as he looked over their handiwork. He smiled as he thought about how far medicine had come. Several hundred years ago, skin grafting on this level would never have been possible. Now doctors could replace the entire body of skin in a day and the healing rate was almost immediate. It was all due to the alien technology of the Danaraja space craft that his family had found about twenty years earlier, hidden under the ground of the area known as Rosenburg's Ranch.

"He is so handsome," Jaime Rosenburg said as she looked over the naked body.

"Don't get any ideas," he told his daughter sternly. "I will inform Tan personally. Wait here for me and do nothing. I will be back soon and we can begin the procedure to transfer Tan's brain patterns into him."

"Did we ever do this before, daddy? I mean, did our grandfather or Uncle Cush ever take a cloned body and imprint another person's brain patterns into it?" Maggie was curious. She had been young when Cush had been executed. She had also been kept at a distance from her grandfather as his lust for his own daughters was well known. Matthew had been most vigilant in protecting his daughters from the lust of the lecherous old man. When he began to have children of his own, Matthew had his own mansion built miles away from his father and had installed a security system from the Fenster Corporation so that his father could not gain access. Due to the separation from the other family members, Matthew and his wives had complete autonomy in the education of their children. Accordingly, Maggie only knew what her father and mothers had taught her.

"We will speak of this later," Matthew promised his

curious daughter. "Wait here and I will bring back General Tan for the procedure."

"When do we leave this place, daddy?" Jaime wanted to know.

"Soon, my dear. Very soon."

Boland 'Quarter' Miles had been monitoring the computer system in the dormitory room of Harumi Shigeta with twin sisters Nola and Lola Belzyt. The computer was running a program attempting to find a match for the eyewitness description of the potential kidnapers of Dirk and Therese Fenster. Miles had written a separate program to cross reference the descriptions with individuals that had criminal charges over the prior two-year period. They had little else to do ever since the soldiers quarantined the dormitories and placed orders on all of the cadets to remain in their rooms.

Miles looked out the window and could see the bodies of Dean Warren and her husband hanging by their necks on the one-hundred-foot high flag poll that had the Academy flag waving proudly in the wind. He watched the entire event when the soldiers killed the Warren's and hung their bodies for all to see. The children of the Warrens were taken into custody and charged with treason. Miles shook his head. Most of the Warren children were not even teenagers yet. Miles knew that if the new military leaders had their way, the Warren family would be eliminated within the next calendar day.

Lola Belzyt was asleep on one of the beds. She was wearing a white sweat shirt with the Clovis Academy logo on it. Her black shorts were wrinkled and her long hair was covering the pillow. Miles smiled at Nola who was stretching out on the other bed. She was nude. After Lola fell asleep, Nola and Miles had sex on the floor on the other side of the bed just in case the sister woke up she would not see them in action. Due to the forced lock in there was little else to do but engage in sexual activity. Miles had seduced her by telling her the tale of how he had earned his nickname "Quarter." When Miles had turned sixteen he participated in an intramural basketball league. In one of the earliest games of the season, Miles hit five three point shots, three two point shots and all of his free throws. For the quarter he was perfect and had scored twenty-seven points. The remaining three quarters of the game Miles missed every single shot he threw up. So, his teammates began calling him Quarter since he was only good for twelve minutes.

Miles slid onto the bed with Lola and cupped her bare breasts in his hands. He kissed her nipples and she encouraged him by running her fingers through his thick hair.

"I love it when you do that," she whispered to him.

She slid her hands under his baggy shorts and took hold of his manhood. They began kissing each other. She pulled his shorts down as he positioned himself on top of her.

The computer began to make a beeping noise indicating that it was ready to print its findings from a search that one of the three had programmed.

"Quarter!" Lola Belzyt jumped up from the floor where she had been sleeping. "We have something!"

She noticed that Quarter leaped to his feet and was naked. He was trying to find his shorts to put on. Lola saw that her sister was also nude and quickly deduced what was going on between her twin and Miles. She crossed her arms and glared at them.

"Don't lecture me," Nola said as she pulled on a Clovis Academy purple t-shirt.

"You always get the guy. Always. Why, Nola? Can't you let me have fun just once?"

"Lola, you were asleep. Things just happened," Nola said as she pulled on her panties. "And why am I always having to justify everything to you? We're twins. You're as pretty as me; you could get guys as easy as I can. Jeez, sis. Quit being a joy kill."

Miles found his button down black shirt and pulled it on. He smiled as he listened to the twins fight over him. If he could have his way, he would sleep with them both at the same time. That could be an adventure worth experiencing.

The three young cadets crowded around the printer and

waited. The eight by ten paper slowly dropped to the printer tray and revealed the image and name of Boris Ilyasova. His long resume followed on several separate sheets of paper. Lola grabbed the resume and began reading it. She smiled at Miles and Nola.

"Former ace pilot on the Colorado, and kicked out of the service for conduct unbecoming an officer." Lola read from the paper. "We need to get this information to Klaus, Elektra and Harumi! He might be one of the kidnapers!"

Miles looked at the face on the paper. "Yeah. You are right. This might be the breakthrough we have been hoping for."

"What do we do with this information?" Nola asked.

Miles rubbed his chin and felt that he needed to shave. He pondered the question and remembered that Klaus, Harumi and Jen Staszko had told him to use his own judgment if any useful information came through. Miles smiled as he had an idea.

"We post his face wanted dead or alive on all of the satellite services. Send his identity to all of the social media out there and offer a reward for ten thousand dollars, dead or alive, in connection with the kidnaping of Dirk and Therese Fenster."

"What if he had nothing to do with it?" Lola asked.

"Then he will contact us to set the record straight." Miles shrugged. "From the rap sheet on this Ilyasova he is a rogue. Post his face everywhere and let him come to us."

"We might want to let the others know we are doing it."

Lola said.

"I will call Klaus and April," Nola announced as she picked up her multi-colored communication and flipped it open. "They seem to be the only two Gorski Gang leaders around. Where the hell did the rest of them go to?"

Lola walked toward the door and straightened out her clothing and her hair. "I'll leave you two alone. I am going to find a man in the rec room and see if I can get laid, too."

Before the door shut behind Lola, Nola and Miles were already kissing and removing each other's clothing.

"We have to hurry," Nola said as Miles lifted her in his arms and carried her to the bed. "My sister is picky. She'll never find a man good enough for her to fuck and she'll be back in a pissed off mood."

They both forgot that the Holographic-communication device had been activated. Klaus Rhinehard was yelling: "Hello? Hello?" as Miles and Nola made love.

From her cushy apartment in downtown Clovis City, Nydia Rosenburg enjoyed reading the news as part of her daily routine. She sipped her cranberry juice and savored the flavor as much as she did the destruction of the Second Fleet. Now that Admiral Khan, Captain Allen and their rebellious crew members were nuclear waste, the rest of humanity would be foolish to continue with their protests and uprisings. The people would finally accept that they could live in peace only if they submitted to the Royal Family completely. She viewed her three-dimensional computer screens before her, using her fingers to move some articles aside so that she could view new ones.

She took another sip of her juice and gasped. She dropped her glass to the floor and heard it break into pieces on impact. Someone was posting videos of the events that were ongoing on the planet New Edinburgh. There were uploaded videos of innocents being raped by MI soldiers and other innocents being killed because they had the audacity to rush in to assist the rape victim. Nydia could see the video posted by an unknown person of the hangings of the Warren's. She read the postings of those that watched the videos. Over ninety percent of them were calls for the Glorious Leader and the Royal Family to step down. Nydia cursed and stood up. She was motivated to contact her sister, Rebecca, and find out why their soldiers were so out of control. Nydia stepped over the broken glass on the tiled floor and found her gold-plated hand held holographic-communication apparatus lying on a table nearby. She flipped the device open and ordered it to patch her into a personal conversation with Rebecca.

Rebecca Rosenburg was enjoying her status as the leader of planet New Edinburgh. She had all that she could want or desire given to her whenever she asked. She stayed out of the way of the Generals and Admirals that had arrived to purge the disloyal as they were doing an amazing job of wiping out their enemies. The Rice family had been apprehended and were all raped on live broadcast by soldiers and Babbcottiatta as a warning to others. Most of the Rice family perished during the multiple violations. There were a few teen-age females from the Rice family that had been sent to die in the arena and their deaths would be shown live for the entertainment of the citizens of New Edinburgh.

Rebecca met and gave the Medal of Valor to Corporal Angus McWilliams for killing the traitor Seward. She found him to be handsome and made some inquiries so that he could be reassigned as her personal body guard. On his first day of duty she seduced him and made love to him on her desk top. He did not disappoint her with his performance and quickly dressed after the session of lust as she was late for an address to the new General Assembly. She walked quickly down the tiled halls with her high heels clacking and her tight fitting business attire hugging her close, McWilliams was in his uniform walking two steps behind her with his laser rifle ready.

Rebecca cursed when her holographic-communication mechanism indicated that she had an incoming call request from her sister Nydia. Rebecca stopped and leaned against the metallic walls as she flipped open her own device. Nydia had always been annoying and offered little to the advancement of wealth or power for the family.

"What is it, Nydia? I am very busy."

"I expect you are, but this is critical. Your soldiers are committing wanton rapes and murders in the streets, Rebecca! We were supposed to purge the leadership, not turn the average citizen against us. The public opinion is not favorable. People are calling for you to resign. Many others are wishing that Rice, Ward, Gorski and Collins would be given their old positions back. This needs to stop!"

Rebecca sighed, "Well we can't give positions back to the people that are dead or condemned to die, can we? What would you have me do?"

"Those soldiers are like ambassadors to the people. They should behave themselves, dammit! Every time they commit an atrocity it pisses people off. Do you want riots in the streets? What if the people that are angry get riled up enough to attack us? What then?"

"Then our slave Saharakaree and Babbcottiatta will slaughter them. This is my solution, dear Nydia. We find out who the traitors are that are posting those videos and kill them. They are spreading the seeds of revolution and should be silenced."

"Rebecca, that is ridiculous. Kill the messenger? That is your plan? Why don't we stop the problem and discipline the soldiers that are out of control? That is the problem!"

"No, the problem is that people think that they can post such films in the first place. People need to learn their place. We rule and they follow. If our soldiers do something, then they should just take it. Fuck the people. Father always said that they were just sheep. You need to trace the recording uploads to the satellite system, find out their Holographic-communication devices or computer ID codes and arrest and kill them. I don't have time to put up with it."

"Rebecca, you need to listen to me."

"No, you listen. There are also pictures of your lover boy, Boris Ilyasova, all over the satellite system that accuse him of being in on the murder of the worthless Calderon girl and the Fenster kidnappings. His face is out there because of the very people I am telling you need to die. Boris is outed, Nydia. His face is everywhere. We need to kill these people and make them stop with their ridiculous notions of free speech or free communication. Nothing is free and the people need to pay for their insolence." Rebecca was livid, screaming into her device.

"Who is accusing Boris of this?"

"We don't know and I am frankly too busy to research it. Why don't you? All you two are doing is sitting around doing nothing but calling me and complaining because some stupid working class girl got beat up on camera. Leave me alone!"

Rebecca slammed her sparkling red holographic-communication device shut and glared at McWilliams. "You weren't out there raping any women, were you?"

"No way. Not me," he responded. Her cheeks were flushed which made her look more attractive to him.

"Good, I don't want to see your face associated with any of that nonsense. We're late. Let's go."

Nydia was even angrier than before. She sat down behind her keypad and began searching the satellite services for pictures of the man that was asleep in her bed. Within thirty seconds she found him, his face was all over the servers. Posters of Boris Ilyasova wanted dead or alive, with the promise of financial rewards, due to his participation in the kidnaping of Dirk and Therese Fenster as well as the murder of Lupita Calderon.

Nydia screamed out her frustration loud enough to wake Ilyasova from his synthetic cocaine high. He came stumbling down the stairs, wearing only a bathrobe.

"Have you seen this?" Nydia was shrieking at him. "Everyone in the Eight Solar Systems will know what you did now! Ulla Ragnarsson may come here and slit your throat just to keep your ass quiet! How could you be so careless?"

Ilyasova focused in on the pictures of himself and read the words which stated the accusations against him. He rubbed his unshaven chin. "Who the hell?"

"Who the hell is the right question, you idiot! Who could

have recognized you while you were there?"

Ilyasova slumped down into the couch behind him, "The Gorski Gang. Mejia, Frazier, Rhinehard, they were all there. They must have remembered me from the bar fight."

"What bar fight?"

"On Space Station Cy-7, when I was still an officer on the Colorado. They remembered me. Damn."

Nydia stood up and walked over to him, thrusting her index finger into his face. "Then they all gotta die, Boris. Like right now! If Ulla comes back and finds we didn't deal with those punk cadets, she will kill us first. Get a shower. You stink. We are going hunting for them. We can take my slave Babbcottiatta and Saharakaree along."

"Killing them might make this worse," Ilyasova stood up, scratching his testicles underneath his bathrobe.

"It cannot get any worse. And stop doing that. You know how disgusting it is. Go shower. I will have some vitamin injections ready for you when you get out."

Ilyasova stumbled back up the stair case.

CHAPTER FIFTEEN

Vezpucci finished his shower and wrapped a large white towel around his waist as he marveled over the view on his bed. The Lynott family hosts had left for him a freshly dry cleaned tuxedo, shirt, bow tie, black dress shoes on the bed. There was a hand written note that instructed him to wear the tuxedo for dinner that evening. It also informed him that there were several sets of clothing in the large walk in closet connected to his suite and in the two sets of cherry wood desk drawers. Vezpucci felt much better after the shower and the nice set of clothes on the bed brought a smile to his face. The last time he wore one was at his older sister's wedding. He checked the drawers and found underwear, socks, nicely pressed shorts and t-shirts. He moved to the closet and discovered that the Lynott's had stocked it full of shoes, slacks, jeans, dress shirts, short sleeved shirts, sweaters, jackets and a black leather jacket. He checked the sizes and found that everything was in his size.

He sat down on his bed and put on the white ruffled shirt. He buttoned it up and looked at the cuff links for the sleeves and cursed to himself. He always had trouble with those. He heard a knock on his door.

"Come in," he beckoned.

Jessica Ward opened the door and walked into his room. She was wearing a black dress that was backless and showed plenty of leg. Her black high heeled shoes matched the outfit. She had on a platinum necklace and matching loop earrings. "Did you see all the clothes that they brought to our rooms?"

"Yes, I can't believe it. I feel like royalty." Vezpucci could not take his eyes off her. She looked lovely.

Jessica blushed when she saw that he was standing before her in only the ruffled shirt and his underwear. "Is this a bad time?"

"No. No. I have a lot of sisters that barge in on me all the time. At least they used to before I started living at the Academy dormitories." Vezpucci smiled at her and held out the cuff links to her. "Could you put these on for me?"

She laughed and took them from his hand. "I'll make a deal with you. I put these on for you if you put on some pants. My father already gave me a lecture about you, so we need to keep things on the up and up."

Vezpucci pulled on the tuxedo pants and buttoned them. "Lecture about me? Why?"

She began working his right sleeve and fastened his cuff link as she spoke. "Look, my father is a political animal. He does everything with one goal in mind and that is to achieve political victory. As a young girl, I watched my father marry off some of my older sisters and brothers to others so that he could obtain an advantage. My father married all of his wives because they came from families that could help advance his political objectives. I doubt he ever loved my mother or any of her sister wives."

"So what has this got to do with me?"

She began working on the left sleeve. "Well, I guess my father can see in my eyes that I like you. I mean I really like you. My father says that you have no value to our family politically. He told me to stay away from you and forget you."

"I could be political."

"You are a cadet pilot. You will be in school for a few more years and then you have to serve six years in the service. You cannot be political until all that time passes."

"So, then, why are you here with me now, defying your father?"

Jessica finished with his last cuff link. Her face was inches away from Vezpucci. "I am here because I am an adult and I do as I wish."

She leaned into him and softly kissed his lips. He wrapped his arms around her and kissed her back. She quickly unbuttoned his dress shirt as his kisses grew more passionate. His hands were roaming over her body. She pulled away from him and laughed out loud.

"What's so funny?" Vezpucci asked.

"I am just a little bit nervous," she responded. "You sure got erect while you were feeling out my ass."

"You have a great ass."

"I am glad you like it," Jessica told him as she unzipped the back of her dress. She allowed the formal gown to slide down over her shoulders and drop to the ground. She was wearing no bra and her underwear was covering very little.

"I really like the rest of you," he stammered as he looked over her body.

"We have to hurry. Everyone will be in the formal dining area soon," she said as she pushed him onto the bed and lay down on top of him.

They kissed and assisted each other on removing the remainder of their clothing. Vezpucci surprised her by performing oral sex for her. She moaned pleasurably as she felt his tongue exploring her vagina. Vezpucci made a comment about how amazing she tasted as he continued kissing and licking her sex organ. Jessica eventually orgasmed and let out a musical moan from deep in her throat. Vezpucci intended to mount her but she pushed him onto his back and she took control by having intercourse with him for their first time while she was on top. Vezpucci did not complain and eventually exploded inside of her.

Ensign Kia Marble finished her shower and dried off with one of the large towels she found in her bathroom. On the bed in the suite supplied to her by the Lynott family was an off-white cocktail dress with matching shoes and a gold herring bone necklace and one carat diamond earrings. Marble sat on her bed and inspected the outfit. She absent mindedly gazed out of her window and saw the Harcourt woman with two of the Lynott grandchildren escorting Jason Ward back toward the mansion.

She glared at Ward and recalled how he had killed her friend Meelia in cold blood. Marble wanted revenge for her friend. She quickly dressed in the outfit that was left for her, left the jewelry, grabbed her laser pistol from the web belt that she had thrown on the floor and stepped out of her room. She kicked off her shoes so that she would make virtually no sounds as she ran across the tiled floors barefoot. She made it to the stairs and saw that Ward was walking up with Lesa and Saia Lynott on either arm. Marble eavesdropped on their conversation. She learned that Jason Ward agreed to marry Lesa and Saia, accepting the request of Patrick Doyle Lynott.

Marble hid behind some gold and burgundy colored drapes and resolved to follow Ward to his room and kill him now. The rest of the mansion was silent. Marble assumed that all of the cadets and other Ward family members were sleeping or getting cleaned up for the promised feast. She held her breath as Ward and the two Lynott women passed by her. Marble waited for a few seconds before following them. She would never get a better opportunity to get to him than this.

Ward followed the two Lynott women to the next stairwell and they began walking up to the third floor and then the fourth, fifth, sixth and stopping on the seventh. Marble walked slowly behind them, breathing slowly and hoping that the stairs would not creak and give her away. She set her laser pistol on kill. She moved up behind Ward and shoved the barrel into his back.

The two Lynott women moved to opposite ends of the wall in stunned silence. Marble grabbed Ward by his left ear and whispered into it. "Your room, now!"

Ward led her to the third door on the right. Marble motioned with her head for the two Lynott women to follow her inside. The four were soon inside a massive suite that was ten times the size of the one that Marble had been in. She focused in on her prey, Jason Ward, as the door to his suite closed.

"Time to answer for Meelia," Marble growled and pushed him away from her and kept the barrel of the laser aimed at him.

Jason had his hands up. "Ensign, please. You are upsetting Lesa and Saia. Put down the weapon and let us reason together."

"You killed my friend!" Marble hissed.

"Fine, fine. Saia, Lesa, you should both stand aside. I don't want my blood and body parts spattering all over you when she pulls that trigger." Jason spoke softly. His demeanor indicated that he was not surprised that Marble was there. It was as if he had been expecting her to move against him. "For what it is worth, Kia Marble, I am sorry about your friend. I just ask that you put yourself in my shoes and ask yourself whether you would have acted the same way as I did? It is possible that I just made a horrible mistake. But if you feel killing me is justice, then please get it over with."

Marble glared at him as he spoke. She wanted to pull the trigger and kill him. But she lingered on his words and began to conclude that perhaps his actions had been reasonable. She shook her head and slowly lowered her laser pistol to her side.

"Thank you for seeing it my way," Jason walked over to the bar at the far end of the suite. "Would you care for a drink?"

"Yes. Thank you." Marble placed her laser pistol on one of the counter tops as Jason began mixing some vodka and cranberry juice drinks. Lesa and Saia took one to Marble, and soon all four of them had a drink. Marble drank hers in two gulps due to her desire to calm her nerves.

"I am sorry if I scared any of you. Meelia was my friend, my closest friend. I don't know what I was thinking by doing this. I am not a criminal." Marble told them as Jason made her a fresh drink. She finished that one quickly as well. "I just cared about my friend an awful lot."

"We understand that," Jason said as he mixed her a third drink. He handed it to Saia Lynott who in turn gave it to Marble. "We all understand. Good friends are hard to come by. Now, I want you to understand our dilemma here. We are currently on the run from a government that I will be seeking to topple. If we succeed, who do you think the people of this planet will turn to for new leadership? Who will rise up to become the new Secretary General of the Security Council?"

Marble drank from her third drink. She began to feel dizzy and assumed that Ward was mixing strong drinks for her. She sat down on a long, red leather couch and felt as if the room was spinning around her. "I suppose that you or Sean Collins would be the likely candidates to become the new leader."

Jason smiled as he heard her voice slurring. He slowly walked over to Marble and sat down next to her. "Yes, my dear. Collins has never cared about seeking elected office. He is all about the court room. He loves to litigate cases, the tougher the better for him. He has no interest in political life. Therefore, I will be the one unless there is negative publicity about me that would enable a rival politician to exploit against me. Shooting an officer in the chest as I did to Meelia is a very, very bad political bag full of poggie dung that I stepped in. That cannot get out. You understand? I cannot have that information being given to the news reporters or the people. I have to appear to have the highest caliber of character to take office in the highest position.

It is due to that sad political fact that I must do what I must do."

Marble realized she had been drugged. She could not move. She watched helplessly as Jason accepted a six-inch blade from Lesa Lynott. She had been set up and her moment of forgiveness was about to prove fatal.

"No, please." Marble was able to say with effort.

"This will hurt me more than you. I read your resume. You took the deep space training and passed with flying colors and you were in the top ten percentile of your graduating class. Your professors gave you recommendations for a good station. You would have been a good servant of the people. That is why killing you is not easy for me. But I have to weigh the fact that I am more important to the people than you are. I can bring fundamental change to those that suffer soon. You will not be able to make a difference for at least a few decades. So, given my life has more value, you must die for the common good. Think of your death as a way for the poor and forgotten to achieve greatness through me."

Jason stuck the knife into Marble's chest and cut into her heart He twisted the knife up and down to ensure that he exacted a killing blow. Marble's blood poured out onto the lovely gown she was wearing as she looked upon Jason with a stunned look on her face. As she bled out, she realized she should have killed him.

Jason stood up and addressed the Lynott women. "Get rid of her body and clean up the blood. I will inform your grandfather that there is a possibility we may have to eliminate all of the others."

Marble died as the Lynott women began to lift her legs off the floor. Her last thoughts were that there was no justice in life.

CHAPTER SIXTEEN

The purple spider had her small army ready. They had surrounded the east mansion that contained the humans that had killed so many of her offspring. She watched a female woman with white skin exit the mansion and order two men with weapons to do something. The three humans were walking away from the mansion and down the large steps toward the paved walkways that led to the other larger buildings. The three now had their backs to the spiders. The purple matriarch squeaked an order to the others and they pounced upon the strange colored woman and the two males. The ones with weapons were targeted first. Several brown spiders leaped onto them and impaled them with their rear stingers. The men and women screamed as they fell to the ground and succumbed to the poison.

The white woman turned and glared at one of the charging brown spiders and concentrated. The other spiders shrieked when their fellow spider spontaneously exploded. The woman had the ability to use her mind as a weapon, the purple spider concluded. She urged the others to take her down immediately. The Harcourt wife of Patrick Doyle Lynott tried to use her Child of Athena mental powers one more time to destroy another spider. She never had the chance to do so. She was overwhelmed by other spiders that began to sink their fangs into her flesh. She could feel herself passing out from the effects of the venom. She slumped to the ground with a whimper. The spiders dragged the corpses back into the tree line to feast on the men. The purple spider planned on using the white woman to plant eggs inside of.

Inside the east mansion, the occupants were unaware that the spiders had attacked. There were several pitchers of beer being passed around, roasted meats were spread out on many kitchen tables for the guests to select from along with vegetables and fruits. Basil Varek thought that the feast was prepared to feed a king and queen. He spied upon the several rows of tables filled with food. Must be good to be a Lynott he thought to himself.   All of the men were dressed in black tuxedos with white ruffled shirts and dress shoes. The women were all wearing form fitting cocktail dresses. Some of the dresses were backless and others had plunging necklines. Varek admired Wanda Essex in her dark purple backless dress with matching high heeled shoes. Her hair was up which exposed the string of pearls necklace around her neck and matching earrings.

Varek found a table filled with pre-poured glasses of champagne. He picked up two glasses and approached her. "You look amazing."

Essex smiled at him and accepted the offered

champagne. "And you look dashing, Basil. The Lynott's really went all out for us. All of our clothes were waiting for us when we finished in the shower and we come downstairs to this. It is amazing. You really made an impression on them."

"We made an impression," Varek corrected her. He had grown weary of all the Ward family, the Lynott's and his friends praising him as a hero. He had done exactly what anyone else would have done. And the fact that he had plenty of good help seemed to be forgotten by many. He looked at the far wall where a large black and red brick fireplace was burning some large logs. Sitting around it were Manuel and Serpas, each with a twenty-four-ounce stein of beer in their hands. He scanned the room for the others. Most of the occupants were Lynott's granddaughters and staff. Varek counted all of the Calderon brothers as present. Each of them save Manuel were receiving ample attention from the Lynott women. Even fifteen-year-old Jorge had two attractive Lynott girls speaking with him in the western corner of the room.

He noticed that Klara Ward was on her Holographic-communication device, yelling at someone on the other end of the conversation. Varek had concluded that she was a cold individual. After the Ward's had been rescued, the children and grandchildren shed tears of joy and sorrow for their lost mothers and siblings. That is all except for Klara. She spent most her time scheming with her father. Varek had never been privy to the conversations between Klara and Jason, but the clandestine nature in which they conducted themselves left him with a feeling of suspicion as to their intentions.

Blomquist and Eklund were sitting on an animal skin rug, petting some of the many cats that occupied the mansion. Varek thought that the two engineering students looked amazing in the dresses that Lynott selected for them. They were laughing and drinking from champagne glasses.

Vezpucci had the attention of three lovely Lynott women and they were getting along quite well. Jessica Ward was sitting next to Vezpucci and seemed to like that so many women were flirting with him. Varek noticed that Jessica and Vezpucci exchanged looks that normally two people involved would give each other. Under the table, they were holding hands as they nodded politely to the Lynott women.

Kazembe enjoyed the conversation as she was speaking with Cobb and several of the Ward family members. There were four Asian women wearing revealing dresses present with Cobb and Kazembe. Cobb was ranting and raving about the hundreds of Dozal that they had killed in the Forbidden Region. The younger Ward children were hanging on Cobb's every word. There were six attractive Lynott granddaughters listening to Cobb as he would raise his voice and mimic the growls of the Dozal.

"What's wrong?" Essex finally asked him.

"Tara, John and Kia are not here," Varek observed. "Everyone else is accounted for. Why aren't they here?"

Essex sipped from her crystal champagne glass. "I am sure that Tara and John are enjoying some alone time together. But Kia told me she was starving and could not wait to eat. Odd that she is not here."

"Very much so," Varek agreed. In the short time that he had been around Marble he had found her to be reliable. She had no family around and desperately wanted friends, which she found with Varek and the others.

Jason Ward saw that Varek and Essex were looking over the room. Most likely they were searching for those that were not present. He concluded it was time to conduct some damage control before people started getting too suspicious. Ward took two of the Lynott granddaughters, Lesa and Saia, and walked over to Varek and Essex.

"There is the man of the hour," Jason shook Varek's hand. "Have I thanked you for saving my life and the lives of my family?"

"Yes, I believe you have." Varek smiled politely at Ward. "But it was not just my doing. It was a group effort."

"Naturally," Jason formally kissed Essex on her upper right hand. "You, my dear, look as lovely as your mother."

"You know my mother?" Essex smiled at him.

"I worked with your mother on a subcommittee on immigration issues a few years back. Such an insightful woman. How is she doing?"

Essex sipped from her champagne glass. "I suppose she will be fine as long as the Militzia leaves my family alone. She has been enjoying her writing at home and raising my younger siblings. It is my sister that I am concerned with."

"Your sister?" Saia Lynott entered the conversation.

"Yes. Her name is Felicia. She is a member of the Second Fleet. I read the news on my Holographic satellite computer that the entire fleet went rogue and initiated a blockade around Sikorsky's Planet. My sister is in the middle of it all."

"Then we wish her well," Lesa Lynott told her. "We are in support of the intention behind the blockade. My grandfather is on record stating that it is time for a change in leadership for New Edinburgh and Sikorsky's Planet."

"I think we all agree with that notion," Jason smiled at Varek and pointed his champagne glass in his direction. "If we are successful in freeing the people here, the new leadership will need talented and bold men such as yourself, Basil. Have you given much thought to serving in politics?"

Varek shook his head in the negative. "Never. I doubt I have the stomach for it, sir. Plus, I enjoy flying ships too much. I would not make a good politician."

"I think that you are wrong, Basil. When this is over and I settle into my new position, whatever that might be, seek me out. I could use a good man like you on my side. We think alike, Basil. We believe in fighting for the people we care about. Besides, the fact that you do not lust for power would make you the perfect public servant. I believe you are a man that would always act in the best interests of the people over your own political aspirations. The people will need leaders with that quality. I hope you think about it."

"I thank you for the kind words, sir. Mister Ward, have you seen Kia Marble around?" Varek finally asked, mainly to change the subject of his own future.

"Please, call me Jason. No I have not seen Kia at all," he lied with a smile on his face.

"She left an hour ago, Mister Varek." Saia Lynott added to the lie. "She wanted to return to her Space Command unit. Our grandfather had one of our pilots fly her back to Clovis City."

"That is not like her," Essex said under her breath.

"She wanted to get back to her unit," Jason shrugged. "We each have to choose our own paths. I wish her well."

Varek was about to ask another question when Gauthier and Haddad descended the staircase. She looked stunning in her white backless gown with a long jade necklace and matching earrings. Her long dark hair hung loosely over her shoulders. Gauthier walked with the confidence a major movie star with her on his arm. They were greeted by some of the Lynott servants at the foot of the stairs. Gauthier smiled at his friends.

"Excuse me, Representative Ward and ladies." Varek bowed to them. "Wanda and I had agreed to...dine...with our friends there. And we are very hungry."

"Naturally," Jason shook his hand again. He waited until Varek and Essex were far enough away to hear. He turned to Saia and Lesa Lynott. "You did incinerate the body?"

"We took care of everything. The body, the blood evidence, all traces of DNA and all of her belongings in her suite, just as you and grandfather directed." Lesa smiled at him. "There is no physical evidence that Kia Marble was ever in this mansion. Even her bones are dust. You have nothing to fear."

"Good," Jason mumbled. "We don't need for her name or memory to upset our plans for the future."

The cadets and the Ward family ate and drank together throughout the night. The Lynott family and staff kept the food, wine, beer, ale and champagne coming. The Calderon brothers had attracted many of the Lynott and Tao women. Xavier was sitting in a couch with five women all around him, catering to his every desire. Juanito also had several of the women around him and they would not allow any of the others to join in on their conversation. Some of the younger Lynott and Tao women were interested in Jorge and his tales of bravery in the Forbidden Region. Some of the Ward men were receiving ample interest from the large numbers of Lynott grandchildren.

At some point in the evening, Manuel led Serpas upstairs to his room to be alone. Vezpucci did the same with Jessica Ward. Most of the party did not seem to notice that they were gone. But Jason Ward glared at his daughter as she followed Vezpucci up the stair case. He had previously instructed Jessica to befriend Vezpucci. Her behavior during the feast indicated that Jessica had disobeyed him and became romantically linked to the cadet. In Jason's mind, Vezpucci had no political value and was a waste of time for his daughter to be involved with him. He began to devise a plan on how to separate her from Vezpucci so that she would be available for him to offer up as a bounty for some political favor.

Cobb had increased the crowd of Lynott and Tao women around him as he related his portion of the battle against the Dozal. He had even displayed the severed head that he brought back with him so that he could show it off to the women. Many of the young Ward children were impressed by the head of the creature and each touched the fur as they listened to Cobb. Two of the women were next to Cobb, one with her hand on his shoulder and the other standing mere inches from him.

At a round dark table in the corner, Haddad, Gauthier,

Varek, Essex, Truang and Kazembe made themselves at home. They had spent hours laughing together as they ate and drank. Earlier in the evening, Pepito and Villandiego had been a member of their table. But an hour earlier, the couple had departed for their room.

"I get a sinking feeling that we should plan on leaving soon," Kazembe finally told the small assembly at the table. "Who opens up their home like this to complete strangers?"

"Nobody," Truang nodded. She had eaten beef ribs and salad for the last hour and there was a plate of large rib bones to her left and a large stein of beer to her left. She was drunk and had admitted it several times.

Essex shook her head at the others, "Now wait a minute. Wait. My family has had many strangers over for dinner and libations. So I disagree with your suspicions and rumor has it that the Fenster kids were really giving with their money. So are the Li's and Evart's. So I do not see anything wrong with this. Can you just accept that the Lynott family is generous and warm?"

"I say we enjoy the hospitality as long as possible. There is no doubt that the Lynott family wants something from all of us. We will find out what the something is soon." Gauthier found a large bowl of fried Jumper Tails and began dipping them into a ramekin of cream sauce to add flavor to the appetizer before eating it.

"I thought that the old man himself was supposed to join us," Haddad said referring to Mister Lynott. "Have any of you seen him?"

"Speak of the devil," Varek spoke up as he was looking out the one way windows that surrounded the entire front of the mansion. The others looked in the direction Varek was pointing at and they saw that their host was walking toward the mansion along with several armed guards and a few women that were dressed in nice evening gowns. The guards were all Asian and Members of the Tao family.

Lynott was wearing a black tuxedo that was identical to the ones all of the male guests were provided to wear for the evening. There were flood lights illuminating the area for several feet around the entrance so that Lynott had a clear view of the walkway.

"Do we have to stand for him? I'm too drunk," Truang announced what the rest of the table already knew. Her speech was beyond slurred and she had a bad habit of laughing out loud at things that the others did not find amusing.

Gauthier thought he saw something moving in the light. There were shadows that were seemed to be changing as some objects passed in front of the outdoor flood lights. The shadows seemed to be moving on eight legs and were moving in the direction of Patrick Doyle Lynott and his entourage.

"Sand spiders!" Gauthier recognized the eight legged shadows, leaped to his feet and grabbed his large steak knife.

Varek and Haddad immediately pushed their large chairs back and grabbed steak knives in their hands. Essex and Kazembe did the same. They looked at Truang and noticed she had passed out, her head was hanging over the back rest of her chair. The five cadets began running for the large sliding doors and yelling to the other cadets that there were sand spiders outside. Some of the indoor cats were watching out the window and were hissing as they had noticed the same.

Lynott, his wives and guards all walked as if they did not have a concern in the world. They did not hear or see the twenty sand spiders that were behind them, crawling on their eight legs at full speed. Lynott saw the door to his eastern mansion open and was expecting to receive a loving embrace by all of the Ward family members and the cadets. Instead he was greeted to a group of cadets charging at him and motioning for him to get inside.

"Sir!" Varek screamed at Lynott. "Run!"

Lynott and his wives stopped in their tracks as they looked upon the cadets that were running in their direction with steak knives. His first thought was that the cadets had come to his home to assassinate him. But the screams behind him made him realize that the cadets were running at him in an effort to protect him. The spiders were leaping onto the backs of the Tao family security guards and some of Lynott's wives. The spiders would wrap their eight legs around their victims, trapping their arms so that they could not fight back. The sickening sound of the rear stingers thrusting through flesh and internal organs followed. A brown spider was airborne and almost landed on Lynott's back. But Varek was there first, pushing Lynott to the pavement and swinging his steak knife at the predator. The spider screamed as Varek severed two of its legs. The spider fell to the pavement and was making a strange hissing noise as it faced Varek.

Several of the victims were on their hands and knees, vomiting from the effects of the venom. Their skin was beginning to shrivel up as were their internal organs. They would be dead in seconds. Haddad assisted Lynott to his feet as Varek was locked in a life and death battle with the injured spider. The creature scurried in Varek's direction, baring fangs that were dripping with deadly yellow-orange venom. Varek stepped to the side and stabbed his steak knife into the back of the spider. It screamed and began running in circles as it tried to shake the knife loose. It had oozing yellow blood coming from the wound.

The leader, the purple spider, saw that others were coming out of the mansion with laser weapons. She squealed for them to run for cover. Some of the spiders ran toward the building and leaped on top of the fences and began scaling the walls. Others ran for the cover of the woods. James Cobb arrived on the porch, positioned himself in a kneeling position, and fired his laser pistol at the spiders. He was soon joined by two Tao female guards, Juanito and Xavier Calderon. They killed several of the predators as Lynott and two of his wives were safely helped into the mansion. All of his guards that had been escorting Lynott were dead and he had lost ten wives to the spiders. The attack had taken less than thirty seconds and had exacted a high number of casualties in that short time period.

Lynott looked back to see the three male cadets and Varek defending the mansion from the attack. He smiled as he saw them in action. They were fighters, just as Jason Ward had indicated. If the cadets survived the incident, they would indeed prove useful.

Jose, Raklitz and several members of the Ward, Tao and Lynott family had taken the party outside in the middle of the hexagon designed mansion. They had all decided to go skinny dipping in the large outdoor pool located at that area. Several of the Lynott employees were present, serving drinks to the guests as they one by one leaped into the water. They were loud, as they splashed one another and shoved each other into the pool. Many of them had stripped out of their tuxedos or dresses and were swimming nude.

The spiders that had scaled the walls of the mansion were soon on the rooftop, seeking and smelling for any prey.

They heard the sounds from the center of the building and were attracted in that direction. They ran to the edge of the ceiling and looked down at the food below them. They observed about forty humans in the water and a dozen more outside of it. The spiders began scaling down the wall toward their unsuspecting prey.

Jose practiced the backstroke across the length of the pool as Raklitz was at one of the bars, getting the bartender to make them a few margaritas. Her rib fractures had been healed by one of the Tao medical doctors after her arrival at the mansion. The spiders were about ten feet from the ground and they zeroed in on humans to attack. They leaped from the walls and into the air. One of the Ward daughters was in line at the bar next to Raklitz. She screamed as a brown spider knocked her to the ground. Raklitz cursed out loud and watched helplessly as the large arachnid impaled the Ward girl into her chest with its' back stinger. Raklitz observed many of the Tao servants and Lynott granddaughters being attacked and suffering the same fate. Raklitz picked up a lawn chair and held it in front of herself and began to move toward the large pool. She saw that the bartender was fighting for his life as a purple spider leaped on his head. He flailed wildly as the spider ripped his throat open with its sharp fangs. There was mass hysteria as the spiders would strike one victim dead and immediately set upon another. The body count was rising quickly.

Raklitz ran for the water. She observed that, for some reason, the spiders were avoiding the water. As she ran, she leaped over a brown spider that was thrusting a death blow into the eye of one of the Lynott girls. There were screams all around her. Jose was trying to pull himself out of the water, screaming for Raklitz to get to the safety of the inside mansion. As Jose was on his feet, a black and brown spider jumped at him from his left. It knocked Jose over and then narrowly missed getting a hold of him due to the slippery dripping water from the pool that was all over his body. The spider was hissing and prepared itself to leap at Jose again. Before it could, Raklitz shoved the spider with the lawn chair and sent it spiraling into the deep swimming pool. The creature shrieked out loud as it splashed into the water. The spider sank to the bottom and drowned.

"They can't handle the water!" Raklitz screamed out loud to Jose and the others. "Get into the water!"

All save a lovely Tao woman made it to the safety of the pool. The purple spider jumped on her back and quickly thrust its' rear stinger into her torso. The Tao girl screamed as she felt the eight legs enveloping her and her flesh being ripped open. The stinger tore through her chest. The victim fell to her knees as the purple spider pumped her full of venom. Jose cried out in anger as the flesh of the Tao girl began to shrivel before his eyes. Her eyes began to turn dark yellow as the venom filled her body and took her. Her heart pounded hard in her chest as she fell to her knees and she began to vomit a thick yellow paste. She was dead before her head hit the pavement, inches away from the safety of the pool.

The purple spider was elated with their raid. They had succeeded in killing dozens of the humans in a matter of minutes. But her elation did not last long. The side doors of the hexagon shaped fortress slid open and many guards and cadets, armed with lasers, began firing upon the spiders. One by one the spiders fell to the blasts. The purple spider released the corpse of the formerly lovely Tao woman and attempted to leap up the wall and climb to safety. It did not make it. Jorge fired his laser rifle at the leader of the arachnids and blew a hole through her body. The spider screamed for only a few seconds before it died. Jorge ran to the body of one of the victims to see if there was any chance to save her. When he saw that her skin was leathery in texture and turning a yellow purple color, he knew that he had been too late.

As the battle against the sand spiders went on at the front and the open air interior of the mansion, Jason Ward sat with his daughter Klara and did nothing. The two had made the decision that risking themselves in combat was beneath them. They both had a political future and the rest existed to serve and protect them. As the battles began to wind down with the killing of the invading spiders, Jason motioned for his daughter to stand, take a knife in her hand and act as if they had been helping all along.

In the aftermath of the attack it was determined that fifty-seven died and twenty spider bodies were accounted for. The Lynott body guards began to burn the spider corpses with flame devices. Other Tao guards began to collect the dead humans and list them into the mansion computer system. The fact that Lynott lost several of his wives seemed to have no effect on him. He did not shed any tears as he urged everyone to resume the party. Many of the guests were too stunned to want to continue. Eklund and Blomquist were filled with dread that another attack might occur any moment.

Lynott hugged Varek for being bold enough to risk his life to save him. "Anything you need, my boy. Anything. You saved my life. That means you are like a son to me. Anything at all, boy. Anything."

Gauthier counted his original crew members and learned that there had not been any casualties from their number. Raklitz, Jose and Jorge assisted in covering the bodies of the deceased with bath towels.

As the clean-up of the spider and human corpses continued, the Lynott patriarch urged Varek to join him at his crystal rectangular table for drinks. Varek took Essex with him and sat down across from the man as servants brought him a large plate of meats, sausages and vegetables. Another female Tao servant gave him a stein of ale. Varek and Essex were given ale to drink and watched as several young women sat around Lynott at the table.

"Amazing creatures, those spiders. All of them in fact. The Dozal, the Verburgt. Absolutely amazing." Lynott was speaking while chewing on a Jumper Tail. "Basil, did you ever wonder why those animals attack us? Not just attack us, but continue to attack when we demonstrate that we possess weapons that can wipe them out? Does that behavior strike you as strange?"

"Yes, sir. It does. John was telling me that there were over two hundred Dozal that charged their position. They killed over a hundred before the animals could get close enough to strike. If it had been a battle between humans, the Dozal side would have logically withdrawn the attack." Varek had been wondering what it was about those animals that made them refuse to run to safety when the humans exacted such heavy casualties on them.

"I have a theory," Lynott said while he was smiling as a young Tao woman, clad in a low cut black gown, slid into his lap. "You see, I believe that is not just mere hunger that drives those creatures. Sure, they seem to like the taste of our flesh. But no. I think that they have intelligence about them. They know we are conquerors. They know that we do not belong on their planet. It is as if the Gods gave them an internal instinct to defend their planet, their species, and their sociological society, it one could call the way they live and interact that. They are willing to die to their last number to kill us because we are invaders. Even against all odds. They would rather die in battle than wait for us to slowly take all of their lands and push them to extermination. They want us off this planet."

"Sir, I doubt that they can reason in such a manner," Essex responded. "Yes, they hunt in packs. The Dozal and Jumpers seem to work in some form of tribal level, with leaders and followers. I will grant you that. But to decide that they would fight to the death because they understand, that they comprehend, that we are not from this world, is a huge scientific leap for me to take. I think they are just hungry."

Varek regarded both arguments for a moment. "Well, they are certainly defenders of their specific territory. John's ship crashed in an area that was most likely the hunting grounds of those two hundred Dozal. Perhaps that would explain their behavior."

Lynott took a long drink from his stein and motioned at one of his wives to bring him a refill. "Okay, let's put the argument on the other foot, so to speak. What if the Dozal were the intellectual space travelers and they landed on old Earth, say ten thousand or twenty thousand years ago? And say, for the sake of argument, that they began wiping out large population centers to take control of a continent. Would you agree with me that humanity would have fought such invaders to the death? Even if the invaders had lasers and weapons of mass destruction and humanity only had wooden clubs and sharpened rocks to fight with? Would we have not, as a species, stood and fought against a common enemy that sought our extinction?"

"I think that some cultures might have fought against those odds. But most of them would have run for the mountains to seek refuge." Essex shook her head as she responded. "I think that your comparison is flawed, with all due respect."

Lynott smiled at her as he accepted a freshly filled stein of ale from one of his wives. He drank from it and looked at Essex and then Varek. "Basil, I understand what you see in her. She is smart and very desirable. A good woman is hard to find."

Varek and Essex, up to that moment, had become friends. There had been no sexual activity between them, nor had there been any discussion between them regarding any romantic interest. Varek was about to speak up but Lynott waved at him to keep quiet.

"I lost over a dozen wives tonight," Lynott told them after he took a long drink from his stein of ale. "Some of them I loved. The others were here due to political tradeoffs I made over the years. They were all good women and I know I will mourn most of them. I believe that the attack by those spiders proves my theory. They want us off their planet. But enough of that talk. How many wives do you want, Basil?"

"Sir, we are sorry about the losses that you suffered tonight." Varek was struck by the coldness in Lynott's voice as he spoke about his deceased wives. He wondered if the man was capable of caring for anything or anybody. He considered his answer carefully. "Sir, I am studying to be an officer in the Space Command. Most of us that become astronauts end up married to our ship. So, if I were to take a wife I think one good woman is all that I would ever want or need."

Lynott laughed and pointed his silver fork in the direction of Essex. "Are you saying that just for her benefit?"

"No sir. It is the way I feel. I never really had much time for romance over the years. I came to the Academy with one goal and that was to learn how to fly ships."

Essex remained silent, sitting straight with her hands on the table before her. She was beginning to dislike their host. Several of his wives and children had just died and all he cared about was eating, drinking and making small chit chat with strangers. Although she hoped that the man was capable of some level of empathy for the dead, he was not showing it.

Lynott bit into a large beef rib and wiped his lips and cheeks with a large napkin. As he chewed with his mouth full he continued to speak. "Yes, of course. Almost all of my sons said similar things. And you know what? They have all taken on numerous spouses. Even my gay son married three men and a few women to make babies with. Look around you, Basil. I can call you Basil? Look around at all my single granddaughters. They are all lovely. I need to marry them off so that they can breed and perpetuate my family line. They need good, strong, brave men. You would be an ideal son-in-law, Basil. Of all the men here tonight, I wanted to give you the first shot at selecting a few of them to take back to the Academy with you. You would be doing me a grand service if you took two or three with you. Take more if you like. My security chief, Yung Tao, has many grandchildren and children that are here for you to select from. You seem like you could rise to the challenge of taking multiple women to your bed. I will pay you a handsome dowry for each one that you find fetching. What do you say?"

Varek looked at Essex who was now crossing her arms and glaring at Lynott. "Sir, I thank you for your kind offer but I must decline at this time."

Lynott slammed his stein of ale onto the table. He had never had a man turn him down when he made such a generous offer. "Why?"

"Sir. If I take anyone with me to the Academy, right now with the political climate as it is, I would be placing them in harm's way. Secondly, all of your grandchildren would be much safer living here in your mansions than in Clovis City. I predict that the citizens there will eventually have their fill of the new military leaders and rebel. The battles will be devastating and many innocents are going to be injured or killed when it happens. I recommend that you keep all of your family here, safe, and look for husbands for them after the leadership is changed to a more stable environment."

Lynott nodded with his words. He raised his stein high above his head to begin a toast. "You are a smart lad, Basil. Very smart. When this conflict is over, I will seek you out and see if you have had a change of heart. Now, drink and celebrate that you have survived all of the obstacles that the Gods placed in your path these past few days. Drink to life and toast the memory of the fallen."

Essex raised her stein. "To the obstacles from the Gods."

Varek looked at Essex as the other Lynott and Tao family members began raising their steins and champagne glasses and repeating the phrase: "to the fallen."

Varek raised his stein and Essex followed his example and they both said the same toast in unison. Everyone drank. They were soon joined by several of the Ward kin, one of them was Klara. She sat near the center of the table so that she could participate in the conversation between Varek, Essex and Lynott.

As the evening wore down, Lynott made the offer of his granddaughters to all of the cadet males that were present in his mansion. The only member of the cadet group that took him up on the offer was Cobb. He selected three Lynott girls and was paid ten thousand Empire Dollars per girl by their grandfather. Cobb graciously accepted the cash and took the three women to his loaned suite after he signed the legally binding marriage papers.

Gauthier and Haddad watched as Cobb departed with the women.

"That is a lot of money for a cadet to have," Haddad whispered. "You certain you don't want some of it? I don't mind having a few sister wives as long as I get a cut."

Gauthier looked into her eyes and saw that she had a serious look on her face. "Really?"

Haddad began laughing. "Just testing you."

"Did I pass?"

"Barely."

"I am surprised that the Calderon brothers didn't snatch up some of these girls. With that kind of money, they could build themselves more motorcycles."

Haddad shook her head. "No. I realize that those Calderon's are your friends, which you have spent a lot of spare time with them. But you are misreading them. I mean that they are not men that care only about money. Listen to them when they talk. They are very family oriented. They speak of their father, mother, uncle and their sisters. No, they are not going to bring any random woman into the family. They won't do it for money. They will only do it for the same reason their father and mother are together."

"Which is?"

Haddad laughed. "For love, silly. You really do not understand your friends at all. I mean, sure they will sleep around with a random pick up. But to marry someone? She has to be a woman that they would be proud to present to their parents. That is what I see in the Calderon brothers. You should learn to read people better, John."

"Manuel seems to view LaTania as more than a random hook up."

Haddad sipped from a water glass. "Yes. She is smart, talented, studies and makes decent grades. She has selected a career path. She is pretty. She seems to be a woman that can stand up for herself. I could see Manuel taking her home to meet his mother."

Gauthier considered her words and the few years that he had been a friend to the Calderon family. The brothers never did bring around a woman that they considered a serious girlfriend. They were extremely selective about the women they took to the family cook outs. Haddad was probably right in her assessment of them. "I think you are correct."

"I think it is time for bed," Haddad told him. "We should make sure Winter gets to her room safely."

Gauthier glanced over at Winter Truang who was fast

asleep with her head on one of the tables. One of the younger Lynott children was sitting next to Truang, petting her head and singing to her.

"Let's go get her." Gauthier stood. "A good night's sleep would do us some good after all the stress we have been through."

Jose and Raklitz had departed the pool area and found a table in the vast banquet hall. They were immediately served wine, ale, water and racks of ribs and fried jumper tails. Several lovely, scantily clad Asian women joined them. Jose tried to remember all of their names but it was impossible for him. Some of the names were difficult for him to pronounce in the first place, much less remembering them all. They were soon joined by an older, tall, slender Asian man that was dressed in a black tuxedo. His head was shaved and he had a laser pistol in his right hand. He sat down next to Jose and smiled.

"My name is Yung Tao. I am the chief caretaker of the Lynott properties. You are Jose Calderon and Dominique Raklitz?"

"Yes," Raklitz shook Tao's hand. She noted that he had wrinkles around his eyes which caused her to deduce that he was in his sixties or seventies. "How did you know our names?"

"I am in charge of security here," Tao responded. "It is my obligation to know everything that there is to know about the guests here."

"With all of the deaths that just happened you are still in charge of security? I would have fired you by now." Raklitz smiled as she spoke, searching Tao's face for any reaction to her words.

Tao ignored her and did not take the bait. "So, Jose, my granddaughters here are wondering if you would have any interest in them."

"Interested in what manner?" Jose asked just to be polite. With the things he had seen thus far, he believed the Lynott's and Tao's to be an odd bunch.

"For marriage, of course."

Jose smiled politely and waived at the women at their table. They each waived back at him. One of them blew him a kiss.

"No sir," Jose finally responded. "I am not really in the market for a wife right now."

Tao shrugged, "Too bad. My Granddaughters would suck your balls off. They have each been trained in the art of seduction. They would make fine wives and bear you healthy offspring."

"I do appreciate the kind offer, sir. But I am not in the market right now. I do have three brothers here that are single and might be willing to take on a wife or two."

Tao laughed and slapped Jose on the shoulder as he

stood up. "Very well then. I shall find them and make them an offer. Enjoy your stay here."

CHAPTER SEVENTEEN

The Orka that had been chosen to carry Elektra and her friends back to Clovis City was a state of the art ship. It had reflective metal that could repel a direct laser blast as well as electrical defenses to use against underwater predators. Naval Captain Drimios Zachariades left the command of his ship the *Kirov* so that he could personally see to his cousin stepping onto a transport ship for old Earth. He had conflicting feelings regarding the pending execution of his in law Arch and cadet pilots Regehr and Nehwal.

The six cadets were placed in separate prison cells on the lower level of the space craft. The rest of the crew consisted of three squads of MI enlisted soldiers under the command of Royal Family Member Captain Cheri Rendon and five clones of the Glorious Leader, Vladimir Sikorsky. Zachariades had met the clones and found them to be disturbing. They each had Sikorsky's mind inside the body that seemed to be twenty years old. But they seemed to compete against one another. Zachariades had to break up a fight between two of them as they challenged one another for the rights to enter the cell of Zorana

Mikec and rape her.

Having left the Orka on auto-pilot, Zachariades made his way to the sealed cell that had his cousin, Elektra, sitting on the small bed with her face buried in her hands. She had been crying ever since being locked in the five by ten cell. Zachariades disagreed with the decision that his mother had made regarding the fate of the six students. He felt powerless to do anything about the situation as crossing mother was a dangerous undertaking. His mother had killed her own husband and his brother's years earlier when they went against her demands. Due to her rank at the time, Themis Zachariades escaped prosecution for the murder. But mother did not stop there with her killing spree. She had four step children from the man she killed. She killed all four of them, ranging from the ages of eight to sixteen, by her own hand, so that Drimios and his siblings would be the only ones left to inherit the Zachariades fortune.

Drimios Zachariades had been the oldest of three sons. His mother encouraged physical and mental fitness as a daily aspiration. As a result, he developed the discipline to enter the military schools to become an officer as a teenager. He was commissioned as an Ensign in the naval service by the age of nineteen. He had earned his doctorate in naval warfare by the age of twenty-one. By twenty-three he earned a PhD in hydraulic engineering. He was brilliant and physically fit. He spent time in the gymnasium when he was not studying and looked like Atlas might have. As a result, he had many suitors over the years. He had married a few of them and had children, all back in Corinth and Athens, studying to be just like their absent father.

Zachariades ordered the computer to open Elektra's cell door. As it slid open he could see her wipe tears from her cheeks as she looked at him.

"May I come in, ksadelfi?" he asked her. He had called her 'ksadelfi' for many years which was the Greek word for cousin.

She looked away from him and stared at the grey metal wall in front of her. "Do as you wish, Drimios. Come in, gloat, laugh at us. But do not defend your mother to me. I swear I will kill you if you do."

Zachariades walked into the small cell and sat down on the bed next to her. "I am sorry about all of this, ksadelfi. I could arrange to have your husband in the cell with you so that you can say good bye."

"Why would you care? Does everyone think that I married a worthless man? Do you all really think that low of me? My husband is brave and smart. He has fought against odds that would make most men run away like cowards. He is a man that would have been in legend had he been born in the right century. He has thrassos. I love him." Elektra's voice was full of despair the likes of which Zachariades had never heard from her.

"I will bring him over for you," Zachariades told her softly. His heart was aching for her. His entire life he had looked upon her as the sister he never had. To see her in such pain was taking an emotional toll on the man.

She looked at his face for a moment and then back at the wall. "Remember when we were younger, you always used to defend me. Remember, Drimios? Of all our ksadelfi, you and I were the closest. How could you let your mother do this to me and my friends?"

He rubbed his palms together in thought. This was certainly playing out like a tragedy that would have been performed in the ancient days of their country. "Elektra, you know that no one will stand up to mother. She rules the family with an iron fist. I wanted to just tell you that I love you and wish the best for you. I will make sure they give your husband a swift execution so that he doesn't suffer."

She laughed. "That is supposed to make me feel better? Really?"

Zachariades stood up and began walking to the door. "I will bring him to you. Do not waste any time. Tell him goodbye. Hold him for the rest of the trip. It is the best I can do."

Elektra screamed at him as he left her cell and the door slid shut.

Zachariades walked down the hallway and looked into the other cells. He saw that Regehr was pacing from one end of his cell to the next, turning around and repeating the monotonous procedure. Nehwal was lying on her small bed and had her left arm over her eyes which led Zachariades to conclude she had fallen asleep.

He walked to the next cell and stopped, stunned by the sight. One of the Sikorsky clones was in the cell with Zorana Mikec. He was hitting her across the face and tearing at her clothing. Mikec was doing an admirable job of fighting back, but losing the battle. Zachariades ordered that the computer open the door and found that his voice command would not work. The clone of Sikorsky turned and smiled at Zachariades.

"She is mine to do with as I please, Captain." The clone stated without emotion, sporting a sadistic smile. "Walk away and I might forget that you interrupted me."

"Please, help me!" Zachariades heard Zorana plead with him.

Zachariades walked to the next cell and saw that Jasna Mikec was lying on her bed, crying. He kept moving down the hall until he came to Arch Frazier's cell and ordered the computer to open the doorway.

Frazier heard his cell door sliding open. He sat up on his bed and saw that Zachariades was standing there. "What do you want?"

"I came to take you to Elektra."

Frazier stood to his feet. He wanted to see that his wife was fine. In the past fifteen minutes, he had decided to accept his own death. His only worry was the effect it would have on the woman he loved more than life itself. He followed Zachariades down the hallway and looked into each cell as they walked. He grimaced when he saw the Sikorsky clone pulling the hair of Zorana to force her to lie still on the bed so that it could mount her. She was screaming for help. Frazier balled up his fists at the sight. The Mikec girls had been sweet and innocent before joining them on the failed mission. They did not deserve to be treated so brutally.

"So much for a just world," Frazier muttered under his breath.

He waited as Zachariades ordered for Elektra's cell door to slide open.

"Inside," Zachariades ordered him.

The Fraziers embraced and kissed passionately.

"I love you," Elektra told him in between kisses.

"I love you more," Arch responded.

The couple looked over at Zachariades after a few moments. He stood with a look of guilt on his face. He had never seen Elektra so passionate with a man before. She had always been reserved and cautious with her past boyfriends. But the love Zachariades witnessed was real and powerful. He began to walk away to give them privacy when Arch Frazier stopped him.

"Wait. You can't just walk off like nothing. That clone thing is trying to rape an innocent girl down the hall. You can't just stand by and let that go on."

Zachariades turned and faced them. "My voice security code will not work on her cell. I tried. He must have restricted me."

"Because he knew you would stop him?" Elektra asked hopefully. "Your patron God Poseidon would not stand for a rape under his Seas. You must stop it."

Zachariades was silent as he considered his options. "The cell doors cannot be opened without the voice command."

Elektra smiled. "I can open it."

"How?" Her cousin was curious.

"Take me to the door and I will show you." Elektra flexed her fingers on her right hand. Since she had lost her right arm and it was replaced by the advanced metal works from the Allen Corporation, she had gone through countless hours of rehabilitation to learn how to use the scientifically engineered limb. Her biggest fear was that she might hurt someone by accident due to the ability of the arm to lift a ton or more and crush metal like a normal human could crush a Styrofoam cup. She had held back revealing her hidden weapon but now was the time. They needed to save Zorana and then escape from their sentences.

Zachariades escorted his cousin to the cell door of Zorana Mikec. Elektra looked at the frame and judged the thickness of the metal. She told her cousin and husband to stand back as she planted her feet. With one thrust with her right arm, she smashed a fist sized hole into the door. The clone of Sikorsky was attempting to mount Zorana when he heard a loud clang of metal on metal. He looked over his shoulder to see a hand sticking out of a hole in the door that had not existed before.

"What in the name of Mother Russia?" His eyes widened as he watched the hand withdraw from the hole.

Elektra grabbed hold of the hole with her right hand and began to pull on it. She had her teeth grinding together and her brow was folded as she grimaced. The others watched in amazement as she ripped the metal door from its hinges. The clone of Sikorsky watched the ripping of the metal door behind him and jumped to his feet to face whatever came at him. His eyes were wide when he saw Elektra running right at him. He laughed at her.

She swung her right arm at his head and her fist went through his face and out the back of his skull. His brains and skull fragments were splattered all over the back wall. She withdrew her arm so the corpse of the clone could fall to the metal floor.

Arch was already covering Zorana with the bed sheets.

She was bruised and scratched from the attack, but she seemed to have her wits about her. She began demanding what was going on.

"We are taking this ship. That is what is going on." Drimios Zachariades responded.

Elektra looked upon her cousin. "By Hera, you had better be certain, ksadelfi. Your mother, the MI and the Royal Family will come at you with everything they have if you do this."

"No one puts my ksadelfi in a cage and no one rapes any woman while I am breathing," Zachariades told them. "Let's free your friends. Arch, the clone's clothing has a web belt with a laser pistol. You had better arm yourself. The MI on this ship are the best shooters."

Arch ripped the web belt from the corpse as Zorana stood on her feet. "My sister. Where is she?"

"Down the hall." Zachariades told her. He turned his attention to his cousin. "How in the name of Poseidon did you do those things?"

Elektra flexed the fingers on her right hand. "Some super assassin blew off my right arm a year ago and left me for dead. I got a new arm thanks to a mutual friend of ours. And by Hera I can do some damage with it."

One by one they freed the others. Regehr and Nehwal

hugged and kissed when they were reunited. The Mikec sisters were also hugging one another with relief that they were freed.

Zachariades told the cadets the odds against them. "You will need weapons. The storage room is down the hallway around the dog leg left. There are two MI guards there. We will have to take them out."

Zorana glared at him for a moment. "The way I feel right now, I will gladly kill everyone we run into."

"That's the spirit," Nehwal said as she slapped Zorana on the shoulder.

"Follow behind me and do not reveal yourselves until the guards have their full attention on me. I will engage them in small talk. When I do, sneak up on them and take them."

Zachariades led the cadets down the hall and they were soon in range of sight with the two guards in black uniforms at the front of the weapons section. He walked toward them and they both snapped to attention. It was a female and a male; both sported the rank of Corporal on their shoulders.

"At ease," Zachariades ordered them.

The soldiers relaxed into a parade rest position.

"Wanted to warn both of you that sonar is detecting three Britva off the starboard. They might make an attack on us."

"Thank you, sir," the female corporal responded.

"If they do attack us you will both need to be strapped in."

Before the enlisted soldiers could respond, Arch shot both of them with his laser pistol. They collapsed to the ground without a sound. Zachariades noticed that the two soldiers had no entrance or exit wounds.

"You stunned them?" Zachariades was angry at that fact. "These soldiers are the elite. You need to learn that in war it is either kill or be killed."

Frazier holstered the laser pistol into his stolen web belt. "I only kill when necessary, sir."

Regehr and Nehwal ignored the discussion as they dragged the two soldiers into the weapons room and began removing their uniforms. It was a ten by twenty storage unit with laser rifles and fully charged cartridges stocked on the left wall, laser pistols and knives on the right wall and web belts on the far wall.

"Now what?" Elektra asked her cousin as she was pulling a few laser pistols from the racks and placing them in holsters on a web belt. She wrapped the belt around her and fastened it above her hips.

"We take the rest of the lower part of this ship and then move to the second level," he responded to her and then glared at Arch. "No more stunning. Kill them all."

As he was giving the order, Zorana had a twelve-inch blade knife in her hand and used it before any of the others could protest. She slashed the throats of the two unconscious soldiers on the floor in a manner that suggested she had used a knife on a person before.

"Zorana! Why did you do that?" Jasna's tone of voice indicated that she was surprised by the draconian actions of her older sister. Only she knew how her sister had learned to use a knife so effectively. They had been raised on a farm and cutting the throats of livestock so that they could be butchered for their meat and hides was something their father had taught them to do at a young age.

Zorana cleaned the blood on a green rag she had found on one of the ammunition carts in the center of the room. "They held me, beat me. Stood by so that freak could try to rape me. Captain Zachariades is right. They all should die. Anyone that treats someone like that has no value or worth. The galaxy is better served if we kill each and every one of these barbarians."

Zachariades smiled at Elektra. "I like her."

"You would." She laughed, recalling that he always liked the tough girls.

Nehwal had found that the uniform of the female soldier fit her and was standing before them as a Corporal in the MI. She smiled and pulled the web belt over her shoulders and fastened it. She then went about the task of arming herself with a laser pistol and some knives for close quarter combat. Regehr and the Mikec sisters were finding weapons for use and trying not to slip in the growing pool of blood that was growing larger from the slit throats of the soldiers. Jasna located their personal communication devices and began to pass them around to their respective owners.

Soon the group of seven was armed and ready to proceed to the next set of rooms. The lower level had several small sleeping quarters that were located down the other side of the curved hallway.

Zachariades cautioned them that there was quite possibly a dozen or so MI soldiers to contend with in those rooms. "With any grace from Poseidon, they may all be asleep and we can kill them silently."

They crept single file down the hallway with Zachariades in the lead with Elektra behind him, Zorana was third, Jasna fourth, Nehwal was fifth, Regehr sixth and Arch Frazier bringing up the rear. They passed several empty ten by ten rooms with beds that were unused. The fifth room had a woman asleep in the bed. She was in a black t-shirt and shorts. Zachariades walked into the room, pulled his large knife from it's' sheath and slit her throat.

The sixth room had a male and female soldier cuddled together in the bed. They were naked and only a green bed sheet covered some of their bodies. Zorana and Zachariades crept into the room and covered their mouths just seconds before slicing their throats open.

Elektra counted to herself that there were five dead soldiers out of a possible maximum of twenty-three. As her cousin and Zorana were killing the soldiers in the second room, Elektra walked toward the next room. She found a female soldier sitting on the bed, reading a book off her hand held computer. Elektra aimed her laser pistol at the woman, pulled the trigger and blew the top of her head off. The corpse slid to the metal floor, making very little noise.

Regehr, Nehwal, Jasna and Arch cleared out the other rooms, stepping into the doorways and firing a laser burst or two, killing the occupants. Elektra noticed that Jasna fired her laser pistol five times and stood at her doorway with a dour look on her face. Elektra walked quickly to her side and looked into the room. She saw four women in black t-shirts and underwear with their heads blown off or their chests open from Jasna's laser fire.

"Four of them," Jasna said to Elektra without looking at her. "Did I do good?"

Elektra put her arm around Jasna's shoulders. "You did great. Keep it up. There are more. Can you do it?"

Jasna kept staring at the four dead soldiers and nodded. "I can do it."

Arch Frazier walked to the doorway of the last of the living quarters. As he looked into the room he was taken by surprise. One of the Sikorsky clones leaped out at him and kicked him in the chest with both feet. Arch stumbled backwards against the far wall and dropped his laser pistol. Nehwal was the closest to him and began running to his defense. She stopped running when the clone that had attacked Frazier leaped out of the room and charged at her with a twelve-inch blade knife in his right hand. He snarled with rage as he came at her.

Nehwal fired her laser pistol at the clone two times. Her first shot hit his upper left shoulder and seemed to reflect the laser energy from the body up toward the ceiling. The second shot hit him in the chest. The laser energy sparkled on impact but it did not penetrate the body as Nehwal would have expected. Nor did either shot slow the clone down. He raised his knife at her and prepared to plunge it into her. The clone did not get the chance.

Zachariades shoved Nehwal aside and fired his laser rifle at the clone. The blast caused it to stumble backwards a few steps, but he remained upright and smiled. Zachariades saw why the clone was not dead. The lasers had torn through the clothing and the flesh to reveal a metal skeleton all around the Sikorsky clone.   It began running at Zachariades, holding the blade in front of it, ready to plunge it into Zachariades.

Arch had regained his composure and was able to run at the clone and leap onto it from the rear. He locked his arms around the chest of the Sikorsky clone and pulled the arms back as he locked his fingers behind the neck. The Sikorsky duplicate howled with rage and began to twist in circles in an attempt to throw Arch from his back. Arch held on as if his life depended on it. The clone grabbed Arch's right forearm with it's' left hand and began to squeeze. Arch screamed in pain as he felt his bones being crushed under the iron grip of his opponent. He let go of his grip which Sikorsky used to his advantage. He flipped Arch over his shoulder and into Zachariades, sending both men sprawling to the floor.

The Sikorsky duplicate was smiling at them. The others could see the shiny metal on his chest and shoulder. "Now you all will die."

Elektra stepped forward.

"We can take him together," Regehr whispered.

"No. This one is mine." Elektra began circling the metallic clone.

"You are very brave," the Sikorsky duplicate told her as it circled with her. "The brave always die young."

Elektra watched Sikorsky closely as she moved him away from her injured husband, Nehwal and Zachariades. "Really? So the real Sikorsky that is over two hundred forty years old was a coward then? Since he lived that long he certainly is not brave."

"Do not speak to me like that!" The clone screamed at her.

"Why? The truth hurts? You spent your life getting others to take the risk for you? You are not a real man. A real man would fight. You are a sniveling cretin. You are a coward, Vladimir Sikorsky."

Sikorsky growled and leaped at her. She sidestepped his charge with ease. Elektra could feel her heart beating hard in her chest. She would only get one shot to kill the clone-metallic construct before her. She smiled when she saw that the Mikec sisters were treating her husband by putting a splint of two long knives around his broken arm.

"The rumors are true, Sikorsky. You betrayed everyone that sought to be your friend. You are a coward that rapes defenseless women and murders millions for your own gain. You care nothing for the people. You are not fit to be a leader. You should be indicted for all of your crimes."

The Sikorsky clone had all of the memories of the original. He also had the same personality traits, narcissism being one of the many negative ones. He sneered at Elektra. "No more calumny about my character! I am going to rip out your heart and then I will kill all of your traitorous friends!"

Elektra saw that the clone was waving his arms around, just as the real Sikorsky would do while giving one of his speeches. She stepped into her opponent and slammed her right palm into his face. Her guess was correct. The head, just like the clone she killed earlier, was not reinforced with metal. Her blow crushed the nose, cheek bones and forehead of the clone. She watched as the clone flipped backwards from the impact of her attack. She pressed her advantage and hit him in the back of the skull with a balled fist which went through the skull and crushed his brain matter. She pulled her fist free and wiped the chunks of skull and brain onto Sikorsky's uniform as the other watched in silence.

"How many more of these are there?" Elektra asked her cousin.

"Three more," Zachariades told her. He looked at Regehr and Nehwal. "It would seem that their creators did not protect the skull. When we run into the others, we shoot them in the head."

Elektra ran to the side of her husband. "Arch, your arm?"

He smiled at her. "It is broken. Don't worry, I can still contribute. Let's take this ship."

Zachariades motioned to the engine room. "Let's move out. Remember the engine room staff are unarmed and are not to be killed. Stun them, bind them and we move on."

The cadets followed Zachariades to the most important section of the ship, the engine room. Inside the forty square foot room was a series of oxygen regeneration tubes, solar power cells, and nuclear power cells, rows of computer panels that went from the floor to the ceiling, tool kits, extra solar batteries, a dunkle materie converter and the all-important engine in the center. The engine was in the shape of a large rectangle that extended from the floor to the ceiling. As it ran it sounded as if it was humming. There were two female engineers inside that were checking the oxygen levels when Zachariades and the cadets walked into the room. The engineers looked to be in their late twenties. They were not surprised to see the Captain, but the sight of the others disturbed them.

"Captain, are the prisoners supposed to be walking around like this?" Lieutenant Charon Kiesbye spoke up. The other engineer was watching as the prisoners surrounded them.

"Sorry, Lieutenant." Zachariades told her as he aimed his laser at her and pulled the trigger. Kiesbye cried out as the laser beam hit her. She slumped to the floor. The other engineer tried to run but did not get far. She spun to the floor after being hit by Nehwal's laser shot. The cadets bound the arms and legs of the two women quickly. Regehr was keeping watch on the hallway that led to the engine room.

After the two women were bound, Zachariades looked at the cadets and sized them up. "Regehr and Nehwal, you two know how to fly this ship so you stay by my side. Elektra, Zorana, keep up with us. We are going to the second level where the other soldiers are. I expect there to be stiff resistance."

"I am coming along," Arch insisted.

"Your arm is broken. You are staying here on the lower level to help protect the engine room. Jasna, you stay here, too. The medical storage room is down the hallway. Frazier, you need some pain injections and fast. Jasna, you must hold this section of the ship at all costs. You understand what that means?" Zachariades barely looked at the cadets as he spoke. He had walked over next to Regehr and was glancing up and down the hallway to determine whether or not it would be safe to move to the second level.

"I can do it," Jasna assured them. "Be careful."

"You be careful." Zorana embraced her younger sister.

Elektra kissed her husband on the lips and ran her fingers through his hair. "Don't go anywhere. I'll be right back."

"I'll be here," he promised as he watched her leave with Regehr, Nehwal, Zachariades and Zorana Mikec.

There were a few seconds of silence before Jasna informed him that she would return with some pain medication for his broken arm. Arch watched in silence as she left him alone with the two unconscious engineers. Arch pulled his sweater off and grunted with pain as he did so. He inspected the fracture on his arm.

"Poggie dung," Arch muttered to himself as he looked at the swelling. The pain was bearable, but he was anticipating how good it would feel to have the pain killers injected into his arm.

He paced the engine room impatiently, praying that Elektra and the others would return soon.

Jasna walked quickly down the empty hallway. Although they had either killed or incapacitated all of the other occupants on the floor, she was still cautious. She had her laser pistol in her right hand and kept her eyes scanning each of the rooms as she passed them by. She passed the cafeteria and moved into the medical area that was next door. She inspected the room which consisted of two beds and several metal cabinets that extended from the floor to the ceiling which were filled with operating instruments and drugs. She sat her laser pistol down on top of one of the beds and began opening the cabinets, searching for any pain killers. She had to climb up a four step ladder to reach the top cabinet. She did not look long to fins what she needed. She located a row of twenty-four hyper dermic needles that were already full of pain medications. She grabbed two and began to step down from the small ladder.

As her feet touched the ground she heard the sound of a person clapping their hands. It was enough to startle her and she turned to see one of the Sikorsky clones standing in the doorway, clapping his hands in a deliberate manner and shaking his head.

"Bravo. Bravo." He said as he smiled at her.

Jasna was terrified by the look in his eyes. She glanced over at the bed where her laser pistol was lying on top of.

"I would not try to get that if I were you. You people forgot to watch your rear. I came down to take my rightful place in bed with you. Imagine my surprise when I found that you and your friends had escaped. I found one of my duplicates with his face smashed in and several of my soldiers shot dead. And you people dirtied my clean ship by cutting people's throats. Quite barbaric if you ask me." The clone inched closer to Jasna as he spoke.

"What do you want from us?" she managed to ask with her voice quivering from fear.

Sikorsky picked up her laser pistol and inspected it. "I want to breed. You see, I have all of the brain patterns of the Glorious Leader. But in the cloning process I and my four brother Replicants that are on this small ship were enhanced in many ways. We were given metal skeletons as opposed to normal human bones. We were also given downloads of memory into our brains of exact details of the greatest battles in the history of man. And we were given an enhanced sex drive so that our DNA of the Glorious Leader would be spread all over the galaxy. So, Jasna Mikec, we can do this the easy way or the hard way. The choice is yours."

Jasna still held the pain killer hyper dermic needles in her hands. "What's the difference between easy and hard?"

"The hard way is that I will have to force myself on you. I will have to beat you into submission. I really do not like that option because you really are beautiful. I would hate to damage your fine skin and perfect cheek bones and lips. The easy way means you submit to me, right here, on one of these beds. You escape the beating with that option and you might even enjoy letting me have my way with you. But you need to tell me which way, because I am full of animal lust for you."

Jasna quickly considered her options as the Sikorsky clone approached her. She could see the way he was staring at her that he meant business. She looked at the closest bed and nodded toward it. "Okay. I don't want to be hit. You can have me on that bed."

"Very smart girl. You will produce amazing offspring for me."

Jasna did not struggle as the clone began to kiss her with passion. She kissed him back and allowed him to lift her up and sit her on top of the bed. She held both of her hands behind her back and released the liquid inside of the two hyper dermic needles in her hands. As she did so the Sikorsky clone was undressing her and nibbling on her neck. She slowly pulled the syringe back and filled them with air. Soon she was ready with her ruse. She looked at Sikorsky and saw that he was oblivious to the two medical instruments behind her back as he was concentrating on the pleasure that awaited him after he succeeded in removing her clothing.

Jasna brought both hyper dermic needles up in her hands and swung them both at opposite sides of Sikosky's head. She slammed each needle into his temples and injected the oxygen into his brain. The clone screamed and fell backwards from her, reaching for the two needles in the side of his head. He spun several time around, his arms flailing wildly as he fell to his knees. Jasna leaped to her feet and ran for her laser pistol.

Before she could reach the weapon, Sikorsky grabbed her left ankle and tripped her. She screamed as she fell face first toward the metal floor.

Zachariades walked up the ramp that led up to the second level of the Orka and had the cadets behind him wait for his signal.   He smiled at a few of the MI soldiers that were sitting around the hexagon shaped command station. Captain Cheri Rendon was reading some reports that were on some of the computer screens before her. There were two clones of Sikorsky sitting across the room from one another, drinking coffee and glaring at one another. Zachariades had sensed a tension between the exact duplicates that had been on the ship. It was as if they were wanting to be the one and only but neither had the fortitude to attempt to kill the other. There were a few soldiers in the adjacent computer station and a few more in the weapons section. Zachariades was certain that there would be no one in the upper pilots' section as he had left the craft on automatic pilot and he had been the only member of the crew that knew how to fly the Orka.

"How are the condemned?" Rendon asked.

"One is being raped. The others are cursing and promising revenge," Zachariades lied. "What news from the Government Broadcast Service?"

"The Second Fleet is finished," Rendon announced proudly. "My great uncle developed a master plan and took out Allen and Khan first by concentrating all of his efforts on their ships. The remaining three were commanded by lesser qualified commanders. They were easy for the kill. All that is left if to pick off the Allen Fighters and the Raumschiffs. The victory for the Glorious Leader has been complete. The rest of the disloyal members of humanity will soon suffer when the Red Javelin weapons hit them. Billions will die. But, billions will live. Those that do survive will remember this wonderful day and never even consider standing up to my family again."

Zachariades had slipped a grenade into each of his hands as the soldiers and Rendon seemed to trust him completely. "Why not allow the rebellious humans on the other planets to just surrender? Why kill billions of innocents that had no part in the insurrections?"

Rendon turned her attention away from the numerous screens and glared at him. "You as an officer and commander should know better than that. Examples must be made. If you execute one traitor, he or she will be forgotten in no time. You kill all the traitors and the innocents that gave them shelter or aid, then it will be remembered for a century or two. By killing them all we will buy another two hundred years of rule for our family. The billions about to die will be replaced since the survivors will breed, make babies and repopulate the regions. All humans are replaceable. They are pawns to be used in the bigger game of domination of other solar systems. Your mother understands these concepts. She accepts and embraces them. Do you?"

Zachariades concluded that the entire Royal Family was crazy and needed to be the ones that were hunted down and killed to the last of them. And now they were cloning one another which made the safety of the rest of humanity more perilous. They all had to die.

"I do understand where you are coming from," he assured her as he pressed the detonator buttons on his grenades.

"Good. You and your mother will go far." Rendon turned her attention back to her computer screens and began reading. "Just don't forget who rules."

Zachariades rolled the grenade in his right hand into the weapons section and the one in his left into the computer section. One of the Sikorsky clones was the only one that noticed what he had done. He growled and leaped at Zachariades and tackled him to the floor of the command station. Rendon looked up from her screens as she heard the noise and stood up as did the other soldiers with her.

The grenades exploded.

The three soldiers in the computer section never knew what had hit them. Their torn bodies were thrown from their chairs and slammed into the walls. Shrapnel from the devices peppered the computer banks all around where they had been working.

The weapons room technicians fared no better. There were four of them and three died instantly when the grenade erupted. The fourth lost her right arm and was thrown against the wall, screaming in agony as she slid to the floor. Her loud screams echoed throughout the ship.

Elektra, Regehr, Zorana and Nehwal heard the explosions and charged up the ramp as Zachariades had instructed them to do. Each of them had laser pistols in hand and began firing at the soldiers that were standing up.

The Sikorsky clone that was closest to the entrance ramp grabbed Elektra by the arm and flung her effortlessly across the command station area. She hit the ceiling and then the far wall before slamming hard to the ground. She dropped her laser pistol due to the stunning impact. As she hit the metal floor she could see that her uncle and the other Sikorsky clone were grappling on the floor. The Sikorsky clone was able to use its' armored skeleton mass to pin Zachariades to the metal floor. The clone reared his right arm back and brought it down with significant force onto his chest. Zachariades cried out as he felt his rib cage being crushed under the blow and his right lung damaged beyond repair.

Nehwal threw one of her large military knives in the direction of a female Lieutenant. Before the MI officer could react, the blade hit her in the left eye and sank several inches into the socket. She fell backwards screaming in pain from the loss of her eye. Her screams lasted only a few seconds as the knife had cut into her brain. She was dead within a few seconds after her body hit the metal floor.

Regehr and Zorana were on their knees, firing their laser pistols at the lower torsos and legs of the other soldiers in the command area. Captain Rendon dropped behind her chair and narrowly avoided a blast fired by Regehr. Rendon drew her laser pistol and began returning fire, using her swivel chair as cover between her and the cadets. One of her laser bursts hit Zorana in the left lower arm, burning the skin and causing her to cry out as she dropped her laser.

Regehr fired on Rendon, forcing her to hide behind her chair. Regehr then turned his attention to the injured Zachariades. He ran and dived across the room to assist Zachariades as the Sikorsky clone was about to deliver another damaging blow. Using his body weight, Regehr was able to cause the duplicate Sikorsky to roll backwards away from the prone Zachariades that was coughing up blood onto the floor. Regehr did not allow the clone to regain his footing as he fired three laser bursts right into his face. The head of the duplicate exploded brain and skull onto the far wall.

Rendon began to stick her head up and aim at Regehr. Nehwal had inched close enough to the woman and kicked the laser pistol out of her hand. Rendon growled and pushed herself to her feet and faced the cadet. They began hitting one another with closed fists and crescent kicks across the body. Each woman was giving the other as good as they were receiving. Their fight to the death seemed evenly matched.

Elektra had her hands full with the other clone. She was trying to catch her breath as the clone charged at her, his head and shoulders lowered as if he were a linebacker in a football game coming in for a sack on a quarterback. Elektra rolled to her right and watched the clone slide to a halt. He growled and began running at her again. Elektra recovered and was on her feet. She waited to time her punch to the head just right. She took in a deep breath as the clone got closer and swung her balled fist. She connected with the chin and drove her metal arm in an upward swing. The impact of her metal fist ripped the front of the face off the clone. He flipped backwards and slammed onto the metal floor. There was blood and brain matter oozing out onto the floor from the opening in his head. He did not move again.

Despite the wound to her arm, Zorana had found another laser pistol and kept firing at the soldiers. She killed several as she used the corner of the wall at the ramp to partially cover herself.

Rendon deduced from her position that the majority of her soldiers were either dead or falling fast. She kicked Nehwal in the stomach and leaped for the ladder that led to the ceiling of the command station and the upper level exit hatch from the ship. She decided that if she was going to die that she would take the cadets with her. She grabbed hold of the wheel shaped hatch seal and began to turn it. The alarms on the Orka started a loud warning that the upper level hull hatch was being opened and that the water pressure outside the ship from the ocean posed an immediate danger to all life on board.

"Holy Hera!" Elektra yelled as she saw Rendon straining to open the hatch to flood the ship. Elektra ran and leaped into the air and grabbed Rendon by the legs.

"You are all going to die!" Rendon shrieked out loud as she tried to turn the hatch seal harder. Water was now leaking into the ship as the hatch was now loosened enough that the seals between the metal were not stopping the ocean water.

Elektra felt the cold water splashing onto her face and shoulders. She used her mechanical right arm and crushed

Rendon's left upper leg. Rendon screamed and held onto the hatch with all her might. Her knuckles on her hands were turning white from holding up her own weight and Elektra's at the same time.   Elektra rammed her fingers of her right hand into Rendon's spinal column and grabbed the bones. She squeezed as hard as she could and could hear the bones crushing under to pressure of her mechanical hand. Rendon cried out as she felt her spine being broken. The pain was too much. She let go of the hatch release and fell to the metal floor. There was more water flowing into the ship from the hatch.

"We have to seal the hatch!" Nehwal stated the obvious.

Elektra leaped upward and grabbed hold of the hatch sealant wheel and began turning it to the right to tighten it closed.   The water slowly stopped flowing inside. Elektra let go of the hatch when the alarms ceased and landed onto the metal floor with both feet. She turned to see that Regehr was on his knees next to Zachariades, holding his left hand in his own. Nehwal was helping Zorana with her wounded arm. All of the cadets had a somber look on their face.

Jasna screamed as she fell face first to the floor. The clone had grabbed her legs and tripped her as she had attempted to reach for her laser pistol. She reached out with her arms to grab hold of a metal table leg and frantically kicked her legs into the face of the clone. She was horrified that the two hyper dermic needles filled with oxygen did not kill him when she stabbed him in each temple.

"You will not escape!" Sikorsky growled at her. His voice sounded hoarse and tortured.

Jasna looked over his shoulder and saw that Sikorsky's skull circumference had doubled in size. The injections had not killed him, but they had caused a reaction to the cloned body. She kicked hard with her left foot and connected the face with her right heel. She screamed as his skin popped like a water balloon might when pricked with a pin. Flesh and blood spattered over the walls, floors and her legs. She pulled harder to free herself from the grip of the part human part metal clone. She could see the skull underneath the shredded flesh and blood. To her relief, the clone finally released her legs and the skull collapsed to the metal floor. She ripped her feet free and stood up. She grabbed her laser pistol and began firing into the body. Her hands were shaking as she fired. After ten laser shots into the back of the skull and neck of the clone she stopped. She saw that the head was obliterated from her multiple laser blasts. She slid to the floor and cried. After a few moments she regained her composure, recalled why she had come to the medical area in the first place and stepped over the headless corpse of the clone to retrieve two new hyper dermic injections for Frazier.

Elektra knelt down next to her cousin and took his hand. "Drimios. Hang on. We can get you to the medical area; put you in cryo-sleep until we can get to a hospital."

Zachariades shook his head. His words were labored as one of his lungs was torn and useless. The other was filling with blood. "No, ksadelfi. No. Take my grey security card in my top breast pocket. You will need it. Take it. I love you, ksadelfi. Tell my children..."

He was not able to finish the sentence. Elektra watched as his eyes were staring at her but no longer functioning. She could see the life go out of them. His head slumped to the side. She held his head in her hands and wept.

Regehr motioned for Nehwal to join him in the pilot section so that Elektra could have a private moment and mourn her cousin. Zorana silently walked toward the weapons section and inspected the damage to the controls caused by the grenade that Zachariades had thrown to kill the occupants. She closed her eyes and stepped over the legs of one of the dead soldiers. She was grateful to be alive even though she would sport a long scar on her arm for the rest of her life. She looked over at her shoulder at Elektra. The woman was so strong and had amazing leadership qualities. She hoped that one day she could be more like her.

Regehr sat in the pilot's seat and Nehwal the co-pilot. Nehwal had taken a dark blue security card from the upper left breast pocket of Captain Rendon. She showed it to Regehr.

"Wonder what it will get us into?" She asked him.

"We seem to have a good knack for getting ourselves into deep poggie shit. All I care about right now is getting us the hell out of it." Regehr was speaking as he was making safety checks.   The two grenade blasts and the attempt by Rendon to open the outer hatch might have caused some damage. He hoped to bring the rest of them home safely.

Jasna returned to the engineering room and found Arch lying on the metal floor, holding his broken arm and grimacing in pain. She knelt down next to him and injected the first shot into the injured arm. She tried not to react to the swelling. She gave him the second shot in the opposite shoulder.

"You sure you gave those to me in the correct locations?" He finally asked.

"If you were a poggie going to the slaughter house, yes." Jasna responded. "I do it all the time at my family farms. But this is a first for me, giving pain killers to a human."

"Well, the pain is going away," he smiled. "I suppose you did it right. Any word from the others?"

"No. Perhaps I should go up and check on them."

"No. Wait here. You heard what Drimios told us. We hold this room no matter what."

"I am worried about my sister."

Frazier nodded. He could feel the medicine making him drowsy. "I am worried about my wife. They will be fine. Think positive."

Jasna watched as he slowly fell asleep. She spread him out on the floor so that he would be comfortable. She found some white sheets and covered him to keep him warm. She pulled out her communication device and saw that she had several messages from her family waiting for her. She began to watch them, one by one, as she waited for the others to return.

Nehwal began calling up the tactical screens as Regehr flew the Orka at full speed to the surface of the ocean. She narrowed her eyes as she spied upon something that she had not expected to be a part of the armament on a ship the size of a Raumschiff.

"Derek? You won't believe this."

"What is it?"

"This Orka has nukes."

Regehr looked at her with a look of surprise. "You mean nuclear weapons?"

"Yes. Four of them. Armor Piercing Rosenburg Corporation Nuclear missiles. Range of launch is one million kilometers. We could really fuck some things up."

Regehr sat back in his chair and began to speak of their options out loud. "The space station is under the control of neutrals. The lunar base was overrun by the enemy. And then there is the Battle Cruiser, the Lysander. The two nuclear submarines that we just left behind. We could fire a missile at each of the four targets. Strike a blow for the good guys."

"We would kill a lot of people that way."

"All bad people."

Nehwal was twirling her hair through her right index finger as she contemplated the suggestions. "If we blow up the Lysander and the lunar base then the enemy would no longer have the ability to control the skies, especially if Reynita, Dino and John secure enough space ships to fly cover for the ground forces. Maybe we should nuke them."

Elektra covered the body of Captain Drimios Zachariades with a flight jacket that was lying over the back of one of the numerous seats in the command section. The news reports that Rendon had been following were still being shown. Elektra wiped the tears from her eyes and watched the reports. She began to conclude that the rebellion was over. Seward was dead and the Second Fleet was annihilated. She decided that it was time to strike a blow for freedom. She climbed up the ladder to the pilot section and saw Nehwal and Regehr speaking about what location to fire nuclear missiles upon.

"What nuclear missiles?" Elektra asked as she poked her head through the open hatch to the pilot section.

Nehwal pointed to the tactical display on the far left of the pilot section. "Those nuclear weapons. We have four on this ship. All we need to do is find the security code to activate them. Then we can hit them back and hard."

Elektra had the grey security card in her pants pocket that she had removed from Zachariades' body. "He knew."

"Who knew?" Nehwal asked her.

"Drimios, my cousin. He knew that we would need his security card to launch those nuclear missiles. That was why he made such an effort to tell me about it before he died." Elektra pulled the card out of her pocket and inspected it. "He knew that we would need the weapons to even the playing field with the Rosenburg's and Sikorsky's."

"And that grey card is the way to order this ship to override the security codes and launch them?" Regehr raised his eyebrows. "Sounds as if your cousin wanted us to use them."

"My cousin was a smart man. I am sure that he deduced that our only chances for success were to blow the Lysander to hell. Hopefully the magnetic pulses from the explosion and the radioactive clouds will leave the lunar base useless for the duration of the battle. Yes. He had probably planned on launching them himself had he lived." Elektra twirled the grey card between her fingers. "How long before we are out of the water?"

Regehr checked his instrument panels. "Thirty minutes. Why?"

"When we get into the air, prepare to launch. It is time

that the Glorious Leader suffered a major setback on his little war on freedom." Elektra told them. "I am going down below to check on my husband and Jasna. When I come back, this war begins for real."

After an hour of silence on the craft, Derek Regehr slowly brought the Orka ship above the ocean surface and into the sky. Elektra had awakened her husband and brought him and the Mikec sisters up to speed on the fact that they had possession of four nuclear devices. The six cadets were crowded into the tight confines of the pilot section as she spoke to them. Each of them filled with emotions ranging from dread to refusal to accept the situation they found themselves in.

Elektra broke the uneasy silence by stating: "Launching those weapons is not something we can do lightly. Not one of us can make that decision alone. We will have to cast a vote as to whether or not we fire them and where we fire them at. I propose we do this. We all know that the Battle Cruiser Lysander poses the greatest threat to us all. It is in orbit and if it suffers a nuclear strike, the radiation will dissipate over time in the solar winds. If we fire on the lunar base, we will destroy all of the buildings there with one blast. In fact, it would be overkill."

"And the submarines?" Zorana asked her.

Elektra placed her hand on Zorana's shoulder and responded to her concern with a soothing tone of voice. "I know my aunt much better now. She understands force and power. If we show her that we are going to prevail, she will do nothing to stand in our way. When she learns that Drimios was killed by his own crew, she might want to join up with us. We do not need to be concerned with her two subs at this time. So, I propose that we fire two missiles at the Lysander and blow her and her crew to hell. Just like the Glorious Leader did to the Second Fleet."

"I am down with that," Nehwal responded quickly.

"I vote no," Zorana said slowly. "What if there are innocents in that Battle Cruiser? I could not live with myself. No."

Jasna thought of the cloned creatures that had attacked them and how close they came to all being dead. She glared at her sister. "I vote yes. We have to show them that we are going to fight them. Yes. We should blow up the Lysander."

"Three to one," Elektra said. "Arch, Derek?"

"Honey, Zorana might be correct. There could easily be non-combatants on that ship. You know that I will support you in anything that you decide to do. But consider this. What if that Battle Cruiser has prisoners on her, like us on this Orka, and we blow them all up? What if someone nuked us to kill the MI soldiers on board? We would have died as well. I do not think I could live with that on my conscience if we did this thing and later learned that there were innocents on the ship. I am sorry my love, but I respectfully vote no," Arch announced.

Regehr saw that all eyes were on him. He extended his left hand toward Elektra. "We have all known fear and we came to face those fears. Those that created the fear we all share mutually arrived on New Edinburgh on the Lysander. I have been listening to satellite chatter and the civilians are each afraid. They are waiting for a signal that they might one day have their lives back, on this adopted world they all call home. Give me the security card. The time has come for the enemy to live in fear. Admiral Seward was a good man. I am sure the Second Fleet was staffed with equally good men and women. If we are to achieve freedom from the current regime, then we must fight back and kill them. I vote yes. I have already programmed in the coordinates into the ship computer. Two nuclear missiles are armed and ready to launch."

Elektra smiled, "Fire when ready."